HIGH JOHN THE

Jim Younger is well known as a musician, playing mainly fiddle and mandolin. He plays and records with his wife, Gail Williams. He has worked as a teacher, but is now a government official. He lives in London.

JIM YOUNGER

High John
the Conqueror

VINTAGE BOOKS
London

Published by Vintage 2007

2 4 6 8 10 9 7 5 3 1

First published in Great Britain in 2006 by
Jonathan Cape
Random House, 20 Vauxhall Bridge Road,
London SW1V 2SA

www.vintage-books.co.uk

Addresses for companies within The Random House Group Limited
can be found at: www.randomhouse.co.uk/offices.htm

The Random House Group Limited Reg. No. 954009

A CIP catalogue record for this book
is available from the British Library

ISBN 9780099492740

The Random House Group Limited makes every effort to
ensure that the papers used in its books are made from trees that
have been legally sourced from well-managed and credibly certified
forests. Our paper procurement policy can be found at:
www.randomhouse.co.uk/paper.htm

Mixed Sources
Product group from well-managed
forests and other controlled sources
www.fsc.org   Cert no. TT-COC-2139
© 1996 Forest Stewardship Council

FSC

Printed in the UK by CPI Bookmarque, Croydon, CR0 4TD

For Gail and Luke
With thanks to Mark, Gill and Lucy

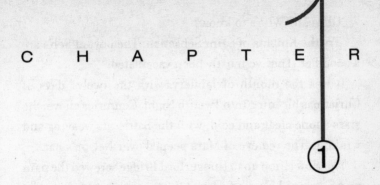

CHAPTER 1

Coming on towards a cold midnight, I had about all I could take. The pain was easing off. Time to risk a move.

I pulled the hood over my head, pushed aside the stinking mattress and crept out into the alley and down towards the lights of Trafalgar Square. There were kerb-crawlers about, Yanks mainly, festooned with bandoliers and holsters, very unappetising in wraparound mirrors, the season's fashion for cruising nighthawks. Last year sideburns and moustaches were all the go. Now their faces were scraped clean as doss-house plates.

I was limping into the Strand, teeth clenched, head down and my third eye open for the military police, when a pedishaw slewed across the sidewalk and two GIs jumped out with the usual offers — *beaucoup* dickey, a fistful of dollars and a bed for the night. The money and the bed I could use, but dickey *nein danke*. I look young for my age, so I told them I was three months off fifteen. The mirrors flashed in the search beam of a scudding helicopter, sparking the thought that maybe I'd said wrong, marking me a chicken like that. No telling what stiffens a tickling stick.

'Oh yeah? Who's to know?'

'Try the Knights of Saint Sebastian. The boys at Seb's are a good bet. They've mostly been vaccinated.'

It was the month of January, with the twelve days of Christmas bleeding into Twelfth Night. Centuries above, the stars shone clear and cold, with the battlesats weaving and winking. The red eye of Mars peeped over Nelson's hat.

The slow climb up to Hungerford Bridge screwed the pain up a notch and I leaned against the parapet, unable to move. My scrotum sack was on fire. I broke the tab off my last amp of morphine and drank it down.

Eastward on the river, sodium and starlight mingled in the flood. A siren keened downstream, panning across the river from Waterloo. Flashing blue lights bobbed in the siren's wake, a procession of graveyard wisps. Two years before, I climbed up here to lob my father's ashes into the Thames.

Two years before, I'd been waiting for Dad to come home. I waited and waited, but he never came.

A man banged on the door one morning. I was asleep and heard the knocking on the edge of a dream, like a prisoner waking to the bustle of chippies raising a scaffold.

'This is 99 Crawford Mansions and you are Lingus McWhinny?'

I said yes. He said, 'I have a package for you and I need a signature.'

I went into the kitchen and tore the wrapper off the parcel. A black urn with Dad's name, the royal seal, date of execution and the zigzag lightning flash of the Homeland logo.

Organ John McWhinny RIP

I unscrewed the lid and sifted the ashes through my fingers. Tiny grey shards, warm from the oven.

I did nothing with the remains till the next morning. The urn stood on the mantelpiece in the front room overnight, next to the silver trophy inscribed *Victor Ludorum* that Dad had won in his schooldays. I slept in there on the sofa as usual. I had an idea it was all a joke and Dad might come home and want his bed, so best to wait a day or two before doing a Goldilocks. About three in the morning a footfall on creaking boards woke me up. No one there, then the throb of a motor-taxi. The street lamp flickered through the grimy window. At daybreak I scooped the ashes into a tea caddy and went down to Hyde Park and through the subway by Wellington's house. I came up by the memorial to the Machine-Gun Corps.

Saul hath slain his thousands, but David his tens of thousands

I watched the flamingos in Saint James's Park for a while and then went down by the river and along the Embankment, where the dossers were stirring for the morning nosebag. A Cockney street-singer was wailing a come-all-ye, to the tune of 'The Croppy Boy'.

We were defeated, and shamefully treated.

I climbed up on Hungerford Bridge and hoyed the caddy into the river.

Rent was paid up for another ten days. There were books and other trash that could be sold – stuffed birds and furry things, relics of Dad's exploits as a taxidermist, and a few tools for doctoring from the days when he was still allowed to doctor. I could sell his clothes and most of the furniture. I brewed up with a handful of used tea bags and sat down to make an inventory. How much for the painting in the bedroom? It was a dark, oily smear of Noah and his boys building the Ark. I stared at it for a while and decided to sell the books first.

The next four days I stayed home. I still had an inkling it was all a joke, that he might come home without his key and need me to let him in. Once at twilight I saw him on the corner, hunched like a buzzard in his black overcoat, but it was only the local rabbi scouting for a cab. I slept at night fully dressed now, upright in the armchair with the lights on. I woke to see Dad in the mirror, but when I blinked he was gone. I heard his footsteps on the tenement stairs. I looked up 'bereavement' in one of his old textbooks. Well, here I was, morbid and bereaved – and all through someone that deep down I was glad to see the back of. Prognosis was good, though.

Hunger drove me out at last. I found a few coins down the side of the couch. I went over to George's and bought six slices of bread, an ounce of lard and a bottle of Johnny-Jump-Up. On the way back I met Sadie, our neighbour from across the landing. I nodded and made to walk past, but she gripped my wrist.

'Sorry to hear about your pappy.'

I made an appropriate noise. She pushed her sherry-scented face into mine and mumbled, 'Some mix-up over the amnesty, I expect.'

The lard was softening in my hand.

'I have to go.'

I ran upstairs. That night I dined on fried bread, got drunk on Johnny-Jump-Up and slept in my father's bed.

I sorted through his bits and pieces — scrapbooks and photo albums and such. No picture of Mum anywhere and no memories of her either. But here was a snap of Dad in younger days, dressed in his penitent's robes, standing beside a crony, also togged up in brown sackcloth, with fearsome pointy hoods on the two of them. It was taken in Spain. They each had an arm over the other's shoulder and knotted scourges in their hands. Despite the purgatorial get-up, they had the relaxed stance of two working chaps on a beano. There was a sequence of photos in a brochure, showing the right way to use a scourge. You could tell it was Dad's hand by the ring he always wore — gold and black signet, with an emblem of a masked satyr grinding a serpent's head with his heel.

Another photo, taken in the early days of the London Commune, showed a platoon of Flagellants, robed and hooded, rifles in one hand and disciplines in the other. Dad stood at their head, receiving the new colours of the Flagellant Faction from Manley Stanley. Manley was wearing a lilac suit and a panama hat. His face was prickly with the stubble of a new beard. In the background, turning away from the camera, was a blurred image of Errol Sachs, the dilapidated and dishevelled ex-Prime Minister. Suffering from piles, he was scratching his arse, unaware he was being framed for posterity.

I remembered a snap I took later the same day. A delinquent Flagellant, sentenced to Field Punishment Number Two for raping a hostage, was crucified on the overturned chassis of a burned-out milk float. His robes and hood were dark with sweat, but he still managed a thumbs-up for the camera. Around his neck Dad had hung a placard.

WHAT DOES NOT KILL ME MAKES ME STRONGER

These were the days before the United States declared its hand, when it seemed that the rebels might still be beaten and the coup d'état reversed. The days when the army was wavering, and every freak and deviant took up arms and flocked to the ousted government's colours, and the Coalition of Saints became the London Commune. When raping a hostage was still punished, in the days before the First Terror.

At the bottom of a shoebox was the grubby pamphlet Dad issued during the General Election: a manifesto from the Coalition of Saints, setting out the terms of their support for the thin-as-piss social democracy of Errol Sachs and Manley Stanley. I'd peddled these for pennies on the street.

Here in the bedroom cupboard were Dad's robes, hanging up where he left them, and a rack of scourges and flails. I laid the robes out on the bed. A few rents here and there, only to be expected really, but otherwise in good nick. I tried on the hood and peered through the eye-slits into the mirror. Not my style.

One afternoon I came home from the flea market, where I was selling a chair and the last of the scourges, to find my key wouldn't fit the door. There was a brand-new bright and chunky lock. I was moping about on the landing when Sadie came out of her flat.

'Bad news, amigo. Your gaff's been reallocated. You don't have enough points. The council man said to tell you to scram. They've given it to an American chap – a poet or a pop star or something. Never mind, you can share with me. If it's points you need, I can give you ten out of ten.'

Sadie pinned me to the wall, licked my nose, tickled my crotch. I ducked and ran downstairs. Out on the sidewalk I hung about for a while, wondering what to do. A van pulled into the kerb. An old man got out and began giving orders to some workmen. A crocodile of crates and leather luggage monogrammed 'T.L.' crept up the stairs to my home. The man snatched a bottle of beer from a passing crate. He jerked the cap off the bottle and tilted back his head, squirting beer on his tonsils like he was hefting a fire extinguisher. I went up to him and told my story. He wiped his mouth and shook his head.

'The embassy warned me this town is full of panhandlers and con artists, but I never thought to meet with one so soon. Your shit is up there? Ain't nothing up there now except a silver piss-pot belongs to some spic called Vic, a stuffed eagle and a picture of some weird-looking guys taking a boat to bits.'

He tucked a banknote in my shirt pocket.

'Now beat it. Go buy some candy or your first piece of ass.'

Sadie was leaning out of her window. She shouted, 'He can have that free!'

I pleaded with him. Some passers-by took up my case, saying it was a shame a boy on his own should be evicted. A patrol car came by and he flagged it down. A bobby in shirtsleeves jumped out, waving a truncheon at no one in particular. I turned casually into Homer Row. Behind me a siren started grinding.

So, two years on from eviction, blown about in the gale of the world, here I was on the lam, clinging to the parapet on Hungerford Bridge. The pain was still crabbing away down below in what was left of my balls, but the morphine was beginning to take the edge off. Now the blue flashing lights had crossed to the north bank. They clustered in Lancaster Place, the attendant sirens throbbing out of sync with the blood beating behind my eyes. I limped across to the southern shore and climbed down to the Embankment wall where a bevy of drunks cursed each other round a gallon jar.

Outside Satan's Kitchen I saw the bandwagon, with its back doors open and Shamela McToddy and Bruiser Barford loading gear. I tapped Bruiser on the shoulder.

'Jesus, Lingus! Don't creep up like that!'

'Hello, Bruiser. Hello, Sham. I claim sanctuary.'

They looked terrified at first, scanning the street for milipols, and then they relaxed into just plain scared. I asked could I get in the wagon. They were eager to oblige.

I climbed in the back and slid across the floor, whimpering as the cold metal seared the tender stripes etched in my buttocks. Sham threw her threadbare artist's smock over me, propped her beret on my head and sat beside me while Bruiser went back into the club for his guitar and to pay off the drummer.

'Comfy?' said Sham.

She stroked my hair and I squeezed her hand, while a regular police car pulled in behind us and flashed in our rear-view.

Bruiser came round the driver's side and waved to the bobbies as he climbed up. He started the engine and opened the heater.

'We'd better go,' said Sham.

Bruiser nodded and stamped on the pedals, swinging the wheel hard round.

Sham chewed the top off a bottle of Abdication Ale with her metal teeth. 'Any point me asking if you got anything worth tasting?' she said.

I pulled a crumpled envelope from my pocket and shook a medley of pills and spansules, some whole, some broken, all some variety of speed, into my palm. I took a couple and shared them round. Sham licked the dust off the envelope and we washed it all down with the ale. I lit one of Sham's 5/11s and we chugged through the night, waiting for the tingle. Wired as I was, and with the little extra nothing to write home about, I still felt it hit with a shiver, smack in the middle of whatever was impersonating my consciousness.

'If God made anything better he kept it for himself,' said Sham.

I tickled her ear.

'The Devil made the world, so I guess we got Satan to thank for this shit.'

'That's blasphemy,' shouted Bruiser over the roar of the engine.

'No, it's heresy. But it's the truth.'

We chuckled slyly, then whooshed with laughter, rushing upward like fugitive balloons.

'What's the new drummer like?' I asked, as the wagon rumbled east and the morphine and speed bathed me in grace.

'Not as good as you,' said Sham. 'But I guess it'll be Doomsday afternoon before we get you back rattling the traps.'

'I figure on resting for quite a while. How's Good King Wenceslas these days?'

'Same old, same old,' said Bruiser. 'Wence was really sorry to hear you got captured. He says he knows now that you had nothing to do with the kidnap. He'll see you're okay. Plenty of room to hide away. You're going home.'

Home. The place where, when you have to go there, they have to take you in.

'Nearly there,' said Sham. 'Just hold on.'

We scooted across the causeway. The marsh sparkled with frost under a silver blaze of stars. Ahead, peeking through the trees on the shoulder of the lake, was the Victorian bulk of the Refuge, once an asylum for the criminally insane. A green glimmer from his study testified to Wence's vigil. Like Napoleon and many another sad captain, Wence didn't get much sleep.

Bruiser skidded the bandwagon to a stop, as close to the front door as he could. The green light in Wence's study went dark. My legs were stiff now and I had difficulty getting out. Sham and Bruiser linked arms with me and gently glided me across the gravel and up to the baronial front door. The door creaked open and Wence appeared, holding a dark lantern. He slid back the aperture and a narrow beam of yellow light dazzled my eyes.

'Lingus, how good of you to come home. And on Twelfth Night, too. There's someone here, familiar with your misrule, who is keen to renew his acquaintance with you.'

In that moment I knew my candle had finally guttered. Sham cursed Wence for a traitor, and Bruiser started babbling some speed-freak gibberish of an excuse that I was nothing to do with him, and then let go my arm. I wanted to run but my legs said crumple. As I went down, with Sham still holding on, a man stepped out from behind Wence.

'Glad to see you again, Lingus,' said Mister Sweet. 'We

knew you would come home at last. I think, Mister Razumski, that we may as well take the boy away now. I'll have one of my men call ahead to Governor Galopede. The Governor will have a tender ready on the quay to whisk young Lingus here across the estuary to his home for the very foreseeable future. His Majesty's Hulk *Vindictive*.'

'Where there's just the sort of correctional programme a prodigal son like Lingus will benefit from,' said Wence.

They sounded like a well-rehearsed double act, but who was the comic and who was the feed, I couldn't tell. I didn't feel much like Top Banana myself. I wanted to go with the morphine flow and shut down my station but the speed circuit kept me in the loop. I floated above my body and looked down with curiosity at my banshee-moon face, with eyes like flying saucers and, despite everything, a wide grin.

'Looks like a satisfactory outcome all round, Mister Razumski,' said Mister Sweet.

'More than satisfactory, I should say, Mister Sweet,' said Wence.

CHAPTER 2 ①

Wenceslas Razumski was the American son of a Bohemian mother and Polish father. Wence was Director of the Refuge, now a community arts centre and bolt-hole for art freaks like Bruiser and Sham, and a sanctuary for waifs and strays and drummers like me.

The Refuge was home to a shifting population of shady characters who worked with stone and chisel, paper and scissors and paint, light, words, sound and music. In return for a plot of studio space in a disused day-ward, dormitory or padded cell – where they distilled the essence of their private nightmares – Wence marshalled them in huge outdoor extravaganzas where tightly drilled routines and the weather combined in his hall-of-mirrors distortion of history. Day by day and through the night, Wence's acolytes shinned up scaffolding, scurried across catwalks and teetered on beams and spars. They carried pots of glue, coils of rope and canvas sheets, like tipsy sailors about to rig ship. Come sun or snow, wind and rain, the structures reared up, as though mushroom-crazed tepee dwellers were on a cathedral jag. The climax of every show was death by fire. The Tower of Babel or the Towers of Ilium, the battlements of Camelot, the Colosseum, all tumbled in flames while the crowd shrieked and sparks flocked overhead. A marching band busked the arena. Smoke blotted the moon. Wence appeared high above the crowd, garbed as Achilles or King Arthur or Nero. Martian fighting-machines smote Weybridge with heat-ray and green smoke while Wence hectored his people, limelight on his fish-mask face and megaphone in hand.

Everyone came. Like some medieval dancing plague or crazy crusade, punters swarmed over the causeway and into the park, where the grass was thick with booths and Chinese lanterns festooned the trees.

It was all there in the Refuge library, squirrelled away in multimedia, the documents of Wence's steady career. He'd done time in the Marines, was a post-Situationist in Paris, had worked Prague, Warsaw and Damascus for the CIA. Then he got into the arts racket over here. At different times governments called him in. Inner city in flames? Send for the fire brigade. Send for the police to protect the fire brigade and then arm the fire brigade. Let the great and the good mull it over and send for Wence. It was a good living for Wence but it was the cheap option.

Not much bread – plenty of circus.

Late on Christmas Day I'd been sitting in the library, gently nodding over a wad of press cuttings, when Wence startled me with a hand on my shoulder.

'You voted yet? Come on, Lingus. The voice of Demos will be heard in the land.'

I slouched across to the screen and accessed the referendum. Why the hell not? Put me down as a yes. Wence leaned over me, breathing brandy fumes.

'You missed the King's speech. He's accepted the petition of Congress and says okay to becoming King of America too. No more presidents with hog-nuts for brains. And, once again, the unification of the English-speaking peoples.'

'I thought you spoke Spanish over there now. You know there's still people here in England not too keen on Andy One's move. They see it as cover for colonisation by the Mob.'

'Yeah, diff'rent strokes I guess. Say, I ran another trace on your mother, but nixes. We got shit for data.'

I shrugged and told him thanks for trying.

'Don't forget: you may be an orphan, but you're one of the family. If you ever need help, come to me. The Refuge is your home now. There's a heap of love in this house and I want you to dive right in and snuffle up. Share. Enjoy.'

Amen to that, I thought. As of Christmas Eve, I've been *sharing* and *enjoying* with Jude, your wife.

2 ②

It was Jude who first brought me to the Refuge. I took a shine to Jude right from the start. She was Wence's lawful-wedded and a good bit younger than him. I was starving when she found me and what clothes I had were in tatters and my skin was covered in sores. Sixteen months on from eviction and settled into orphanhood, I huddled in Soho, drinking rainwater and scavenging food from the bins. Life isn't easy for a boy on his own. You compete with the gangs for the juiciest bins and unless you get taken into the pecking order you're on slim pickings.

I landed lucky at first, running with the Meek up Shoreditch way and then chumming with the Sons of Onan, out of Shanty Town. But I got greedy one time with a load of dooby-doobs we hoisted from a Yankee sailor in Limehouse, and that put me beyond the pale. Word was out I'd welched and I learned the hard way that you don't fuck with the Sons of Onan. I still had my purloined stash, which I eked out, but they rotted my head and I was stalking pigeons by the end. It's not easy picking a live one among a flock of hallucinations. At last I grabbed a one-legged veteran and crawled under a bush in Soho Square to tuck in. I dozed for a while, letting my dinner go down, when a bunch of urchins woke me up screaming, 'Missy, Missy,' and then there was a pair of grown-up moccasins and I was dragged out. The woman knelt down and felt my pulse, then she opened her handbag and held a mirror to my lips. Before it misted I saw my face, eyes like slashes in a vandalised canvas and mouth smeared with blood and feathers.

I woke one morning soon after dawn. I was in a big attic room with birds twittering and scratching in the eves. I felt weak in a healthy sort of way, like after a long swim, and then I heard the sound of a drum, a steady cobbold-like rapping, and the shrill note of a flageolet. The tune was only a few notes but with peculiar angles and turns. I slid out of bed and over to the window and hauled myself up.

Through the glass I looked out on a river with mist clearing from a shallow valley and a shimmering lake. Between the river and the lake was a half-dug canal, awaiting completion of its last fifty-metre stretch.

I unlatched the window and leaned out. Below me were terraced lawns stepping down to a round pond with a sparkling fountain. Further away, towards the lake, the rising sun clipped a sycamore grove. Among some rhododendrons near the pond a man stood playing a flageolet with one hand and beating a tiny drum with the other. Ten paces off, a woman danced, the froth of a white petticoat surging around her heels. She had long red hair. She danced while the sun cleared the sycamores, then the music stopped and the two of them walked back towards the house. She looked up and saw me, calling up for me to get back to bed and stay there. I did as she said and then I heard her footfall on the stair and the rattle of the doorknob. She flounced into the room and sat on the bed, told me her name was Jude and asked mine. She put her hand to her mouth and coughed and asked about my family. I told her Dad was dead, a victim of the Terror. I gave her the rest of my story, sticking to the truth where it suited.

'You poor boy. And you never knew your mother?'

'She's alive somewhere, at least I think perhaps she is. I want to meet her someday, more than anything in the whole world.'

17

'Then I shall ask Sister Vincent to set her convent praying for that very intention. And I'll have a word with Orlando – he was the one playing the drum while I was dancing – to see if there's a spell he can work. It's only prudent to get the Devil on your side.'

She laughed. Her face was warm as butterscotch and her bottom lip plump as a cushion.

'When I'm better I want to learn to drum. Orlando can teach me. Then I can play for you, and you can dance for me.'

'Perhaps he might when you're properly on your feet.'

Convalescence was short and every day I got fatter. I stayed where I was and let myself be cosseted, and then one night I told Jude I was afraid of the dark and asked would she stay? She chucked me under the chin and giggled.

'You're not as innocent as you make out, are you?'

But she bent down and gave me a lingering kiss before she switched out the light, leaving me the dark and my phantoms.

All the time I lay in the room Wence never came near me. Jude talked about him from time to time and told me I'd see him soon enough when I was fit to go downstairs. She and Wence had me in mind to play Boudicca's cup-bearer in the Christmas show. Jude was to be Boudicca and I said I looked forward to it. She told me about the Refuge. As well as shows in the park, Wence sent teams of outreach workers into the city and surrounding country.

'I've just started work in Shanty Town,' she said. 'I love the warmth of the people and the humour they bring to their lives; they're so rich. And when you see what they create out of nothing, so inspiring. It's true what Wence says: there are no poor in spirit.'

She babbled about Wence for a bit and I felt there was something she was trying to tell me in a roundabout way, but loyalty wouldn't let her come out with it. Things could be better between them and it obviously wasn't money trouble so it must be sex. She rambled on and on while I listened politely, all the while wishing she'd take her clothes off and hop into bed. I gave her a touch of the Oliver Twists, burying my face in my hands and sobbing, letting her know I was crying for my mother. Jude gathered me in her arms and hugged me. Peeking through my fingers, I saw she was crying. Her plump bottom lip quivered and a bead of drool was welling in the corner of her mouth. Her eyes were closed and she rocked me to and fro. The drool on her lip brimmed over and trickled down her chin.

One morning I was woken by the skivvy coming in early for the chamber-pot. I felt fit and strong, a newborn Adam, but she pushed me off. Looking out the window, I saw a man walking below in the garden. He was stout and bearded and dressed in olive-green overalls with 'Wence' picked out in diamanté on his back. The rising sun shone on his bald dome. He walked among the rhododendron bushes, now bereft of blossom, parting the branches and peering through the foliage. Jude had told me there was a posse of feral cats in the grounds and that Wence had set some traps. Maybe he was checking them. Later in the day, when I got in the garden to take a look, I saw nothing out of the ordinary, except among the bushes towards the pond a child had lost her doll, a hand-crafted mannequin of plaited straw. I plucked it from a bush and held it up, filtering the evening sun blood-red through woven, empty eyes.

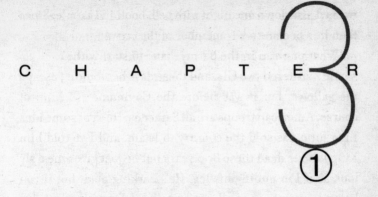

I found Jude on the lakeshore cutting withies by an old weeping willow. She looked me over.

'I told Orlando formal dinner tonight. He's kitted you out for a barn dance. No use complaining. Law unto himself.'

She shut her clasp knife.

'There, that should be enough. Be an angel.'

I took a bundle of withies from her and we walked back towards the house. She asked me what I made of Orlando.

'A bit peculiar. Why does he talk in that funny way?'

'Because he's mad and a warlock, I suppose. He was an inmate in the Refuge when it was an asylum, before we took it over. The other patients were shunted off and turned into soap or something. He hid in the cellars and drains. No one missed him; the place is a warren. He haunted the house after that and for a while we really thought we had a ghost. All a bit odd of course, because the Refuge was a Victorian loony bin and the ghost was a medieval court jester. That's what Orlando is, or pretends to be at any rate. He juggles, tumbles, does magic, fire-eating and escapology and he plays all manner of instruments. He's a wonderful drummer. Anyway, Wence tracked him down one night with bell, book and candle. Since then he's become a key member of the crew.'

'What put him in the barmy-kane to start with?'

'He murdered two GIs, and these days he wouldn't escape the gallows, but it was before the Commune. To him, of course, American troops are all Saracens. He's got some idea King John has sold the country to Islam, and I've told him King John is dead these 800 years but he just gives me a sly look as if I'm pulling his leg. He's barking mad, but if you listen long enough it all begins to sound quite logical and convincing.'

'How about Wence? Does Orlando have him figured for a Saracen?'

'No, he thinks Wence is a Crusader, some sort of Christian knight from Bohemia. Well, he's not far wrong, apart from the Christian bit. His mother was from Bohemia and there's talk of him getting his knighthood for all the community work he's done. That's one of the reasons the Homeland Controller is coming tonight.'

She made a sour face.

'That, and his stage-struck daughter wants to join the company. Kind of a quid pro quo.'

As we were crossing the terrace Orlando came towards us, wringing his hands. He said nothing but gave me a queer look as he passed. His teeth were long and yellow, his nose red and shiny and his face was pitted with scars. His cheeks were mottled mauve and pink. Strands of greasy black hair trailed across his forehead, where an angry eruption of yellow plukes clustered above his right eyebrow. The bells on his cap jingled as he nodded our way.

We went indoors and stacked the withies.

'What do you do with these?'

'They're ever so versatile. You can weave all sorts. I'm helping the residents make some frogs for an ornamental garden, in one of the better neighbourhoods in Shanty Town. Orlando's a dab hand at bending the withies. You should see his corn dollies too. They're quite a craze up in Shanty Town, as sex-magic fetishes. If the man's gone off the boil, or the woman is barren, they send for an Orlando corn dolly and Bob's-your-fertile-uncle.'

'I already saw one. I found it in the bushes and hung it up. I thought it was a child's doll. It was gone when I came by just now.'

Suddenly Jude was annoyed and told me I should have left well alone; the dolly was hers and it had to be placed in a sacred spot. Now she'd have to do the ritual all over again. I apologised and she calmed down. She went back to Orlando.

'He once got a cat to climb a rope and vanish into space. I saw that myself. And he claims to have the gift of prophecy but all I ever get in that line is a ragbag of riddles.'

'You say he's a warlock?'

'Yes, that's what I said. Perhaps he is.'

Wence stood outside his study, a waxwork smile on his face.

'Jude has told me all about you. Stay with us as long as you like, maybe help out when you get your head together. My wife needs young people around her. As you see, I'm getting on in years. Tonight you eat with us, like family. You know who's coming to dinner?'

'Jude says the Homeland Controller.'

'Sir Lionel Dingwallace. He's the man who dusted your daddy. But he isn't a monster, he's a patriot. Not a scoundrel patriot in the narrow nationalist sense, but a man with higher loyalties to the wider Anglosphere. You'll see for yourself. There's a lot of hate in this country, a corrosive bitterness over what happened, with the coup d'état and the suppression of the Commune. But all we need is love and reconciliation under the oceanic sovereignty of Andy One. Am I right?'

'Yes sir! Andy One is the king for me all right. What happened to Dad was just one of those things. I won't bring it up.'

'That's the spirit. But for tonight you're John Doe. I guess Sir Lionel can't remember every malcontent he snuffed but you've got an unusual name. I don't want his nose put out of joint.'

'Understood.'

'There's a countryman of mine coming to liven things up, Tatum Liotes is the name. He just got made Poet Laureate, God save the King.'

'What happened to D'Arcy Peever? My dad used to say his end-stopped couplets were the business.'

'He blew it with a poem about the Abdication. His argument was that the old King embraced the Whore of Babylon by turning Catholic the way he did. Andy took offence on his brother's behalf and Peever had to go. It seems like conversion to Rome is a sore spot with English poets.'

'The roots lie deep in our unwritten constitution. But I'm a Scotchman, by descent if not by birth. Whatever happens we lose out.'

Wence laughed.

'You lose out? You have to be Polish to know about losing out. But hey, maybe Jude can find you a better outfit for tonight. You look like a cowboy. Jude?'

'Sorry, I was miles away. Yes, best bib and tucker.'

We shook hands again and Wence went back into his study. A green light came on over the door.

3 ②

The dining-room lay beyond Wence's study, with places laid at a round table. A log fire burned in the grate, taking the chill off the early autumn air. The wall lights were dimmed and there were candles on the table. Around the room half a dozen waiters waited. Four bodyguards stood, one in each corner, sharp swivel-eyed men, packing heat. At the table we were nine. Anti-clockwise from Wence came Sir Lionel Dingwallace and his daughter Leah, then Jude and an Anglican vicar who went by the name of the Reverend Obadiah Bartleby. His daughter Sarah, who was a girl of my age, sat next to me. Then another youth, whose name was Art, was introduced as the son of Tatum Liotes, although he looked nothing like him and mumbled in an English accent. On Wence's left hand was Tatum Liotes himself, who sported 'T.L.' monogrammed in golden filigree on the lapels of his dinner jacket. He wore a toupee – quite a tight weave, and not a bad fit, but obvious. He was already drunk and he fanned an inebriated leer around the company, settling on me. For a moment I thought he recognised me.

Wence introduced us all round, and then the waiters stopped waiting to wait and began to wait, passing round soup or melon to start. The sommelier flashed a ritzy white at the Homeland Controller. Bottles were opened and the drinking began. Wence began to praise Tatum Liotes.

'Tate here is my good ol' buddy from way back. Tate kept the evildoers off till the chopper came in.'

'Shooing flies is all it was. Hey, this wine tastes like piss. Will anybody get to raisin' Cain if I go straight to the brandy?'

After a lengthy suckle on the brandy bottle, Tatum pushed away his untouched soup and asked the Homeland Controller if he had trouble with liberals.

'Not any more. Once Demos is embarked on the ship of state via the referendum, you'll find the liberal consensus was just a mirage all along. It melts away like the jolly old *neiges d'antan*. You'll get the odd liberal survivor here and there, plus a sprinkling of malcontent mavericks, and we cull those for the good of the herd. Have you ever thought of buying office back home, Mister Liotes?'

'No sir, boss! I'm a poet and a Greek, and that's enough for me. I'm an American too, to the tip of my Colt .45, but my Parnassian line goes back to Mount Olympus. My people made the first poetry, they invented it, and it suits me fine to be one of the unacknowledged legislators of the world.'

The Reverend Bartleby hoisted his face from his melon and said, 'Ah, Ariel. The divine Shelley!'

'Pardon me, padre, but Shelley my schlong. You know who spun that legislator riff first?'

'Do tell,' said Sarah Bartleby. 'Was he a Greek?'

'No ma'am, but I guess he knew Greek better than I do, I'm ashamed to say. It was Little Johnny Milton. An Oxford man, like yourself I'd guess, padre. And you too, boss?'

'Yes, indeed, the Reverend Bartleby and I were up at Balliol together.'

'Okay, get this. When Milt was cruising Oxford, back in the Black Death days, his buddies called him "the Lady of Christ's", that's a college-type joint, right? He was a stud, right fine and handsome. I saw a movie about him once.'

He made a pumping motion with his forearm, suggestive of coition. The Reverend Bartleby beamed, oblivious.

'My moral tutor, dear dead Doctor Boggs, asserted more than once that Milton's verse mimics the throb and swell of organ music.'

'You're on the money there, padre,' said Liotes.

Plates were cleared away and we hit the venison, and at the end of that Art was reluctant to let go, scouring the rim of the serving dish with the heel of a loaf. Liotes rebuked him for his manners, which coming from him was a bit rich, and Art told him to fuck off. While this was going on, I saw Leah making eyes at Wence. She was a big girl, beef to the heels. I put her in her early twenties.

Sir Lionel said to Sarah Bartleby, 'I understand you've been taking part in one of Mr Razumski's charades?'

'Daddy and I have been playing a Victorian vicar and daughter. Pre-Darwin, to avoid doctrinal complications, so it's been a most relaxing week. We've been waited on hand

and foot, so I've really had a chance to crack on with sewing my samplers.'

'Mister Razumski tells me one of my bright young men has also been here this week, playing a scullion. Sweet's the name, an Oxford man. Perhaps you ran into him?'

'Possibly,' said Sarah. 'But of course he couldn't come out of character, so one wouldn't know.'

'It's one of our sidelines,' said Jude to Art. 'Between the *son et lumières* we run holiday weeks where we resurrect the life of a bygone age. Marvellous therapy. So many of us long for a more organic society: the rich man in his castle, the poor man at his gate.'

'If he got a gate he ain't so poor,' said Liotes.

A trolley trundled up and puddings were passed round. Art was shovelling spotted dick into his gob at high speed, Liotes was on his second bottle of brandy. Jude was talking in a drunken monotone, but no one else was listening that I could see, as she banged on about the miracle of Shanty Town but how having a baby was the greatest miracle of all and chance would be a fine thing. Wence slobbered over Leah and told how his parade of images was an attempt to resurrect the soul of man, to find the truth behind the veil.

Then the Reverend Bartleby said, 'Ah, what is truth? Pontius Pilate asked the question almost at the foot of Calvary itself from where the road leads down to the tomb and the risen Christ. I find myself sometimes envying Thomas the Doubter who saw Jesus die on the Cross and who later was invited to probe the palpable wounds of our immortal Saviour. How lucky were the men of those times. I do so long for signs and wonders. In all my years of ministry, I have never been vouchsafed the shadow of the tiniest miracle. Does that make me an unsound churchman?'

Sir Lionel pinged his glass with a fingernail.

'I shouldn't emphasise the "unsound" business, Bartleby, not when I'm putting you up for Inspector of Chaplains in His Majesty's Hulks. It was trouble enough burying your connection with Brandreth.'

'Every family is entitled to one black sheep, and Jeremiah is merely a brother-in-law.'

'I'm glad to see you so unattached to him. I will keep the connection buried, and come New Year I shall bury Brandreth. He's proving stubborn but we'll break him yet.'

The talk got around to Japan, where Wence was sending a show on tour. He said that the best person to lead the crew was Jude, but she wasn't keen. She shook her head and mumbled something about how Wence just wanted her out of the way so he could fuck Leah. No one paid attention.

Sarah said, 'I wouldn't mind a trip to Japan. It would make a change from Saint Sepulchre's and ladling soup into those gummy mouths. I know charity is a sine qua non in our business, but it does so interfere with me getting on with my samplers. There's quite a demand for homespun artefacts among the more pious members of our congregation. I think it's the combination of an uplifting motto with exquisite embroidery that appeals.'

'"The poor will always be with you",' said the Reverend Bartleby. 'That's your bestseller, isn't it, my dear? Goodness knows, Saint Sepulchre's has more than its share of paupers in the surrounding parish. I sometimes think that's why we don't attract a better class of worshipper.'

'If you're looking for a change,' said Wence, 'you must go to Shanty Town with Jude. Jude says it's a melting pot of faith, with all sorts of new cults springing up.'

The Reverend Bartleby gazed across his zabaglione and sucked his spoon.

'The risen Lord walks where he will in the cool of the day. Perhaps that is where I might find my signs and wonders – *de profundis in extremis*, as it were – rather than in the flesh-pots of Babylon.'

'Darling Wence and Jude, I would love to take you up on your offer,' said Sarah. 'But Daddy goes green round the gills if I leave him alone for any length of time. We have no curate, you see, because we can't afford one, although thanks to my samplers we managed to scrape enough for a locum to cover for us while we're here on holiday. Gosh, I hope he's all right. He turned up at the last minute and I didn't get a chance to explain properly about Makepeace. He doubles as verger and churchwarden, and he lives in, as our general factotum. Makepeace is an old family retainer on Mummy's side. He was ever so devoted to her while she was alive.'

'I shouldn't worry, my dear,' said Bartleby. 'I have noticed a distinct improvement in Makepeace this last month or so. By all means, go into the depths with Mrs Razumski. I have often felt your horizons are painfully circumscribed.' He mopped his brow and loosened his collar. 'Just make sure you leave Makepeace detailed instructions about the soup. I should prefer not to face a hungry mob. Also, please ask him *not* to dust my Admiral Lord Nelson toby jugs and figurines in your absence. The last time you were away, on your advanced embroidery course, he waved his duster too vigorously and Nelson lost his remaining arm. And try to dissuade him from making me quite so much custard. I am partial to it, but not at each and every breakfast-time. Otherwise, go when you wish. Take time off from your samplers if need be.'

'Come the day after tomorrow,' said Jude. 'One of the Sons of Onan was killed, falling drunk from his pedishaw. I'm sure you'll find the funerary rites most exhilarating.'

Time for the guests to go home. I stood on the fringe of the throng, while people were milling about shaking hands and sucking faces and Wence announced that Leah was staying the night so he could run the video of *War of the Worlds*, the most recent show, to give her an idea of what she was getting into. Sir Lionel nodded consent and offered the Bartlebys a lift. Jude took out a glass-stoppered bottle with an eye-dropper in the cap and squeezed drops of something or other on her tongue. Tatum Liotes was almost legless and clung to Reverend Bartleby. Art circled the table, snatching scraps. I went outside to the limousines, where the Poet Laureate was now sprawled on the ground. I lent a hand to stow him in the leading car, face down in case he was sick. As the convoy drove away, Sarah leaned out and waved.

'It's a wrap,' said Wence. 'Jude, you and the boy make sure the skivvies clean the room up proper. I don't want it a pigsty like last time. Me and Leah have got work to do. Don't wait up.'

Wence led Leah away and they crunched across the gravel into the dark. Jude began a crazy, cackling laugh. She draped herself round my neck and sagged against me, almost dead-weight. She spoke in a baby voice.

'You know Wence's trouble? He can't come. Erection, yes. Penetration, yes. Ejaculation, no. I spoke to Sister Vincent. She tells me you need all three conditions fulfilled for consummation. So we're not really married, not yet, after all this time.'

She ground her lap against my crotch. I could feel Condition One take hold. I had to get inside her or I was going straight to Condition Three. I dragged her over the gravel. She said she wanted another drink, so I lumbered her back to the dining-room, figuring she'd forget about it once I got going. She tumbled to the floor, unconscious, which on balance probably suited me better. I heard a noise. I went through to the kitchen. A couple of waiters were left, playing pontoon. I told them to scram and I'd clear up. When they left, I locked all the doors.

I was halfway out of my trousers when a face peered out from under the table.

'Wotcha,' said Art. 'Any chance of seconds?'

C H A P T E R 4 ①

'First thing, the name's not Art, it's Arthur. And Tatum's not my real dad: he's adopted me and it's all legal, he showed me some papers. What I am is his catamite, what the likes of Bartleby call a sodomite's minion. It's not so bad if you're queer like me. And since Tatum's been top-gun poet it's a high old life, getting pissed in nobby saloons and meeting the likes of Lady Halitosis and that geezer tonight, Sir Ding Wallace or whatever he's called. I was never one for poetry as a nipper but I can see now it has its points. But I've had enough now. He's fair worn me out; you can see what he's like. It's not just drink and poetry, it's pills as well – uppers usually, but up, down or sideways it's all the same to him. So if I can stop here tonight, tomorrow I'll scarper.

'It all started for me when the Commune was on. There was a lot of fighting down our way, bit of a sideshow to the main event but nasty enough and you can still see the bullet holes in the walls and bombed-out houses. You see places where the bloodstains never seem to shift, where the mass executions happened. Tatum and I drove through last week. He's got an epic poem in mind: the story of the Commune.

Sir Ding is keen on the idea, tell the story as a fratricidal tragedy and end up preaching love. Make a national totem of the whole shoot.

'Anyway, we got out to scout about and I seen something I thought had died out. A little posy of flowers in a jam jar with a photo of some boy, in a hole in the wall where the brick was eaten away. Sort of a shrine, a war memorial, like Tatum's poem's going to be.

'You hear some stories. At the finish this Captain comes across a kid, no more than eleven, loaded pistol, big knife and a bag of squaddies' scalps. No chance, so it was drum-head court and then straight to the wall. The Captain was in charge. They were standing round waiting for the cardboard coffins to come up when the boy whistles the Captain over, shows him a watch and asks can he be shot with the next batch because he'd like to nip home to give it to his mum. The Captain thought of his own boy, I suppose, if he had one, so he puts him through a rigmarole of parole and lets him go, thinking all the time that's the last he's seen of him.

'They were shooting them wholesale and the first lot had been coffined up and the next lot were sorting themselves out in front of the wall and the squaddies were throwing down another few bags of sawdust when the boy comes tearing round the corner. "Here I am," he says. "Told you I'd be back."

'My dad went out to try to get food for us, and I reckon he got rounded up and shot for a looter. If he had a sackful of grub that was enough to punch his ticket. Maybe he just got sent to a camp. Ten on the rocks or cooking the waste in a nuke. Mum faded away after that, just sat in the kitchen with a face like a kicked-in telly; you couldn't get her to blink. Joan, my sister, went for help and while she was out Mum wet herself. She was pissing all down her legs and over the floor. I shook her so hard she fell off the chair and fetched up with her legs under the sink. Doctor Drain come and took her away, up Saint Helier he said. We walked up there later in the dark but when we got there we found they'd never heard of our mum. The hospital was full of soldiers from the fighting. Two coppers come and searched us for explosives and then they split us up and I got taken away for a good kicking.

'After a bit they let me out the cupboard and there was Joan, lying on a bench. Her eyes were blacked and she was all cut and bruised, legs scratched and blood under her fingernails. I asked her what happened and she didn't say, just they were letting us go. It took ages to walk back; Joan couldn't walk too well.

'We tried all sorts to find out what happened to Mum and Dad but we got nowhere and after a bit we just agreed to give up. We had to stand on our own now, and we had a bit of luck when Joan got taken on at a canteen for all the Yanks swarming in at the time. I used to go along and help out – there was always plenty of scoff on the go and I was like a mascot to the Yanks, gave them a bit of cheek. One night we were working and it was a darts match, Yanks against Carshalton Police. Joan was in a funny mood, staring at this big fat copper and muttering under her breath. She nipped to the lav and when she come back she looked like she'd been sick, she was breathing real hard. She went out front to collect glasses but she didn't pick any up.

'The big fat copper was at the oche, lining up a double, when Joan made a rush at him with what looked like a dagger in her hand. She stuck it in his eye and he went down screaming with Joan on top. It was a dart she had. They all rushed in to pull her off and it was bedlam. Two coppers had her up against the wall and they were punching her in the gut. A Yank tried to interfere but the coppers formed a cordon and kept him off, and they kept punching until Joan was puking blood. I picked up the knife we had for cutting lemons and next thing I was running through the cordon at a crouch and I come up on one of the blokes doing my sister and he's grunting and I can smell his filthy unwashed arse and I stuck him in the hole. Then I got kicked in the head and it was lights out.

'Joan and me were lucky to get out alive. If the Yank police hadn't come in with their dogs we'd have got mashed up good and proper. Funnily enough, the canteen being under American law done us a bit of good, took the edge off the sentences. Joan got twenty years at a camp for stroppy women up in Cumberland, cooking the waste, and I got five in Wakefield for the git I stuck.

'Wakefield wasn't so bad. I met this bloke in there, name of Dunford, inside since he was a nipper, and he put me straight about things. Old bloke he was and we shared a cell. He carried a book of Byron's poems everywhere, with a picture of Byron in the front. When he was a lad he looked a dead ringer for Lord Byron, so his teacher told him.

'I settled down to a nice, safe routine, three squares a day and cocoa at night, but there's a fly in every ointment and in our case it was the new screw they put on the landing, two weeks before my first Christmas inside. By this time I was going to Chapel on Sundays with Dunford. It was a nice break. Dunford was a Catholic and me bugger all, but I soon picked it up. The screws didn't care if I worshipped the man in the moon and the old priest who come in to work the oracle was well past it. He had one of the lags up on the altar with him to give him a prompt.

'One Sunday they had an extra thrash in the afternoon, where they show off this bit of bread that's the body of Jesus and they get all moony over the bread and grovel about. So I was grovelling about like a good'un, not wishing to appear the proverbial spare and joining in this song they have about the bread, when I notice the new screw giving me and Dunford a real dirty look.

'The grovelling came to an end and we all went off for tea. Fish-paste sandwiches on a Sunday usually but today was a pasty, cold. I'd eaten mine and was starting on Dunford's – he had a dodgy tum so I swapped him a fag – when the screw comes up and starts on about dirty old men buying favours and if ever he caught us at it Dunford would be in solitary for the duration, which in his case was life. He mouthed off a bit and Dunford sat there ignoring him, puffing away. That cheesed the screw. He told him to put his fag out. Dunford kept on smoking. The screw took his stick and cracked it across Dunford's knuckles and I thought he must have broken his hand but Dunford just sat there as if nothing was happening. Didn't even drop his fag. Then he looked at the screw and there was something hidden in that look, powerful like the body in the bread. The screw put up his stick and backed off.

'He left us alone for a couple of days, but he started getting cocky again, pushing us around in small ways you couldn't afford to argue about. After lights out I whinged on to Dunford about it but he said let it ride.

'Christmas come on and we made the cell look nice. Dunford had a crib and some wooden animals he'd turned out in the workshop and a Jesus he'd carved with a knife he kept hidden in his mattress. He had decorations made out of bog paper and cards from the time his mum and dad were alive. There was a fresh mash of hooch on down by the sties so we were all set for a merry Christmas.

'Christmas Eve was the first hint of real trouble. We got back from the carols to find the old dingly-dell in a right fine mess. The decorations were torn down and Dunford's baby Jesus was missing. In the crib was a turd with a sprig of holly in it. Even I know that's blasphemy. Dunford went white. He got his knife out and started whittling another Messiah while I cleaned up.

'That night the screws had a party. You could hear them singing and shouting their lewdness, sexing up the carols. Dunford was asleep, with a new baby Jesus gripped tight in his fist. On the stroke of midnight the new screw opened the Judas and told me to get dressed, I was wanted by the Guvnor. Trust me to fall for it. Coming by the jacks they jumped me and bundled me in. They shoved a bag over my head, twisted my arms and held me down the pisser, and pulled my pants down and stuck a truncheon up my hole. Then I was lying in the pissy old conduit while they pissed all over me. They wished me merry Christmas and then they fucked off.

'I took the bag off my head and the truncheon out of my arse and then I crawled out to the landing. All over the nick you could hear the sound of lags tapping out season's greetings on the plumbing. My cell was open. I crawled in and woke up Dunford.

'Christmas Day the new screw wasn't on duty. On Boxing Day, Saint Stephen's Day Dunford called it, the screw walked into the recreation room while we were sitting playing draughts. Dunford told me to go ponce a fag off Skel while he sussed the next move. I wheedled the snout off Skel and I was skinning up when the room went quiet. There was the screw on his knees, head lolling to one side and a faceful of agony, clutching at the knife in his chest. He fell down and started calling for someone, his wife or his mother I suppose. He sobbed and gurgled a bit and that was that. Dunford was back at the board, making his move.

'I had the cell to myself for a bit after that. The powers that be were doing away with people right, left and centre – well, left and centre anyway – and for a bit, during the First Terror, the nick was as safe a place to be as any. They had a couple of referendums by now to sort out who got what and Dunford wasn't a sex fiend or traitor, he only croaked a screw, so he got a private send-off instead of a public show. If the vote had gone a different way he'd have had his first outing in years. But I think he was happier the way it was. He wasn't the outdoor type.

'The Sunday after he was scragged I went to the chapel to say a few to the bread-man for his soul. After, I asked the priest if he'd say a special mass for Dunford. For a bit of snout he was agreeable.

'Dunford left me his book of Byron's poems. He'd written in it "To my good friend Arthur. We will meet again in Heaven." Some hopes!

'I did my time and one morning I was standing outside the gate with a few bob and a travel warrant and a tooth-brush. I didn't have Lord Byron. I'd used the pages for rolling snout. I sort of hoped there'd be someone to meet me but the road was empty. Except for the old woman who stood there every morning waiting for her son who'd snuffed it years since.

'I started for the coach station but they said they weren't taking warrants from lags any more. I stuck my thumb out for the south and got to Newark pretty quick, but after that the traffic thinned out and what there was was police and army mostly, with more Yanks than I remembered from previous. I tapped a couple of Yanks in a jeep in a lay-by, but they said no chance of a ride. Regulations. Too many outlaws about. It wasn't safe to be a Yank.

'I fetched up in Peterborough. I went to a convent and the nuns showed me to a warehouse packed with all sorts. Families, old folk on their own, orphans, mostly in rags. A few nuns were there, keeping order. They gave me a blanket and I kipped down next to a bunch of wandering players, sort of a circus. They were busking the town. We got talking and I chummed in with them, humping the gear and that. We dodged about the Fens the best part of a fortnight and I worked up a mind-reading act with one of the lads.

'We got down to Ware and set up in a derelict trouser-press factory. Then we come down with the flu real bad. I was first back on my feet and then the fire-eater, so we teamed up on the streets to get a crust. She did her act and I played a bit of a tune I learned on the hurdy-gurdy. That's when I met Tatum. Wence got wind of our outfit and come for a butcher's, looking to poach any likely talent. He had Tatum with him. They ran into us on the street. As soon as the fire-eater heard the Yankee voices she spat and did a runner, but me, I wasn't so choosy. We went for a drink together and they got me pissed in about ten minutes. I was sliding under the table when I sussed there was a sort of auction going on over me. I got the impression Wence was bidding by proxy for someone nobby. Tatum upped the ante by offering to adopt me, so I lifted my arm and shouted, "Sold!"

'I went off with Tatum, hurdy-gurdy and all. He had some idea of chanting his poems while I droned away on the snoring beast but we never got it together. I never learned more than the one fire-eating tune and folk soon get tired of that without the fire-eating. Poems don't suit. Maybe I could never prosper with it on account of filching it from my mates.

'Like I say, if I can kip here tonight, I'll be off in the morning and no bother. Sandwiches for the road? You're a gent. Cor, your lady friend here, Missus Whassname, she's dead to the world all right. If you want to go ahead, don't mind me. I can always go back under the table. No? Well, it is a bit late. Come on, I'll give you a hand with her.'

That was Wednesday night. Next day Arthur showed no sign of wanting to go anywhere. He lay holed up in my room, dossing down on the floor.

'What do I tell Tatum if he comes looking?'

'Say I've gone north. But he won't show. He's on a crystal-meth comedown. That's why he couldn't hold his drink. I reckon he'll burn opium a few days, then mandy-up and hug his twanky. Every speedhog got to slow down some time.'

Arthur unwrapped his packet of sandwiches. I went to the sink and squeezed toothpaste on my brush. In the mirror I saw Arthur open his mouth and post a sandwich, driving it home with the heel of his hand.

I rinsed and asked if he ever used dooby-doobs himself and he laughed a choked-up, masticated sort of laugh.

'What you mean is, have I got any? Sorry, mate, never touch 'em. They put you right off your grub. Besides, I'm high on life.'

I went to look for Jude. She wasn't about, but down on the lakeshore I found Orlando skimming stones. His flageolet lay on the ground beside him. I picked it up and blew a few notes. He smiled at me with a mouthful of tusky teeth.

'Jude says you want to learn music.'

'I want to be a drummer.'

'You don't fancy the flageolet?'

'I just want to drum. The tune you were playing for Jude was nice though.'

'Two tunes. The first is "The Cowcumber".'

'And the second?'

'"Well-Dressed and Thrown Away".'

I skipped a stone over the lake. 'Medieval pieces, I suppose.'

Orlando sighed. 'Someone's been filling your head with nonsense about me being a lunatic. I don't really believe we're living in the Middle Ages, and even if I did, I'd scarcely refer to them as such. I know the Refuge is a Victorian asylum, at least it was. My sense of history is quite healthy. The trouble with Jude and Wence is they have too much imagination.'

A cold wind ruffled the lake, scattering spangles of autumn sunlight. We sat in silence for a while. Orlando took a pouch from his pocket and rolled a fag.

'Want one? Here, take as much as you want, and while you're smoking with me, reflect on the peculiarity of a psychic refugee from the Middle Ages having such a post-Raleigh habit.'

I busied myself with the makings. Orlando blew out smoke.

'Ah yes, Wence and Jude. Nothing they like better than a mystery. Life would be so dull without. Take you, for instance.'

'Me?'

'Don't come the innocent with me. I've seen the way she lets you rub against her like a rutting tom.'

'You've hardly seen us together at all.'

'I've seen plenty, my little Kasper Hauser, my little peach of a foundling. Hauled into the world by strong, womanly arms, face all bloody and feathered, an innocent orphan. But you're very far from innocent. And of course, as you'll find out soon enough, you're not an orphan either.'

'Is my mother alive?'

Orlando cocked his head. 'Your mother? No idea. It wasn't your mother I was thinking of.'

* * *

That night I stared through my reflection in my bedroom window, out into the stormy sky. There, grafted on a black thunderhead of cloud, was dear old Dad, grinning. No doubt it was him all right, the man who died and rose again, who faked his death to forestall the vengeance of the Second Terror.

Arthur was snoring on the floor among a litter of crusts and milk bottles. I stepped over him and climbed into bed. I sat propped on my pillow for an hour or so, watching the night. Dad and the storm moved on. A silver boiling of fretful cloud flickered across the pale scab of moon.

4③

I was fidgeting about, trying to drop off, when there was a knock at the door. It was Orlando. He was wearing a long, gabardine raincoat smeared all over with blood and feathers. His hands and fingernails were bloody and clotted. A chicken-shit smell hummed around him. He perched on the bed.

'I've brought you a present. I thought it might cheer you up. You looked quite down in the dumps earlier. There are worse things than finding out you've still got a father. If you come over to Shanty Town tomorrow with us you'll see I'm not having you on. They say if you stand at the crossroads outside Percy's Cantina long enough you'll see everyone you ever knew.'

'I'd rather it was Mum. But I'll come.'

I kicked Arthur awake. He sat up, rubbing sleep from his eyes. He clocked Orlando.

'Who's this? Sweeney Todd?'

I introduced them. Orlando apologised for not shaking hands. He waggled his mitts to show why and the chicken-shit smell went up a tone.

'I've been doing the entrails. Everyone round here wants their fortune told on the hurry-up. I've done three tonight.'

He rummaged in his gabardine.

'Here's the present I brought you. With this you can wheedle Jude into bed and give her a right royal seeing-to. No need to wait till she's unconscious.'

I cradled the corn dolly and tickled its ribs. It grinned at me with thick, plaited lips. An erection of tightly woven stalks lurched up over its belly.

'Coochee coo,' said Arthur. 'He's a cheeky chappie, ain't he just?'

The Midden loomed over Shanty Town, a truncated cone of clay maybe a hundred metres high, topped with a plateau. Local legend said it was the leavings from the excavation for a government bunker. The lower slopes were pitted with craters and tangled nests of scrap jealously guarded by the scavengers who made their living there. Higher up were terraces, landscaped by the shanty dwellers and planted with bushes and stumpy trees. At night you could climb high and watch the lights of London. I'd lain up there many a time.

Now Bruiser pounded the gears and hauled the band-wagon into a clear patch of cinders on the flank of the Midden. Nearby, Sons of Onan guarded a bonfire, waiting for the signal to torch it. A ramp led away from the bonfire to the summit, looping the Midden like the chute of a helter-skelter. The side of the chute was bounded by a wall of tyres. We climbed out of the wagon. Bruiser handed binoculars to Jude. She studied the summit for a while and then passed them to Sarah Bartleby.

'Gosh,' said Sarah. 'Just in time.'

I stood behind her with Bruiser, Sham and Orlando. A mournful procession was dragging across the rim of the plateau. A garish painted banner fluttered in the wind and a melancholy chant wafted about us, blown down from the heights. Jude told Sarah to give me the glasses.

'Go on, take a look. You used to know these people.'

I raised the binoculars and focused on the procession, scanning the ranks for dear old Dad. Nowhere in sight. The procession halted and a four-wheeled luxury pedishaw was pushed forward, teetering on the lip of the ramp. The dead jockey was tied to his machine. He'd been stuffed and mounted, quite a neat job, and two white identity discs were screwed into his eye sockets. Orlando had a spyglass of his own.

'Looks like they broke his limbs and splinted him.'

He was about to go into the finer points of the taxidermist's art but Sham shut him up, out of respect for the dead jockey. The singing petered out. The banner dipped and at once the bonfire was ablaze. Up on the heights they turned the pedishaw loose and it took off fast, whizzing round the Midden lower and lower, bouncing off the tyre wall until it rattled round the last curve and hurtled across the cinders with the dead jockey rocking in the saddle and the wind humming fiercely through the spokes. The last few metres of ramp were set up at an angle and the pedishaw took off, somersaulting into the maw of the fire. Black smoke flecked with fierce sparks filled the air as the fire collapsed around the dead jockey and his rig. Bruiser cheered.

'Kinetic cremation!'

We backed off. There was silence as we watched the fire flare up and then damp down to a steady blaze. A deputation from the Sons of Onan approached us, their right arms raised in greeting. I recognised Arnie but none of the others. They were wearing some kind of uniform these days, a bit like the Scouts, with shorts, khaki shirts and berets. They wore lanyards draped across their chests. Jude ran up to Arnie and gave him a smacking kiss.

'Beautiful, Arnie, beautiful. Inspirational.'

Sarah said to Sham, 'It was rather moving. A bit unorthodox, but none the worse for that. I wish Daddy could have seen it. His funerals have been getting rather dreary of late.'

Orlando and I stood by with dumb smiles. Arnie bid us welcome, at some length, finishing with, 'Now we feast. All are welcome in the Lodge of the Sons of Onan.'

Arnie looked gravely at me and offered his hand.

'Even those who turn renegade from our tribe. Today, all are kin. Surely we will feast together and drink the Good Oil.'

Jude took out her glass-stoppered bottle.

'Speaking of which, I could do with a refill.'

'Do I get a taste?' asked Bruiser.

'All in good time,' said Arnie.

It looked like we were set to party. Bruiser went to the bandwagon and came back with a gallon jar of Johnny-Jump-Up. He took a slurp and passed it round. Sarah looked doubtful but didn't want to be left out. She heaved it down and came up gasping.

'Gracious, what's this?'

'It's a cocktail,' said Bruiser.

Arnie told a Son to guard the wagon and we set off for the Lodge. When I lived here, the Lodge was only an idea of Arnie's that we kidded him about. Now it was done, a long, timber-framed hall with proper glass windows and a pitched roof made of corrugated zinc. Arnie took us inside and through to a veranda overlooking the back yard. On the way I clocked the roof timbers hung with banners and a dais at the far end of the hall with a big book open on a lectern.

In the yard a dog-roast was in full swing. Over the white heat of a barbecue pit, skinned and jointed hunks of dog were broiling on a griddle. A red-faced Son in a white overall was busy with a prod. Close by on a wooden pallet another Son was carving genteel portions of dog, done to a turn. He crammed the meat into pockets of bread and topped them off with dandelion leaves. Thirty Sons waited in line. One by one they took their dog-meat parcels and sloped off to the liquor stand.

From a death row of kennels in the corner of the yard came snuffles and whines and a furious scratching. An Alsatian skin was draped over a hurdle to dry. Two small urchin boys were cleaning a dog's head in a bucket of caustic soda.

'How about another drink before we eat?' said Bruiser.

'How about another drink, period?' said Sham. 'I've never seen anything so disgusting in all my life.'

Orlando hunkered down to give the boys a hand with the dog's head. In a few minutes it was ready. Arnie took the gleaming white skull and mounted it on a pole outside the Lodge.

'Our totem!' he said proudly.

'How frightfully jolly,' said Sarah.

Arnie went over to the liquor stand to get us all a snifter. Meanwhile we polished off Bruiser's jug. Passing it to Sarah, I said, 'Two dinner parties in three days. It's becoming a habit with us.'

Sarah looked scornfully at me.

'I think this counts as luncheon, actually.'

The smell of roasting dog, rich and greasy, wafted over us. Jude stood with her hands on her hips and sniffed the air with gusto.

'This is the life!'

Drinks came up on a tray, clay pots decorated with verses from Proverbs and brimful of volatile hooch. My motto was, 'A strange woman is a narrow pit', so Dad was around somewhere. That was one of his favourite saws. I scanned the throng, but still no sight of him. Arnie proposed a toast 'to our dear departed' and we tossed off the liquor. Through the blur I saw a platter of dog-meat sandwiches heading our way. Arnie signalled the bearer to hang back.

'Eat later. Now it is time for the Offering.'

On the other side of the yard was a hut, partly hidden by bushes. There was no window or door but a low hatch at ground level. The party quietened down. A Son approached the hut with a tray loaded with bread and meat. He knelt down, bowed his head reverentially and knocked on the hatch. I nudged Orlando and took his spyglass. The hatch opened but no face appeared. The tray was pushed through and the Son got to his feet. A hand appeared and beckoned with a long, bony finger. Here was the hand that wielded the scourge, here the third finger and the gold and black ring with the masked satyr's foot crushing the serpent's head. The server inclined his head to the aperture to hear my father's words. He stood up and shouted, 'Chilli sauce, and lay it on thick!'

An acolyte dashed forward with a ladle.

'Now Our Father will surely eat!' proclaimed Arnie.

The party began to swing. Arnie said apologetically, 'He only walks by night.'

There was a dreamy look in his eyes, as he said, 'Surely the time will come when he walks by day.'

'Amen,' said Jude.

Arnie snapped to attention.

'Come. Feast with the Sons of Onan.'

We squatted in the dirt. Dog-meat sandwiches went round.

'You're not eating,' said Jude.

I grunted and nibbled a dandelion stalk. Sham excused herself and went to find the latrine.

The food was soon gone. Orlando joined the urchins who were playing jacks with a handful of doggy testicles. Sarah wiped her mouth and took a mighty swill from a jug decorated with the motto, 'A whore is a deep ditch'. She toppled over and Bruiser caught her on the way down. Arnie declared it was time to go into the Lodge and taste the Good Oil. Sarah sat up and clapped her hands.

'Good Oil. Good-oh.'

Leaving Orlando playing cat's cradle with a length of intestine, we went in, and Arnie invited us to sit on a dogskin quilt. He took Jude's bottle and filled it from a can. He twisted the stopper and handed it back. He handed round the can and we all took a couple of beads on our tongue. It came up quick, warm in the throat and deep-sea cold in the bowels. My legs felt heavy and a rushing wind filled my ears, fading until there was a sharp, clear silence like I was on top of a mountain. I tried to shut my eyes but the lids were frozen open. The walls of the Lodge no longer met at right angles and pulsating blisters were forming across the dogskin quilt. I looked round. My chums had hairy faces and pointy snouts and ears. When Arnie spoke his voice wobbled like jelly on springs, a thousand echoes clamouring in chorus with him.

'Blessed be the name of High John, whom we call the Conqueror, who furnishes the Good Oil and takes away the sins of the world.

'Blessed be High John, who walks by night, tending the sick, who succours the dying with the Good Oil.

'For we are one tribe, lost in the wilderness these countless years and party to no Covenant. Therefore make we a Covenant of Blood with martyrs gone before and martyrs still to come. And the seed of our tribe shall not wither.

'For behold there comes One greater than I-and-I, who leads His People from the brink of the Bottomless Pit into the Paradise prepared for our tribe, and His Coming is surely prophesied. So says High John, whom we call the Conqueror.

'All Time shall be redeemed and all abominations and demons cast into the Bottomless Pit, from whence they come with legs above their feet, to wander through the world for the ruin of souls.

'Our tribe shall sit alone in Glory. So says High John, who calls himself Daddy, whom we call the Conqueror. And the Infidel shall grovel in the mire.

'The Trumpet of Apocalypse shall sound and the veil of the Temple be rent. So that all shall be revealed by and by.

'A little child shall lead them, born in spirit of man alone and conceived of a virgin. All this shall be done through High John, whom we call the Conqueror, who calls himself Daddy.

'World without end, amen.'

Sham was biting her lip, trying hard to stifle a laugh. Bruiser was catatonic, eyes like a toad and skin all mottled. I put him down as an overdose. Jude and Sarah held hands and rocked to and fro. Arnie stilled them with a touch.

'When can I see him?' said Jude.

'Me too,' said Sarah.

'It is not yet time,' said Arnie. 'Let us pray.'

Jude and Sarah bowed their heads.

Arnie began, 'The mightiest hand of God is always down upon us. My own small tongue is but a stone in size . . .'

I left them to it and staggered outside. Orlando joined me for a smoke. We watched the urchins pass by carrying a stuffed Alsatian, the summit of the taxidermist's art.

'High John the Conqueror, eh? There's a fancy moniker if ever I heard one.'

He whistled admiringly after the mummified dog.

'This place has class. Think I'll come more often. Fancy a sandwich?'

The moon leered through my bedroom window, wearing Dad's face. I crossed the room and closed the curtains.

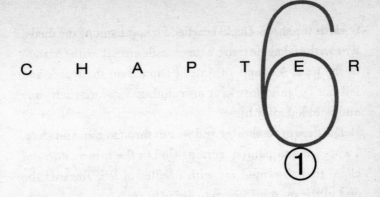

C H A P T E R 6

1

Winter came on fast. Orlando took me running. Under the plooky skin was a strong and supple frame.

'A drummer is an athlete; nearest to it is a boxer, you dig? A real hep-cat drummer need legs like saplings, steam-hammer arms, and his reflexes got to be razor-keen. A cat needs wind and the best way to shape up is roadwork. Remember Newt's Law: what you dish out you get back. You'll find out when you gig for two hours behind a full kit. Sure, what you play with Bruiser and Sham is just rockabilly, a single snare and no tom-tom, but you still need the wind and it's no use looking to those little blue leapers of yours to make up the difference. You need it on-line and intravenous from Big Mamma Nature. You dig?'

I dug. No problem there. Generally I preferred Orlando's beatnik style to his medieval gig, but I had to admit the running kit of hipster shades and beret and Gauloise hanging from the corner of his mouth looked out of place against the November landscape.

The wind blew strong across the lake, whipping waves

towards the shore. Ducks scuttled for cover among the reeds. We ran the lakeside track, a three-mile circuit, with Orlando in the lead. A couple of times I slipped on the leaves and fell but Orlando just kept on running. I got up each time and hobbled after him.

The days grew shorter and we ran through rain and sleet. I wheezed and panted, cursing God in the brown slurry of cloud that showered me with needles of ice. Towards the end of the month I began to enjoy it.

Orlando took me north, towards Epping, through the forest where the ground rose and fell so you got a kind of motion sickness and the branches and creepers overhung the track and smacked our faces. We climbed a hill, slogging through the trees, and reached a clearing where Orlando finally folded, hands on his knees. I sat on a fallen tree-trunk and watched my breath balloon white and smoky in the grey drizzle. Orlando sat beside me. He put a finger to his nose and pressed a nostril, blowing hard. A wad of snot landed at his feet. He rubbed it into the mould with his shoe.

'People have got a down on drummers. We're musical savages, dig? The first music back in the days of old Cave-Daddio was the clack of ribs on skulls to guide the hunter home. Everything has a soul. *Ecoutez.*'

He bunched his fist and rapped his knuckles on the tree stump. Somewhere in the forest a woodpecker was drilling, and beating up from the south was the busy drone of a helicopter. It flew overhead, a stars and stripes tattoo on its belly.

'The Man has a base a mile north of here. We'll run that

way for a bit. There's a folly in the woods, some kind of nobleman dude's whacko idea of a Greek temple. You ought to eyeball it. We can come back round by High Beech.'

We got up and jogged through the trees. The light was beginning to fail. We came to a tangle of brambles on the lip of an old bomb-crater. I swung up into the fork of a tree and looked across. On the far side of the crater was a cascade of rubble where the wall of the temple had collapsed. The severed head of Apollo stared back at me.

We climbed into the crater and picked our way among the rubble, scrambling up the far slope into the ruin. The floor was black and white marble and strewn with leaves blown in by the wind. Around the walls were alcoves where lamps once burned before statues of the gods. The roof was full of holes and the sky was darkening fast with a storm coming on. The rising wind blew through the holes in the temple roof and made a curious sucking and whistling. I had heard much the same coming from chest-wound casualties during the Commune. I looked round for Orlando. He was lurking in a pool of shadow, humming along with the wind. In a far corner something white caught my eye, bundled in an alcove and partly concealed by debris from the roof.

It was the face of a man, an American soldier, snug in the niche, his body wedged tight by swelling limbs. His eyelids were closed and his hands folded over his crotch with his legs tucked under him. There was no obvious sign of violence, but for sure he hadn't hoisted himself up and died of boredom. Orlando crept up beside me.

'Crazy scene, eh?'

He was smiling. I said I wanted to take a closer look, to

see if the soldier still had his dog tag. Orlando knitted his fingers into a cradle and I stepped up to the dead soldier. The young American smelled at home here, among the dead leaves. He looked like he'd fallen asleep in front of a television, except I was aware of the deliberate composition of his limbs, like he'd been in the care of an eccentric undertaker. There was no dog tag around his neck, but I tweaked a white card from the breast pocket of his shirt. There was writing on the card but the damp had made it blotchy and it was difficult to read. We went outside, where the light was better. The drizzle had turned to rain.

'For goodness' sake Orlando, take those glasses off.'

He plucked them from his face and hooked them in his shorts.

'Well, can you dig it?'

I held it up and tilted it to catch the light. In green ink it said, 'How long wilt thou sleep, O sluggard? When wilt thou arise out of thy sleep?'

I said to Orlando, 'Yes, I can dig it. It's the Authorized Version, Proverbs six, verse nine. Here, see for yourself.'

Orlando refused the card.

'I know what it says. Not my choice, I must say. The victim was but not the verse.'

He began to laugh. Suddenly he looked at me coldly and said, 'I don't care much for these new-fangled renderings of Holy Writ, do you?'

I heard a whistle blow three short peeps, away to the north.

'Saracens!' shouted Orlando.

He took off down the slope, leaping nimbly among the

chunks of rubble. An adrenalin shock jolted my heart and I jumped down in pursuit. There was a flash of lightning and then thunder, and a cloudburst beat down the branches around us. We cut into the woods at an angle to our original descent. We stopped for a moment to get our breath and were about to move off when the sharp crackle of a radio came spitting through the trees. On the fringe of the clearing I saw the camouflage stripes of a soldier who was talking a radio argot, bristling with acronyms, while he stared at the sky. A helicopter was coming close. We slipped away and after about fifty metres I sneaked a look from behind a tree. Orlando tapped me on the shoulder and then I heard the rasp of a rifle bolt drawn back.

'You stop right there. Hands up. Higher. On your head.'

My arms felt heavy as I lifted them. The speaker came into sight. He was a forest ranger dressed in oilskins, an old greybeard of seventy, hefting an ancient Lee Enfield. He prowled round us, keeping the rifle to his shoulder and sighting down the barrel at my head.

'What are you doing out here? Black Alert's on and nobody shouldn't be in these parts, excepting them who should. Squaddies are out and the Yanks. I'm surprised you ain't run into them. Dressed a bit light for this weather, ain't you?

'We're out running', I said. 'We're art students.'

'Art students? Oh aye, of course you are, and I'm Robin Hood. I reckon how you're a couple of decoys set on by Control to fox me. I ain't takin' no chances.'

He lowered the rifle to his hip and covered us one-handed while he took a whistle from his pouch. He blew three blasts and grinned, well-pleased.

'What I say is you two are soldiers in civvies. Blue Team.'

I shook my head.

'Afraid not. If there's some kind of exercise going on we're not part of it. Can't we just go home?'

I heard voices approaching and then bodies crashing through the bracken. Soldiers appeared, young men with tidy moustaches and helmets decked with fern. They carried rifles and snub-nosed automatic weapons. They stood around us, silent, suspicious and hostile, while the forester babbled his tale to their Corporal. While he was talking, an officer came up. He was clean-shaven, no older than his men, and he carried a long, silver-tipped cane. He wore a cape over his shoulders. The forester now addressed himself to the officer, who walked up and down while he listened, occasionally prodding the earth with his cane. Now and then he stopped and turned over the soil as if he were looking for something – truffles maybe. He looked sleek and well-fed. My arms were aching and I was shivering with cold. Orlando stood quite still with his hands on his beret and an idiot grin on his face. The forester showed no sign of shutting up, still babbling about decoys. The officer tapped him on the shoulder with his cane and put a finger to his lips.

'Darling, do shush! The way you're going on, one would think our friends here are war criminals. I'm sure there's some misunderstanding.'

He turned to us.

'I don't for one minute believe you're part of this show. You don't smell like soldiers to me. One thought occurs and niggles somewhat, that you're irregulars brought in by Blue

Team. Against the rules, but who are we to talk, with Dorcas here on our side.'

He tapped the forester on the head with his cane. The man beamed.

'Of course, you're free to go if you want, but if you could see your way clear to playing ball for a minute or two, just to nip my niggles in the bud, then I'd be most grateful.'

I relaxed and lowered my arms.

'Put those arms back up!' screamed the Corporal, dropping to one knee and pointing his rifle at my gut. The other soldiers cocked their weapons. The officer waved his cane.

'I say, chaps, steady on!'

He spoke gently to us.

'It's a bind, I know, but for the sake of realism, would you very much mind keeping your arms up for the moment? The chaps need the feel of the real thing.'

I kept still and dumb, signalling with my eyes that it was fine by me. I was suddenly conscious of the sour reek of my armpits.

'Now . . . Name, rank and number? Ha ha, only joking. Where are you chaps from?'

I waited for Orlando to speak but he kept mum. I spoke up and told him we were from the Refuge.

'Of course, that's it. I knew I'd seen your friend before. He's the chap who sends the moggy up the rope. Can't reveal how it's done, I suppose? No, I thought not, professional secret, eh? Well, we all have those buried away. I'm the chap who supplied the bangs for *War of the Worlds*. Remember me?'

Orlando nodded.

'Captain Prometheus, the King's Own Pyromaniacs. No, just having you on. Give my best wishes to Mister Razumski when you see him. Capital chap. Jolly enterprising of him to ask us in to help. Heat-ray, artillery bombardment, green smoke, the lot. The CO was pleased as Punch. Nothing like a spot of community relations for reversing the negative image of the army with you arty types.'

He spoke to the Corporal.

'I think we can bring their arms down now, can't we?'

Gingerly we lowered our arms. The officer looked at his watch and pointed down the trail with his cane.

'You'd better cut along, and so must we. Home after dark, eh? You can always say we kept you out past bedtime.'

Orlando and I glanced at each other. We took a few slow steps along the trail. Suddenly the officer barred the way with his cane.

'You chaps were up in the folly, weren't you?'

My mouth was dry. Orlando grunted.

'Good show you came out when you did. We've got a live firing exercise on.'

He flourished his cane. Out of the east, rolling towards us, came the rising whine of aircraft. Three explosions close together shook the earth. The curve of the hill shielded us from the blast. The Captain slapped his thigh with the cane.

'Ooh what a sexy noise! I do love a good bang.'

He took a silver cigarette case from his pocket and lit a cigarette in the shelter of his cape.

'Don't suppose a couple of healthy outdoor types like you have any time for these, but I must say, after a good bang, I like a good smoke.'

He sucked smoke greedily.

'My chaps saw you go in. They had strict orders to stay outside but even so they nearly went in after you. Thought you might be a couple of loopy conservationists intent on martyring yourselves. When you came out sharpish we let you run into Dorcas, to see what he's made of, and I must say he's made of splendid stuff, aren't you, old boy?'

We congratulated the forester, shook hands with the Captain and said our goodbyes. We set off down the trail. I nudged Orlando and we began to jog. After a shaky and gasping start our breathing hit a steady rhythm. Orlando began to hum, a snatch of modal madness, just the tune at first and then the words until he sang in full-throated exultation.

Sumer is icumen in. Lude sing cucu!

The wind shrieked and the hail set about us like a scourge.

I was bone-weary when we reached the park and began the run up to the house. In the aftermath of adrenalin shock I stumbled head-on into the gale, my body trembling and jerking like a post-mortem demonstration of Galvano's reflex. Muscle tone was almost gone and my head bounced around like a punchball. The horizon tilted at a crazy angle and was constantly shifting until I felt like I was rolling into the troughs of an angry sea.

Orlando set the pace, lifting his long bony legs deliberately, like a wading bird. We seemed to be moving very slowly. Ahead of us, rising up to the house, stepped the terraces, massive now as cliffs. At the carp pond the path branched left and right, changing from gravel to paving-stone. Orlando jinked left but I could do nothing but stride straight ahead, feet scrunching on gravel and slapping on stone, then silence as I sailed out over the water, and then the splash as I hit.

I lay on my back, bedded in slime, staring up through the water, watching bubbles of breath quit my body. I knew I should rise but I had no strength in my limbs, and my will was fading like the ripples above me.

Fat fish slithered across my face.

I lay cocooned in a blanket. A single candle burned in the window where Orlando kept vigil, twisting and twining the straw sinews of a dolly. As he worked he sang softly.

'Six dukes went a-fishing down by the seaside
One spied a dead body laid by the waterside
They took out his bowels, stretched out his feet
Garnished his body with myrtle so sweet.'

The candle was jittery in the draught from the window. I listened to the song and watched the play of shadows on the ceiling. Outside, fog chafed the window-pane. The draught curled about me, chilling my face, hands and feet. I closed my eyes and drifted in and out of sleep. On the brink of a dream I sensed the presence of Jude. I felt her hand on my brow, ice against ice.

Sleep was welling in me, billowing under me and bearing me out to sea in a white, blinding fog. I shouted but my voice was baffled. Naked on an ice floe, I lay prone and breathed the stink of myrtle. Above me in whiteness I heard the creak of vast, outspread wings and the alien groan of birds.

—Has he woken yet, Orlando?
—No, but he's very restless.
—Fever?
—Yes, I've been mopping his brow with this. Catch.
—What a delicious scent. Is it myrtle?
—Yes.
—There, there. Lie still my lovely. Don't fret.
—He's dreaming. See his eyes flicker. A nightmare took him some time ago. He babbled of a park where statues come alive, of a dead body in a grotto and white, swooping birds. He spoke to his dead father as if he were alive, here in this room. I fear for his mind.
—There, my lovely, lie still, lie still.

—Who is the dolly for?
—A barren woman up in Shanty Town. She has waited long but a spell can't be rushed, nor does it always work the way you intend, but nonetheless it works at last. All things are delivered in time.

—This woman . . . Why doesn't she get High John to treat her?
—She doesn't fancy the treatment.
—Oh.

—Have you met him, Orlando?
—High John? No.
—I've tried to get in to see him through Arnie. No luck so far.
—There, that's done. What do you think?
—Nice work, as usual. I hope it works better for her than mine did for me.
—A spell can't be rushed. You gave up too soon on the dolly.
—You couldn't have a word with Arnie, could you? The Sons might listen to you since you're a man.
—I thought you were in their good books, with the garden project and everything. They invited you to the funeral.
—Yes, but it's so far and no further. The curtain always comes down just as it's getting interesting. They won't let me stay after dark.

—Orlando, do wake up. He's terribly restless again and I don't know what to do. Shall I give him a drop of the Good Oil? It is a sacrament after all, a sacrament of healing. Arnie says that High John says it mends the fracture between body and soul.
—You don't have to sell it to me.
—No, but I've seen you give me funny looks when I get the bottle out.

—I don't mean to carp, but if it's a sacrament perhaps it should be administered sparingly, that's all.

—I don't abuse it. Arnie says High John says it can't be abused anyway. A sacrament should be taken at will.

—A sacrament is holy when performed out of piety. Nothing is sacred or profane in itself, only so far as it mediates between us and our god. Our ancestors practised human sacrifice and cannibalism. The light of revelation led them on. Who are we to say they sinned?

—I think we're getting off the point. Give me a hand with Lingus. I don't want him thrashing about and knocking the bottle over. It's too precious to spill.

—Orlando? This treatment of High John's that the barren woman didn't fancy, what is it exactly? Is it the laying-on of hands?

—Not just hands, although hands do come into it. It's a very personal . . . one might say . . . priapic service. He plays Priapus. That's his prescription.

—Goodness, how exotic. Who's Priapus?

—Oh dear, Orlando. I'm not sure the Good Oil was right after all. He seems worse.

—I've seen cases of possession like this. What's he muttering?

—I can't tell. Something about his father again. Lingus, darling, lie still. Oh God, how awful! Quick, give me something to wipe him down with. We'll have to change the sheet;

he can't lie in this. No, darling, it's not your fault, I know. You can't help it. Don't talk, just be quiet and rest. Oh Lord, what a smell.

—What does he say?

—I think you may be right about his mind. He says . . . He says High John is his father. How ridiculous. But at least he's quiet now. Look how peacefully he's sleeping.

—Probably nothing to worry about. I told you he was talking to his father before you came in. It's just the fever working in him, stirring up dreams. And dreams are where we walk and talk with the dead. As for High John . . . Lingus heard us talking about him and mixed him up with his father. If he wakes up saying the same thing, then we worry. When the fever is gone, that's the test of whether his mind is unhinged or not.

—Keep an eye on him, Orlando. If he says anything odd once he's up and about again, let me know.

—You can trust me.

—I'm so glad you've dropped all that medieval business with us, and all that crazy archaic talk. It's as if you trust us now, where you didn't before. Wence and I never believed you committed those awful murders. But once you were framed, I can quite see why you pretended to be mad. Would they really have hanged you otherwise? I suppose they would.

Still, you sound as sane as anyone now. Lingus excepted of course, poor boy.

—Like you say, I'm as sane as you or anyone. Sane as I ever was.

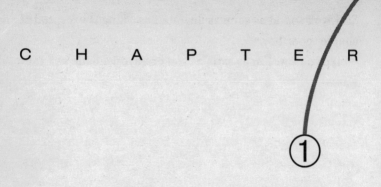
On the morning of Christmas Eve the weather set fair and mild. The rising sun skimmed the lake and by noon the ice was gone. A meek breeze hustled up, whining softly, falling back.

We took a break from rehearsal and sat out on the terrace. Roman soldiers and Ancient Britons fraternised and smoked cigarettes together. Hot tea, infused with navy rum, was available from a steaming samovar and a queue quickly formed. Jude and I sat huddled together on a rustic bench and sipped hot whisky and cloves, thick with sugar.

Ever since she realised Leah was pregnant by Wence, Jude had gone downhill fast. I could see it must be a blow — pride and all that — but even so I thought she was making heavy weather of it. So Leah was up the duff — so what? I talked to her about it but couldn't make her see things my way. I suggested a little freelance tumbling and fumbling with yours truly. As bait, I stressed the advantage of a youthful, virgin lover: no health risk and ardour to the max. I recited the corn dolly rigmarole over old Coochie-Coo three times a day but Jude still wasn't biting.

She leaned against me now and drooped her head on my shoulder. Her hair was dull and unwashed and her eyes were bloodshot drunk. Whisky and cloves mingled with the fumes of brandy and gin. Through the thickness of her emerald-green skirt and layers of starched sugar-paper petticoats she pressed her thigh against mine. She gave me a slobbery kiss on the chin. I tilted her head and planted my lips firmly on her mouth. She closed her eyes. The lids were streaked with crumbling and sweaty mascara. Her skin was pale and greasy, like cold bacon fat. She licked my nose.

'Thank you,' she said.

'What for?'

'For not taking advantage of me, and settling for a cuddle. For being around to listen, even if you think I am an old nag and a bore . . . And for giving up that nonsense about High John being your father. You had me worried for a while.'

'I had you worried? Ever think with the amount of liquor you're packing away, not to mention the good old Good Oil, that I might be the one to worry?'

'Lingus, you're a sweetie. I'm so glad you're sane. You *and* Orlando. My two best friends in all the world are sane. Let's drink to sanity. Cheers. The only way I could be happier is if that bitch has a miscarriage. Or if High John grants me an audience.'

'Well, if you get to see High John, give him my love and ask him what he did with my mother. No, don't hit me, only joshing; don't get mad. Ouch.'

*　　*　　*

You can spell it out to people, but if they don't like the message you're wasting your time. When I came round from my bout of fever, I tried telling Jude about the body in the Folly. I tried telling her about High John the so-called 'Conqueror', aka 'Daddy', and that far from being sane, Orlando was his hit man. Together they were cranking up for a massacre. She heard me out and then said, 'Lingus, you're so very pale, still. Why don't you go and lie down? Do you get headaches?'

'Now and then. Don't you?'

'Ah.'

I tried again. I kept it up for a week. Then Wence approached me to say he'd heard I was ill and maybe he should arrange for me to go into a swell hospital he knew, where an old army buddy of his, now a shrink, ran a thriving leucotomy practice. No need to linger in distress, Lingus ol' buddy, when your agitation is also upsetting the woman of the house, whom I have very special reasons – the reasons of a complaisant and uxorious husband – for keeping sweet and reasonable at this precise moment in the growth of our marriage, blah blah.

In other words, don't give me a hard time. Overnight my delusions vanished. I went back to my drumming lessons with Orlando. He didn't bear a grudge about me trying to tell it like it was and landing him in the shit. He told me he understood, people could get crazy, and he was glad I was better.

I started gigging with 'Done Told Ya', a relentless rockabilly outfit permanently stuck in the key of A major – Bruiser Barford (guitar/lead vocal), Shamela McToddy (double bass/harmony vocal), Lingus McWhinny (drums/harmony vocal) – rattling my traps in seedy shebeens where unemployed labourers and assorted criminals raked broken bottles and razors across each other's faces in time to our retro rockabilly rhythm. Happy days!

7 ②

So on Christmas Eve I sat halfway content, blue-painted cupbearer of Boudicca, with a hard-on thrusting through my breeches-clout and my arm around Jude, sipping hot punch and looking down from the terrace to the pond, where the fountain strewed its pearls and the carp swam complacent and fat.

Wence squatted by the pool, a hand raised against the glare on the water. In his other hand he held a net on a bamboo pole. Leah stood behind him, leaning on his shoulders and holding a croquet mallet. She laughed high and giggly. Wence laughed low and rumbling. He dredged the pool with the net and hoisted a carp on to the path. Leah whacked it with the mallet, once, twice.

'Wence always has carp on Christmas Eve,' said Jude. 'It's an old Polish custom.'

She waved her glass in salute to the carp and its killers.

'Let's go in and have another teeny-weeny drink.'

As we stood up, Jude began to sway. The glass fell and smashed. I steered her through the French windows. Behind us, Wence called her name. She stiffened but carried on walking up to the punchbowl. She ladled out the punch with a shaky, two-fisted grip. Her glass overflowed and splashed her skirt. She scooped out the few token segments of fruit, threw them on the floor and topped up with more liquor.

'Lead in your pencil,' said Jude.

A centurion came through the French windows carrying a tray piled high with plates and cups. Lunch break over. Behind the centurion came Leah, dressed as Boudicca, with a helmet on her head and a shield on her left arm. She framed herself in the doorway and beckoned me with her trident. I waved her away.

'Jude, I have to get back to work. But first I'm taking you upstairs.'

She didn't answer. She gripped the table with both hands and bit her lip. Boudicca called over, raised her wrist and tapped her watch. She frowned and I nodded. I steered Jude towards the door.

Out on the terrace Wence was shouting about the carp. Boudicca vanished and Sham came in carrying the carp. She shouted back at Wence.

'Yeah, yeah, she's here. I'll ask her.'

Sham came up and asked Jude for the keys to the cold store. Jude stared at Sham. She fumbled under her petticoats and came up with the bottle of Good Oil, smeared, sticky and almost empty, but no keys.

'Don't know.'

'Oh for God's sake,' said Sham.

She took the carp out again.

I said to Jude, 'No argument. Bed.'

She let me lead the way, shuffling along holding tight to my arm. Bruiser passed us on the way out.

'Hey, *muchacho*, she looks like one sick *compañera*.'

'I'm taking her for a lie-down.'

'Well, make sure, you know, face down.'

He drew his finger across his throat and mimed a gagging fit, sticking his tongue out over his chin. His tongue was covered in sores.

'I'll be careful.'

'Nearly been a gonner that way myself.'

He breezed off and Jude began to mumble.

'Round here . . . I'm an object . . . I'm treated like a sodding object.'

I blew in her ear. I shepherded her along the corridor to a lift and propped her against the wall. I rang the bell. The lift arrived and I bundled her inside.

We rode three floors to the apartment that had once been home to her and Wence but where she now lived alone. The smell of spirits and stale hashish hit me as I opened the door. I took her through to the bedroom and laid her on the bed.

'My brassière . . . Unhook my brassière.'

I knelt down and did as she asked, kissing her tits and then her eyelids, licking off the remains of the mascara. She sighed and draped an arm over my shoulder. I kissed her on the mouth and felt her tongue flutter. Then she sparked out. I was tempted to do the business there and then but it would have been a bit of a rush with Boudicca waiting downstairs. So I took down a long crocheted shawl that was hanging by the door and covered her. Then I went into the sitting-room to find something to use as a basin, to put by her in case she was sick. In a red enamel bowl by the window two shrunken oranges and a sticky black banana lay festering. I stuck the bowl beside the bed. Back in the sitting-room I opened the window to let out the fug. I scouted about and gathered up a handful of half-smoked stogies with a bit of poke left in them and stashed them in my sporran (Boudicca's cupbearer was a Pictish slave). Three flights down Boudicca howled my name.

Later on, about nine, with the dress rehearsal finished — apart from bickering and recriminations — we gathered in the canteen for carols and *gluwein*. There was a tree in a tub and a heap of presents scattered around. We milled about in civilian clothes, kissing each other and shrieking. In the absence of Wence, who was off in his study dressing up as Father Christmas, Leah made her presence felt, collaring people and barking orders.

I saw Sarah Bartleby come in. Her hands were thrust into a fur muff. She wore a leopardskin pillbox hat. I waved to her and she came straight over, followed by a tall, cadaverous man dressed in a peculiar uniform, all breasts and belts and buttons like an aviator from the Great War. He carried a stack of parcels. A treacly roll-up was screwed into the corner of his mouth, where it burned fitfully. He spoke out of the side of his mouth.

'Where do you want these, miss, by the tree?'

'Yes thank you, Pocock.'

He pushed his way into the throng. Sarah took her hands from the muff, which dangled from her neck by a silken cord.

'That is Pocock, our chauffeur. He comes with Daddy's new job: Inspector of Chaplains in His Majesty's Hulks. It's only a part-time post for Daddy, so we're still at Saint Sepulchre's, but we're allowed Pocock night and day every day of the year. He's so obliging.'

I stroked the muff and smiled at the hat.

'A hefty increase in stipend too, no doubt.'

'Oh these! No, all my own income actually. The sampler business has really taken off. So much so, I've had to contract most of the work out. Luckily, Arnie gets me all the home-workers I need. Super girls, so neat. It was all High John's idea of course, according to Arnie. I was at my wits' end. The arrangement is absolutely super for all of us. After all, what the good folk of Shanty Town need isn't charity, it's work. I'm sick of charity. All that foul soup and gummy mouths.'

Her head bobbed about, looking over my shoulder at the company.

'Where's Jude?'

'Sham has gone to fetch her down. She was a bit wobbly earlier.'

'Was she? Poor dear, I'm not surprised. I suppose you know . . . Yes, obviously you do. The bump won't show for a bit yet — which is a blessing — but what a dreadful busi-ness, and all the fault of that buffoon Orlando, though Jude won't hear a word against him. Corn dollies indeed. That sort of thing is best left to High John.'

'If you can catch him.'

'Ah well, don't tell Jude — it's meant to be a surprise — but I've been having words with Arnie and it looks like High John will grant her an audience before the New Year. Daddy and I have been taking instruction from him, through a screen of course. We both feel the old liturgical forms, tried and trusted though they are, are in need of a freshen-up. The idea that all Divine Revelation ceased umpteen centuries ago, apart from a few mumblings from the Holy Spirit at General Synod, is quite absurd — if you believe in a living God, that is. He's bound to send a prophet or two, especially at a time of tribulation like this. Don't you agree?'

I leaned close and whispered, 'High John is my father.'

Sarah trilled, 'How super that you should feel that way too. He's the Daddy of us all, really, in a spiritual sense. I must say, I took you for an atheist at first.'

'Well I'm not exactly . . .'

'Now don't go saying anything to spoil my nice new opinion of you. Let's leave it at that, shall we? I say, this Daddy business could become confusing, don't you think? From now on, I shall refer to my own dear biological father as "Papa". Much more in keeping with his elevated status as Inspector of Chaplains in His Majesty's Hulks, even if it is only part-time. I do love rolling his title round my mouth; it's so satisfying, so solid. And Papa, bless him, needs solidity. He's been up in the clouds for years.'

Pocock came back, a fresh roll-up burning in his mouth.

'When do the carols start, miss? I like a carol.'

'Soon I hope. I have to get back for a Midnight-Mass photo-shoot.'

I asked if Sarah wanted a drink of punch.

'Fine for me. How about you, Pocock?'

'Nothing for me, thank you, miss. Spiritous liquors give me the vapours.'

I struggled over to the bar. Squeezed in among the tipplers, a glass in each hand and his head over the punch-bowl, was Tatum Liotes. I greeted him.

'*Ave atque vale.*'

Still clutching a glass in each hand, he dooked his head in the bowl and came up with an apple in his teeth.

'Skraagch!'

I rejoined Sarah and Pocock. Bruiser was with them now, chatting up Sarah. She took the punch from me without a word. I asked Pocock how he enjoyed life with the Bartlebys.

'Wonderful, guv. I dare say Sepulchre's-in-the-Mire isn't everyone's ideal posting but it's a real treat to be in a proper pious household after my last situation. I'm not a prude, guv, don't get me wrong – the Good Lord imbued us with fleshly lust so we may propagate each after his kind. His own kind, mark you, guv. But the Lord draws the line at buggery. Congress with beasts, and doing it up the coal-hole, is the loathsome crime of buggery writ large. Stands to reason.'

He became mildly agitated. The roll-up twitched in the corner of his mouth. I was about to ask where he'd last worked but thought better of it. Bruiser was leering over Sarah. She took his hand from her tit and placed it in her muff.

'Sorry, Pocock. I didn't quite catch what you said.'

'Nothing of import, miss. I was merely talking of my last situation with the young gentleman here.'

'Oh yes, frightfully hairy, so Papa says. I say, Lingus, what do you think? Isn't Pocock the most exquisitely deferential chap in all Creation? It's so soothing to have a properly sane and servile servant after all these years with no one but Makepeace. But Makepeace can't help himself, I suppose. Let's hope he remains sufficiently *compos mentis* to profit by your example, eh, Pocock?'

'As you wish, miss.'

'Quiet! Quiet, everyone!' screamed Leah.

There was an outbreak of shushing. In the following silence, far away in the corridors and halls of the asylum, we heard the wistful strains of '*Stille Nacht! Heilige Nacht!*' sung in the pure treble of prepubescent boys. The song drew near and then they were just outside the door. Bruiser switched out the lights and Leah drew the curtains to let in the moon. A procession of boys entered, robed in white surplices. They held flickering candles. We parted to let them through. The boys' hair was cut right into the wood, like they'd come from the penitentiary. Their parchment faces were pale and translucent in the candle glow.

Singing, they gathered by the tree, fanning out in order of size. Sarah nudged me.

'This is all well and jolly, but where's Jude? I've been here ages. Someone went to fetch her, you say?'

The singing stopped and a handbell pealed. A salvo of 'Ho ho ho! Merry Christmas!' burst over us, as Good King Wenceslas, dressed like Father Christmas, came clanging jovially among us. Sham trotted beside him, tugging his sleeve. He fended her off. He told her to scram.

'Beat it, sister.'

The crowd was closing behind Wence in his progress to the tree. I took Sham aside.

'Where's Jude?'

'She's not in her room. There's a basin of sick, two oranges and a banana, but no Jude. I can't find her anywhere.'

Sarah pushed in.

'What's going on? Where's Jude?'

I joined Sham and Sarah's hands together.

'That's what I'm going to find out. I'm going for a rummage round the lake.'

There was a burst of applause as Wence switched on the Christmas tree lights.

'You two wait here and collect my presents. Wence will be giving them out in a minute.'

'I know what I'd like to give *him*,' said Sham.

A cold Christmas moon poured silver on the water. Out on the lake, on a raft, a mannequin with a turnip-lantern head bobbed in the wind. I called to Jude and an owl answered. I walked briskly along the shore until I came to the timber tower and platform from where Wence planned to direct the Boxing Day pageant. Drawn up below it were the galleys of the Roman invasion fleet, rimed with frost.

I climbed the ladder to the top of the tower. A fire was burning over towards Shanty Town. A light was on in my room. The light went out and the window took the glow of the distant fire.

*   *   *

I pushed open the door of my room and switched on the light. No one there, except shadows hunched in corners, frozen in postures that suggested the furniture had been creeping about while I was away.

On my pillow was a sprig of myrtle.

'And there's this,' said Sham.

I put my parcels down on the floor and took the envelope. I broke the red wax seal with my thumbnail.

'Well?' said Sarah. 'We're all agog. Is it from Jude?'

'Go on,' said Sham. 'What does she say?'

The girls were grinning at me. They knew very well what it said.

'You've seen her, haven't you?'

'You've been gone ages,' said Sarah. 'Anything could have happened.'

'You're not going to read it to us then?' said Sham.

'No.'

'In that case,' said Sarah, 'I shall get my kicks at Midnight Mass. Pocock, be an angel and bring the car round. Merry Christmas, Lingus.'

I picked up my parcels and headed for the lift.

I padded along the corridor to my room then put my ear to the door. Not a sound. I knocked timidly, even though it was my door, and then boldly. Still no answer. I twirled the knob and entered. The room was now ablaze with candle-light, with candles in the window and all along the mantelshelf. Jude sat before the mirror, brushing her long red hair. She smiled at my reflection.

'Take your clothes off while I finish my hair.'

I sat on the edge of the bed and took off my keks while Jude teased her hair. She wore a crisp white blouse and a royal blue skirt. I was still wearing my long white shirt. I was about to lift it over my head when she said, 'No, leave it on.'

She came to me and lifted me up from the bed. Her face had lost its lardy look under a dusting of powder. She kissed me. Under the tang of toothpaste was a whiff of bile. She hitched up my shirt and draped it over patient Geordie. She knelt down before him, weighing my stones in her palms. Her bottom lip was swollen and quivering.

CHAPTER

When I woke Jude was gone. The sheets were damp and sticky. I pressed my face into the linen and smelled the blazonry of our coming together: fetid heat of lions and the sour reek of the serpent, cold and insinuating.

The curtains were closed, filtering dusty yellow sunlight. The candles were burned down in puddles of grease. On the floor was a little glass bottle with its stopper lying beside it. It was empty. I lay back on my pillow and closed my eyes. From the terrace below I heard the note of Orlando's pipe and the beat of his tabor. I listened for a while. Then I got up and drew the curtains and pushed open the window. Orlando was playing as before but his dancer was Leah, executing clumsy, ill-favoured steps. She was dressed in grey overalls. Wence sat on a wall, one arm round an ornamental urn, his face pressed against a fern. He looked like he was sprouting a green beard. The dance finished and Leah jumped on the wall. She kissed Wence's bald head. Orlando saw me looking out and waved. I called out 'Merry Christmas' and Wence shouted up, 'My study in half an hour, where you will hear something to your advantage!'

I closed the window and got back into bed. I ducked under the covers and breathed Jude's smell. I rose towards a climax that spent itself in dry, painful jerks. I dozed for a bit, then got up to wash. I sneered at myself in the mirror. A pubic hair stuck to my lip.

My presents were scattered under the bed. I pulled them out and unwrapped them. There was one from Sarah Bartleby, a nicely stitched sampler of haloed angels flapping about and a motto which read: 'My son give me thine heart, and let thine eyes observe my ways.'

There was a card with it:

Merry Christmas, Lingus. Not my choice of verse, but it was done for me up in Shanty Town as a last-minute one-off. Not my idea to get you a present in the first place, actually, but Jude twisted my arm, saying what a sad little orphan you are. She suggested aftershave, but I thought since you don't have much to shave yet there wasn't much point and anyway you'd probably drink it — you or that friend of yours, Boxer or whatever he's called (he does look a bit jowly and canine, come to think of it). Jude seems to think you and I might be friends, but I don't think it's likely, do you? Toodle-pip. Sarah.

From Orlando there was a small but powerful short-wave radio, with a card giving a frequency and urging me to listen alone at three. I switched it on and tried it then and there but found nothing much other than static and heathen jabber. I put it away for later.

There was a lump of opium from Bruiser and a bar of chocolate from Sham. I hadn't tasted chocolate in ages, so I munched it while I unwrapped Wence's present, which was a book of poems by Tatum Liotes called *Seven Ways to Peel a Rainbow*. I thumbed through the titles: 'Behind my Flies', 'Buddy Can You Pull My Wire', 'An Infant's First Smile' and so on. What a feast. I chucked it in the bin. I got the opium and nibbled a bit. Then I tidied up and made the bed. I gathered all the scraps of ribbon and wrapping paper and crammed them in the bin on top of Tatum's book. Last thing I did before going downstairs to see Wence was clear the spent candles off the mantelpiece and prop up my sampler. Quite pretty, all in all, and as good as a Christmas card from dear old Dad. It's nice for families to keep in touch, especially at Christmas. Don't think I didn't appreciate it.

Wence was alone in his study, peering through a magnifying glass at an old dictionary. There was a jug of hot coffee on the side and a platter of freshly baked croissants. He waved me to help myself. While I tucked in, he cut the end off a cigar and lit up.

'I'll come straight to the point. Tatum wants to offer you a job. Part houseboy and part personal assistant. The houseboy angle is no sweat. You skin up for him and get his beer out of the icebox. By the way, Coors are planning a Coronation Ale and it looks like they want Tatum to feature in the promotion.'

'They couldn't get Frankenstein's monster, right?'

'Shut up. Okay, the rest of the houseboy gig is you take out the empties, you bring up a fresh crate, maybe you do a little light housework. This you can handle?'

'What doesn't kill me makes me stronger, I guess.'

'That's the spirit. Now, the personal assistant – or a word I found in this book here, "amanuensis" – Tatum's planning an epic.'

'On the London Commune. Arthur told me.'

'Don't mention that ingrate to Tatum. Oh, in case you're wondering, that's one duty you won't be expected to perform. He'll respect your sexuality, whatever it is, and anyway he's got something brewing with a trooper of the Household Cavalry. Take it from me: Tatum you can trust with your life – even your butthole. Where was I?'

'Amanuensis.'

'Right. It's an oral history angle. You transcribe recordings of survivors, you talk to survivors from both sides if you can find any, you make notes and draw the Big T's attention to anything he can use. The poetry you leave to Tatum.'

'Gladly.'

'What else? Yeah, you keep his diary in order, get him out to readings and what-have-you on time, get him home alive and sponge the vomit off his dinner jacket. Interested?'

'I'll take it.'

'Money you negotiate with Tatum. He goes back to town after the show tomorrow and he wants you with him.'

'Fine. I guess I'd better tell Bruiser and Sham to look for another drummer.'

'Maybe Orlando could dep. Some gigs you could still do. Tatum's pretty flexible about time off. See how it goes. He's recording an album some time in the New Year – *Tatum Liotes Talks Dirty, Volume One* – so don't be in too much of a hurry to ditch the musical career.'

'Is that all you wanted to talk about?'

'That's it. I'll tell Tatum you're on board. Hey, I nearly forgot. Did you read any of Tatum's stuff in the book that Santa brought? What did you think?'

'"The case presents no adjunct to the muse's diadem."'

'Come again? Oh yeah, he writes some swell lines. Got it by heart already, I see. You should do well.'

I left Wence turning green on the end of his cigar and went down to the canteen. The opium was floating nice and mellow at the back of my head. A bunch of techies sat at the bar drinking beer; they shouted me over but I didn't feel like company. I poured an orange juice and sat down near the Christmas tree. There were a couple of uncollected presents underneath and, among the branches, an envelope addressed to Wence. I recognised Jude's handwriting. I took the envelope and scarpered upstairs. It wouldn't take much to open it and seal it again. I got in my room, locked the door and switched on the kettle. I held the envelope in the steam and teased open the flap. Jude had written:

Dear Wenceslas

I've gone away and I'm not coming back. Whatever
it is you want from a woman you obviously don't
find in me, so it's for the best. I can no longer
countenance your pandering to the monstrous ego
of Miss Dingwallace, and I can no longer endure
the public humiliation of your slavering lust for
her weightlifter's thighs. Now she's pregnant and
soon it's going to show. I'm going to stay at the
Convent with Sister Vincent for a week or so
while I think about what to do and where to go
next. Take care of Lingus, it's his birthday next
month. Seventeen candles on the cake, don't
forget.

I resealed the envelope, then I went downstairs and slipped
it back under the tree. Bruiser came over to say that Wence
had told him I might be leaving the band, and he was sorry
to hear the news. I said it was au revoir rather than adios.
We took our opium pipes down to the basement cinema
and spent the next hour companionably rolling little brown
pills and toking away like a couple of Chinese sailors. We
drifted into an opium reverie while the projectionist ran
scratchy old cartoons as a Christmas treat. Bruiser tapped
me on the shoulder and told me it was him who had driven
Jude down to the Convent. It was south of the river, near
the Elephant and Castle. He said Jude had said I should
look her up, no problem. I said I thought she might have
let me know she was going, and why didn't he tell me
earlier?

'Yeah, well, she was pretty upset. It was all a bit of a rush. Anyway, I'm telling you now.'

Up on the screen, in a manic and garish procession, Sylvester stalked Tweetie Pie, Jerry outwitted Tom, and Wylie Coyote took another anvil on the nut.

Two o'clock came and we floated into the canteen for Christmas dinner. Spartan fare, compared with the smells wafting from under Wence's door, but there was plenty of it — more on our table since neither Bruiser nor I was hungry. At ten to three I pulled my last cracker. Then I made my excuses and said I was going to lie down.

Back in my room I locked myself in and switched on the radio, tuning to the frequency Orlando gave me. There was static and a steady blip every three seconds. I fiddled with the tuner. On the right a babble of foreigners, on the left a combo of clarinet, bagpipe, tambourine and a furious strumming on some kind of jangly lute. The tune was wild and fast with a strange limping rhythm. I counted the beats. The underlying time seemed to be ten-sixteen with occasional bars of eleven.

It was close on three o'clock. I tuned back to the blips. They came faster now, until they were a continuous whine. There was silence and then 'God Save the King', played by a consort of what sounded like amateur brass, slipshod in rhythm and wobbly in pitch. The music finished on a bizarre chord, hinting at a wild modulation that never came.

A woman speaking pretty good English — although strained through Balkan inflections — announced the imminent presence of Manley Stanley, Deputy Prime Minister and Minister for Peace, War, Justice, Sport and the Arts in the Socialist Government of Great Britain in Exile.

There was a moment of dead air and then a shuffling of papers. A man's voice said, 'This one?' and after another stretch of dead air and a constant clicking, like someone switching a microphone on and off, the same man began to speak.

'Christmas greetings to you all. Prime Minister Errol Sachs apologises for not being able to address you himself, but a severe case of "Tirana tummy" has laid him low — contracted, no doubt, I assure you and our kind hosts, from an imported tin of infected South American corned beef. Therefore it is I, Manley Stanley, who speaks . . . Is this thing on? Are you sure?'

There was the sound of an impatient finger tapping the microphone, then Manley Stanley cleared his throat and began again. I turned the volume down and pressed the radio to my ear.

'Christmas greetings to the people of Britain. To the many millions upon millions of unemployed and those working for starvation wages, to families who face this special time of the year with a loved one in prison or in the camps — perhaps a husband and father, wasted in body and spirit as he cooks the waste in the nukes of the far north; perhaps a beloved son and brother serving eternity in the Hulks, in the vast grey spaces of our east coast estuaries. Will they see Christmases to come? Or will the Fever bear them away on Time's ever-rolling stream with no glimpse of dearly longed-for faces?

'And Christmas greetings too, to those families who keep evergreen the memory of a son or daughter who fell in the fight for Liberty. At many a table there is many an empty place, and little ones with tear-stained faces pinched and drawn with hunger, who fear for the life of their dear, sainted mother, their sole bulwark against a world so brutal.

'To all these, to heroic Jeremiah Brandreth and to all our comrades in prison, I say: Keep up your hearts! Say not the struggle naught availeth!

'We are banished and in exile, with death-warrants on our heads. Errol Sachs and I, Manley Stanley, were elected by the sovereign people of Britain. Our anointed King bestowed on us the sacred trust of government – but today we are foully traduced by cut-throat pirates who trample Britannia's age-old liberties in the mire. Pirates! Bloody butchers, who offer a libation to our overthrow, quaffed in blood!

'Yes, we are banished, but over land and sea our voice rolls in thunder. Liberty's memory is long and she will not be denied. The hungry sheep look up and are not fed. But as they cast their eyes heavenward, they see a shooting star, *yclept* FREEDOM! In the dark days to come let that star be our inspiration, until the rising sun of democratic socialism brings dawn once more to our dear native land.

'To the youth of our country I say this: Your fathers and

brothers, mothers and sisters, have sacrificed much in the struggle for freedom. Perhaps you yourselves were fighting at the barricades and in the streets, fighting rearguard actions through the sewers, pursued by rats and mice. You have seen your comrades sacrifice life itself, in the hope that others might live free in perpetuity. Oh let not their sacrifice be in vain! Be strong and pure in thought, word and deed, valiant champions of righteousness and upholders of the sacred trust, Promethean Guardsmen of Liberty's sacred flame, marching ten, twenty, fifty, a century abreast – Freedom's phalanx irresistible, a juggernaut of justice whom no tyrant can withstand. From your hand is cast the dreaded thunderstone of Liberty. Even as David smote Goliath, so shall ye cast down the Philistine of these latter days, severing the head of this loathsome hydra and cauterising each budding stump.

'Yes! The time of pity is at an end and compassion in its turn is banished, the Achilles' heel of our party and state. Youth of Britain, be remorseless in your resolve to conquer. Be ruthless in victory. Spare none – no, not one – that your own tribe may flourish. For unless the weeds which clutch and choke be extirpated root and branch, there shall be no harvest in the land, no fruitful pasture where ye may lay down the burden of the beast and drink your fill from Liberty's sacred fount.

'And let us not forget those young GIs, far from their native land, who also long for deliverance. Those who weary of standing guard in this remote and far-flung outpost of Empire where the cold and rainy summers are so short.

'So short is life, so long the tour of duty.'

Manley Stanley coughed, and there was a pause while he slurped a drink. He started speaking again, this time in a queer sort of American voice.

'How are things at home, John? Is the bank about to foreclose the mortgage on your daddy's farm? Have poison rains denuded your forests? Will you ever again see sunset on the prairies, moonrise over the Rockies? When are you going home, John? Maybe you're a city boy and you miss your piece of the action. You can't go out much here in London, John. Is there anywhere left that isn't off limits? And you know why?

'How are you going home, John? In a box? We all know you break the rules, get hungry for a piece of tail that hasn't been fourteen times round the officers' brothel before it lands in front of you. We all know you go slumming, sticking together in packs for safety, well tooled-up in case – in case of what, John? What trouble is a little bitty woman gonna give a hunk like you? What do you have to fear from the fresh-faced boy who turns a trick for a loaf of bread. Oh yes, there are sodomites among you, don't blush now.

'The streets of London are dark. Who can you trust? Maybe you get drunk, lose sight of your buddies. Can you feel that spot in your back, John? Yes, that's it, lower down, where the spinal cord is most vulnerable. Can you feel the knife, so sharp and skilfully plied that at first you think it's just a twinge, reaching too high at basketball maybe. But no, John, sad to say, your legs are buckling and you're going down. You'll never see your killer's face.

'How does the uniform feel, John? Tight around the collar? Think how tight a cheesewire gets. It's agony to die like that, snared in the vile garotte. What's your girl back home going to think when she hears the news, eh John? She'll see you in her dreams. Purple face, eyeballs choked with blood — and the tongue! Oh the times she's had with that tongue! The times you had. Poor man's caviare, eh John?

'Never mind, John — John Clay — maybe she's already run off with a Mexican. Maybe she's getting her skillet good and greasy with a wetback right now. Was there a special way she used to dress? Special things she used to do? Can you feel her run her tongue along your shaft? Maybe she's running her tongue along a Mexican's shaft, right now. He's got a good long shaft, John, and he knows how to use it. Sure, he may be diseased a little, but as long as she don't swallow his stuff, she might, just might, be okay. That's a surefire way of catching the plague, right John? I guess they told you all about that in orientation class before you shipped out. Seems like you no sooner find a cure for one itty-bitty bug than another comes strutting his stuff.

'When you get back home, maybe you'll find a Mexican is doing your job, driving your car. He swam over the border at dead of night. He won't be drafted. No one knows anything about him, excepting your girl.

'And now a big Manley Stanley "Howdy!" to the friends of Private Belusski. Okay, guys, remember how the officer told you Belusski had some bad news and was shipped home on compassionate grounds? How come you never seen so much as a postcard from your good buddy? I'll tell you. He's buried alive in a pit out by Saffron Walden. Well, let's just say he was alive when our patriots buried him. Some of our young'uns got so mad with the way things are they felt they had to make a contribution, and Private Belusski was it. Nothing personal, boys, it might just as easily have been you. Next time it will be. Saffron Walden is a beautiful town. You should visit.

'You and your buddies are riding high, John, ever so high. But the gravity of revolution will pull you down, down into the dust where the conquerors lie.

'Don't go down into the dust and the dark, John. There's still time to seek the light. The nesting gulls have left our northern shores, never to return. They know there's poison in the tide, in the seashore wrack. Time to be leaving. There's poison for you too, John, in the corruption of your own dark deeds. And as you heft the sword you live by, so shall you perish.

'Goodnight, John, I bid you goodnight.'

Another pause, a crackle of static and then Manley Stanley switched back to his English voice.

'To the people of Britain I say these words: Wicked men walk among us, rank strangers in a strange land, and hospitality is no duty of ours. Show them the door, politely but firmly. And never forget why they are here. To serve the oligarchs of an Evil Empire across the sea, whose agents are among us, native British men and women who have sold their birthright for a hill of beans. Yes, they call themselves patriots, but their loyalty is to the hydra-headed octopus of Anglospheric capitalism, whose jackbooted tentacles outreach all national boundaries.

'You may be saying: This is all very well, but what can I do about it?

'There are numerous small ways you can help — by

refusing to collaborate with the enemy, for example. If you are a doctor, refuse them medical assistance. If you are a priest, refuse absolution. Each of you, I am sure, can think of something. And be positive. Remember your native culture. Play soccer instead of American football, cricket instead of baseball. Abandon your formless cavortings at times of celebration – though what have you to celebrate? – and take up morris dancing instead. Remember the folk-songs of old England – 'Down at the Old Bull and Bush', 'Jerusalem', 'Why Does a Winkle Always Turn to the Right?' – speaking of which, isn't it time for a turn to the Left?

'Yes, never forget, your enemy is not merely the Yankee toad who squats with warty bottom on the face of our land. The national struggle must be the catalyst to the wider social revolution which will sweep the capitalist oppressors, British and American alike, into the Dustbin of History, and restore our Socialist Government – now in exile, but recognised here in Tirana as the legitimate Government of Britain – to the hallowed Parliament of our forefathers and mothers.

'Some of you will, of course, already be in clandestine groups such as the band of heroes who kidnapped Private Belusski. To you I say: I salute you. Keep up the good work. Others – and for these no paean of praise can be fulsome enough – are about to commit themselves body and soul to the aims of "Martyr's Torch", the pacifist wing of our movement. Their self-immolation in places of public resort will be the beacons which will surely light the all-consuming bonfire of Freedom! If you feel you have a vocation for fiery martyrdom, do not feel you have to wait to be approached by an agent of the "Martyr's Torch" organisation before you set about achieving the consummation of your heart's desire. Of course, there are many advantages to be had from membership — guaranteed posthumous financial help for your family and professional pre-immolation counselling, to give just two examples. But if you have a mind to do it, why wait? Torch yourself now!

'Remember, all must perish who are your enemies, root and branch. Build the bonfire high!

'And now, all that remains is to wish you once again a very Merry Christmas, and a Happy New Year when it comes.'

There was a click and a crackle, and Manley Stanley was assumed into the ether. In the static that followed a deep chortling bellied out of the radio. Then Sir Lionel Dingwallace spoke:

'What can one say? I hope you enjoyed Mister Stanley's broadcast as much as I did. I have had many requests from citizens asking that I jam these "Tirana tirades", but I honestly feel, and referendum results bear this out, that such an exercise would be counter-productive. No, by all means, let us hear what he has to say. One of the charges levelled against us by Mister Stanley is that we stifle freedom of expression. But the proof of the pudding is in the eating.

'And while we're on the subject, may I remind you that the polls are still open to take your vote on the question: Should public executions be televised? If you haven't already cast your vote, access your screen now or get on down to the polling-station of your choice.'

'Democracy in action. Working for you.

'Now, if you were listening to Manley Stanley – naughty, naughty – then you missed the King's speech, so we're repeating it on this wavelength in two minutes. In his first Christmas message to the nation, His Majesty will explain to you, his beloved subjects, why he has granted the petition of the Congress of the United States. He will announce that from New Year's Day he will be King of America too. *Rex imprimatur* of our beloved Anglosphere. Which rather makes a nonsense of Mister Stanley's anti-American diatribe, doesn't it? His Majesty will extend his thanks to you all for the warm wishes he has received on his accession, and he will also describe some of the arrangements for the Coronation, unfortunately delayed while we deal with an outbreak of death-watch beetle in Westminster Abbey. You can contribute to the cost of this vital restoration work, and His Majesty will give details of a simple-to-follow sponsorship scheme.

'Remember: participate with pride. The fabric of our heritage is the stuff our dreams are made of. Merry Christmas, and a Happy New Year when it comes.'

'You going to say how you voted?'

I walked a little way along the stack, out of range of Wence's brandy breath. I took down another volume of press cuttings.

'That's between me and my conscience and the Homeland Department.'

I scanned the shelves.

'Things are getting out of order round here.'

'Yeah, Jude used to see to it, but she lost interest. Now she's gone, maybe I'd better get someone else to look after things. You would have been my first choice for librarian, if good buddy Tate hadn't snapped you up first. I'm going to miss you. Don't forget . . .'

'I'm one of the family, right? Any time I need help, just get my butt over here. Don't worry, it's on my mental hard drive.'

Night was fallen. I closed the curtains.

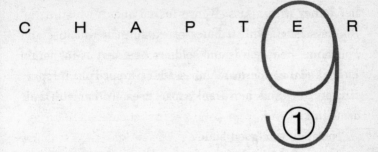
I stood on a raft with Boudicca, shivering in my breeches-clout and sporran. My exposed skin was painted blue with woad, but the make-up artist needn't have bothered. The fierce cold could have turned me blue on its own. The beam of a mighty spot, angled from the timber tower, sealed us both in a cone of light.

Boudicca handed me a goblet of Roman hooch. I took a cautious sniff, then a sip and finally a swig. I grabbed my stomach and rolled my eyes for the camera. I fell to my knees and hugged Boudicca's thigh, then I slid down her leg and died. The spot went dark and we held our pose for a few seconds. Over the lake, another tableau sprang into light. Bruiser began winding us in. Boudicca stroked my neck.

Boxing Day, or more properly Saint Stephen's Day, feast of the first Christian martyr. Down in Hyde Park a floodlit martyrdom was under way – the Deputy Quartermaster of the Commune, in hiding these past few years and finally betrayed, flanked by two emulators of Gilles de Rais. We had a good turnout considering.

The American Ambassador and our Homeland Controller

had arrived before the show by helicopter. Boudicca greeted her father with a kiss. Wence fussed about, whistling up flunkeys laden with tributes of exotic malt whiskies and bourbons. Bodyguards and soldiers hemmed us in. Tatum Liotes and the American Ambassador swopped playful sparring punches and then drank a toast to each other with their arms linked.

'Here's to you, good buddy.'

'And to you.'

Stoked up on bourbon against the cold, Boudicca and I had gone out on the lake to be pulled hither and yon by the demands of Tatum's script and Wence's direction. Now, for me at least, it was over. I jumped ashore and headed for the changing-tent. Bruiser whisked Boudicca along the lakeside in a pedishaw to her next appearance. I scraped off the woad as best I could and wrapped up warm. Sham gave me hot tea from a flask. A carpet-bag was packed and ready with my few belongings. I prodded it with my toe.

'More than I came in with, at any rate.'

'Look after yourself,' said Sham. 'Don't forget, any time you need us, we're here.'

I kissed her goodbye. Two GIs were waiting outside to escort me over to the celebrity grandstand. There was a modest but armour-plated saloon parked by the stand with a young soldier behind the wheel. My escort asked him to open up the trunk. I slung my bag inside.

'You can wait in the chariot or go on up.'

I scrambled up the ladder to the grandstand. At the top I was frisked by a goon. I spied Tatum on the front bench with Sir Lionel Dingwallace. I made my way down and stood by politely while Tatum finished his business and said *sayonara*. Out on the lake a battle was taking place between coracles and galleys. I saw a coracle plucked from the water by two oars, like a pea between chopsticks. An Ancient Briton climbed from the coracle and straddled an oar, inching his way towards the galley. He had a knife in his teeth. The oarsmen desperately tried to shake him off. He slipped but hung on by his wrists and ankles, upside down like a sloth. The crew hastily pulled the oar inboard. The Ancient Briton dunted the ship's timber with his head. The oar was tugged from his grasp and he fell from the end like a piece of meat off a skewer. There was a big splash as he hit the water. I didn't see him come up.

It was pretty noisy, what with the crowd bawling from the shore and the Romans and Britons chanting in Latin and Woadish. Wence's commentary on the action boomed out from the timber tower. Tatum had no trouble making himself heard though. He punched the Home Controller on the shoulder.

'Hey, good buddy! I really appreciate that. If I get to talk to Brandreth, I can get this epic number really rolling.'

'*Pas de problème*, old boy. Just be sure you move fast. New Year's Day I hang him high. My fellow, Mister Sweet, will arrange everything with the Governor of the Tower. New Year's Eve is probably most convenient. My chaps should have finished with him by then.'

'Dinky. Uh, here's the boy. Time to piss on the fire and whistle up the dogs.'

Tatum took a last pull on his beer bottle and lobbed it towards the lake. I had a moment's panic that some trigger-happy *capo* would mistake him for a bomber. I jumped back out of the target area.

Tatum laughed. 'Me too, boy. Makes a body kinda nervous, with all this firepower around.'

I asked him if he wanted to stay for the end of the show. No need to rush on my behalf.

'Nope. I filled the sack with horseshit, so I reckon to know how it stinks when you tip it out. Say *hasta la pasta* to the Boss and let's haul ass.'

Tatum stretched out in the back of the car and I sat up front with the driver. Redcaps waved us through the gates. Tatum began to snore. I asked the driver how long he'd been in England and how long he had to go.

'I done two year nearly and a month short. Then home sweet home on the range and the first piece of hygienic ass since Balaam was a boy.'

'Got a girl back home?'

'You bet. Steady since when. Sweetest cherry I ever had. But listen, buddy, can you figure a dame? Last letter I get, week before Thanksgiving, she tells me she's learning Spanish. Why she wanna do that? All she need to say to me she can say in American, boy, American.'

'Maybe she got an urge to read *Don Quixote* in the original tongue.'

He jabbed a finger in his mouth. 'She'll get plenty of tongue when I get home. Spread 'em, baby.'

'Poor man's caviare.'

'Huh? You bet. Suck 'em and fuck 'em. What else they for?'

We talked about fucking all the way into town. Fucking with women, fucking with men, fucking with beasts. We talked about blow-jobs, hand-jobs, brown-jobs and odd-jobs.

'Ever see a stallion cover a mare?'

I said I hadn't.

'You see that, you gonna have trouble walking upright, you hear? You be the size of twenty men after you see that. You don't get you a juicy slab of prime ass, you gonna have jissom backed up all the way from your nuts to your skull, creaming out your ears.'

'You could always go behind the barn for a hand-job.'

'A hand-job? Naw. No way, buddy. Any dame see a stallion's hard-on, she be pining for it same as you. If you don't take her, why, she gonna give herself to the horse. I fucked my sister that way, to save her bumping her ugly on Old Riley's dick. He was some horse. Boy, I figure I done right, 'cos bestiality is worse than incest in the eyes of the Lord God. What you reckon?'

I shrugged and said I didn't think it was worth fretting over the relative value of two mortal sins.

'I don't fret none, except my girlie studying up on that Spanish fandango. It ain't natural.'

'What's natural these days? Culture shapes everything, according to the professors. Even Nature is a cultural construct.'

'Is that so? Well listen to me. This culture stuff, I got no use for. Tell me, can you fuck it, huh? Tell me, can you fuck it?'

And so on and so forth, all the way home.

Tatum woke up at the last set of lights before Crawford Mansions.

'Hey, driver, you want to come in for a snort? I got all sorts of liquor, all kinds of dope.'

'No sir, I never mess with that stuff. No offence, you go right ahead. I dost my thing, thou doest thy thing et cetera. But I got to get back to base.'

'Suit yourself, soldier, but I reckon with an attitude like that, you'd have had a hard time making it in my outfit.'

'With all due respect, sir, we lost that war. Reckon you gotta be minded to fight or party.'

'Yeah, well, fuck you, soldier.'

'Fuck you too, sir.'

The old homestead looked in poor shape, empty bottles and sticky glasses and coffee cups full of dog-ends everywhere, and the toilet crusted with sick and all sorts.

'Tomorrow I'll give it a good going-over.'

'Aw, that's okay, leave it while you settle in.'

'No sweat. I want to get it looking nice. I used to live here with my dad. Not that that's much of a reason in itself, but I'm tidy-minded.'

'Yeah? Say, do you miss your dad, him being dead and all?'

'Oh, he's not really dead, just shamming. He's under cover up in Shanty Town. Seems like he's starting a gang of psychopathic killers strung out on some brand of home-made religion.'

'You don't say? Takes all kinds, I guess. Diff'rent strokes for diff'rent folks. Say, do you know how to skin a number?'

'Can a swim duck? Pass the makings.'

Tatum said he was going out, don't wait up. I slept on the couch in the sitting-room. At two in the morning Tatum came in. The crashing about woke me up. I heard him go into the kitchen and open the fridge. There was a lot of clinking and a rhythmic muttering that went on and on, a mad ritual stuck in a groove, counting up to seventeen over and over again. I got up and went through. He was counting the bottles of beer in the fridge.

'Ah, just making sure I got enough.'

'The shops are open again in the morning.'

He nodded.

'Fifteen, sixteen . . . Yeah, okay, I guess you're right; there's plenty, unless we get visitors. What happens if we get visitors?'

'It's unlikely at this hour.'

Tatum got up and searched his pockets.

'Say, you ever try one or ten of these?'

He held out a handful of blues. I palmed a couple and fetched a glass of water.

'Please,' said Tatum. 'Be my guest, have a beer.'

'Okay, if you're sure you can spare it.'

'Sure I can spare it. As many as you like. Skin another number. You feel like talking?'

I swallowed the blues. I shook my head.

'No, not much, but I will do soon.'

Amphetamine dawn is the most beautiful dawn in the world. Someone should write a poem about it. Not me, though. I'm too busy talking about the last time I got pilled-up. Which is what I always talk about when I'm pilled-up.

'You're really a great conversationalist, you know,' says Tatum. 'Anyone ever tell you that?'

Speed kills the cynic in you, along with a lot of other things I suppose, but even so, I scan Tatum's words for irony. Not a trace. This man is my best friend. I really like him best of all. Down in the street the milkman's horse clip-clops and whinnies.

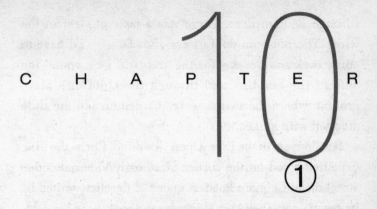

We gabbled six hours straight. At last Tatum stretched and yawned.

'Guess I'll mandy-up now and score some shut-eye. I got a tricky canto to wrap and a signing session at Harrods. What you gonna do?'

'One: check out the Imperial War Museum, see what they have on the Commune. Two: call in the Convent and say hello to Jude. Three: come back here and clean up. Four: transcribe those recordings of survivor stories you got lying around. Five: grab some sack-time. Six . . .'

'Okay, okay, how about some mandies for later? Best way to sack-out after a speed-run.'

'No, I got some opium. Methaqualone gives me the hives.'

A convoluted debate on the relative merits of Mandrax and opium for bringing you down off speed took up the best part of the next hour. Finally, happed up against the cold in cap and muffler, and gifted with a pocketful of mandies, which I finally accepted to shut Tatum up, I was out on the street, whistling for a cab.

I rode a pedishaw to Kennington Road and walked

through Bedlam Park. There was a taste of sleet in the wind. The museum doors were shut fast, so I'd have to come back another day for the archives. I cut round the side of the building and through the children's playground, where the swings were chained up and the slide studded with spikes.

The Convent of the Ever-Open Wounds of Christ the King Crucified stood on the corner of an early Victorian sidestreet off St George's Road. A queue of derelicts waited by its green door. They were shivering and shaking in the cold, heads down against the wind. An old man at the end of the line cuddled a grizzling baby, mumbling words I couldn't catch. The Convent bell chimed the Angelus. The door opened and a nun came out to the portico. She counted heads, then shouted over her shoulder, 'Ten cocoas, twenty slices and a baby's bottle.'

I stood back, out of respect. When feeding was nearly done I crossed the road and said hello. The nun put her hands on her hips and gave a sigh of exasperation.

'I didn't see you lurking there. The cocoa's all gone, and the bread and marge. Let me see, how about some water?'

I was spitting cotton with the blues. She pulled a bottle from her robes, uncorked it and I tipped it back. I ran the back of my hand across my mouth.

'Thanks, most welcome, but I didn't come for charity. I've come to see Mrs Razumski. I understand Jude is staying here?'

'Auburn hair, rather pasty?'

'Yes, that's her.'

'You'd better come in and talk to Mother Superior. Mrs Razumski vanished last night. I was told to make up a cell for her and she'd be here ten days at least. Went off without a word. Mother Superior is most perplexed. I'm Sister Joseph, by the way.'

'Pleased to meet you, Sister Joseph.'

She ushered me inside and closed the door. An old nun sat in a cane chair, a little way down the corridor, with her feet resting on the bottom tray of a tea trolley.

'Sister Malachi, will you collect the mugs? Give them a few minutes to finish. Don't forget the baby's bottle; it's my last one.'

Sister Malachi made no reply. She seemed fast asleep.

'Come on, Sister. No dozing on the job.'

Sister Joseph clapped her hand on the sleeping nun's shoulder and gave her a gentle shake. Sister Malachi slid off the chair and tumbled to the floor. The impetus of her fall sent the tea trolley scooting down the highly polished, black and white tiled corridor. Sister Joseph knelt down and lifted up Sister Malachi's celluloid wimple. She listened to her heart and felt her pulse.

'Oh dear, I think she's dead.'

She peered into Sister Malachi's eyes and felt for the pulse in her neck.

'Yes, no doubt about it. She was rather ancient and drank far too much cocoa. It's a blessing Father Michael is here today. He can dish up the last rites before Sister Malachi goes cold on us. Go and get the tea trolley and we'll use it as a hearse.'

I fetched the trolley and we tried lifting Sister Malachi

aboard. Sister Joseph took the shoulders and I took the ankles. Sister Malachi weighed in heavy. A rosary wrapped round her middle, with beads the size of boulders, didn't help much. We strained and heaved and could hardly get her off the ground.

'Listen, you're doing it all wrong. Close her legs up, for goodness' sake. You're like some gormless rustic with a wheelbarrow. That's it. See, it's much easier now.'

We wheeled Sister Malachi down the corridor. High narrow windows fed us a ration of grey sky. The air was chill. The cast-iron radiators gave out no more heat than a baby's breath. Sister Joseph grumbled.

'This is one more dimple in her wimple for Sister Bariel. She's something of a prophetess. She's blessed, or cursed if you like, with "The Sight". She had a dream the other night where she saw all this happening. It got all round the Convent, of course, though I doubt if Sister Malachi abated her cocoa-drinking by one single cup as a consequence. Ah, there's Father Michael now.'

A priest in a black cassock was stiffly descending the main staircase with a finely wrought chasuble over his arm, stepping carefully, looking down at his feet. He wore an orthopaedic shoe on his left foot, which seemed to be clubbed. His ears looked as if they belonged to a bigger man and stuck out proud. On hearing his name he straightened up and turned towards us, carefully negotiating the last few stairs.

'Yes, Sister Joseph, what is it? And what's the matter with Sister Malachi? She looks quite ill. Are you taking her to the Infirmary?'

'Not much point in that, Father. She's dead. I have to take her straight out the back. The rules of the Order are quite firm. Burial to follow within four hours of death. That gives Sister Arnold and her Pioneers just enough time to dig the grave and make ready. Hard work in this weather, with the ground frozen. They'll need to light a bonfire first, to soften it.'

The man in black smiled slyly and nodded and tried to slither past us. Sister Joseph touched his sleeve as he made to go.

'Oh, but you'll give Sister Malachi the last rites, won't you, Father?'

He shook his head and bent towards us, better to stress what he was about to say. I caught a whiff of his perfumed breath, sickly cachou overlaying a tang of rotten eggs and tobacco.

'Really, this has come at a most inconvenient time. There's a gaggle of Anglican sky pilots downstairs in the cellar, waiting for me to display this fetching example of the rober's art, and I have every expectation of taking half a dozen firm orders. As for Sister Malachi, I'm sure she died in a state of grace. I don't think God looks too severely on the cocoa-abusers of this world, do you? Just leave her by the back door and cover her decently. And no, you may not use my chasuble as a shroud.'

'Oh, please give Sister Malachi the last rites, Father. She's still warm . . . yes, just, but not for much longer. It's terribly chilly in here, don't you think, Father?'

Father Michael unfolded the chasuble for our inspection. His demeanour softened and his voice turned seductive.

'That's where this little beauty comes in handy. You're officiating in a draughty Anglican church with low attendance, so no nice congregational fug to take the chill off, but wrapped in this, you're hot as the hobs of Hell . . . although you need the right undergarments. I've started a nice line in thermals, all the way from Rome – Italian styling at its best, firm support where it's needed, and consecrated by the Holy Father. Here, take a look.'

He fished a pair of drawers from his coat pocket and spread them out on the chasuble.

'See the label? Cross keys, triple crown. They're the real McCoy all right. Here, son, have this pair on me.'

'Thank you.'

'Don't mention it. I'm hoping they'll go great guns with the lost sheep downstairs. You don't fancy modelling them, do you? Never mind, another time perhaps. Oh yes, great guns altogether. The Pope's imprimatur on their drawers is just the fillip some of these impostors need. We'll run them up the flagpole and see who salutes. I'm thinking of having them made over here, under franchise. The trick is to subcontract. I know a very obliging fellow up in Shanty Town, name of Arnie.'

'Yes Father. In the meantime . . .'

'Yes Sister, the last rites. Listen son, nip along to the library and fetch my snuffbox.'

'Father means his Extreme Unction case, hand-tooled in purple leather by me and monogrammed in gold.'

'And quite the nicest Christmas present I had too, Sister Joseph. If you could knock a few more out, I could easily get rid of them for you.'

He tapped the side of his nose with a tobacco-stained finger and winked.

'I haven't the time, Father.'

'You don't have to worry about that. Arnie can sweat them out for you. He has so many nimble-fingered girls on his books. Think about it and let me know. A few shekels more never went amiss.'

'I'll think about it, Father. Now, young man, the library is straight ahead; jink left at the Sacred Heart, hang a right and you're there. You can't miss it.'

I clopped along and brought back the snuffbox. Sister Joseph pointed me up the stairs.

'The Limbo Room is up there, along the corridor and on your left. Sister Vincent will be along directly.'

10②

The Limbo Room was furnished with a table and three straightback chairs. On the wall was a signed portrait of the Pope. Beside it was a grainy photograph that looked as if it had been taken in a rainstorm. It showed the founder of the Order of the Ever-Open Wounds of Christ the King Crucified holding out her palms imprinted with stigmata. Her eyes looked like sections through a hard-boiled egg.

I contemplated Santa Remedios of Oviedo for a while. Her eyes began to divide and multiply like bacteria. Steady as she goes, I told myself, popping another drinamyl tablet under my tongue and wishing I had a bottle of beer to wash it down.

As if in answer to a prayer, the door opened and a middle-aged nun came in, carrying a tray bearing bottles of Abdication Ale and two tumblers.

'I thought you might like a cold libation. I'm gasping myself, and the sun is well over the yard-arm.'

She poured me a beer and took a great gulp herself, straight from the bottle.

'That's better. Sister Vincent is the name and I'm in charge here, though goodness knows I seem to be the last person to know what's going on. But you don't want to listen to my whinging. It was good of you to lend a hand with Sister . . .'

She snapped her fingers twice.

'Malachi?' I offered.

'That's the one. She cost us a fortune in cocoa. No, that's unfair, God forgive me. After all, we're in the business of giving it away and we get something precious in return, so many days' purgatorial indulgence for every mug. Forgive my churlishness, child. It's one thing after another: Mrs Razumski doing a bunk to God-knows-where and Sister Malachi dropping dead like that, without so much as a by-your-leave. And Christmas to contend with on top of it all.'

Sister Vincent took another pull on the beer bottle and poured the remains into her glass.

'Sometimes I think I'll go mad, except we've got one mad nun already. Any more and we'd exceed our quota. If it weren't for Archbishop Cyril and his kindness, I don't know what I'd do. Oh for goodness' sake, what is it now?'

There was a frantic rapping on the door. Sister Vincent got up and opened it. A tiny nun sidled in, arms waving, babbling in the old Scots tongue from a mouth of blackened stumps.

'It's you, McWhinny. The foul maker o' the twa-backed humpty beast. I kenned you were nearby. I spied you this forenoon as in a glass darkly while I was shining the door-plate with Brasso. You swam in the depths of my lustrous sheen, copulating with yon wabbit-looking wumman, Jude. Foul fiend, and fornicators both.'

'You weren't by any chance actually drinking the Brasso, were you?' said Sister Vincent. 'I ought to introduce you before we go any further. This is Sister Bariel, who came to us when we shut our Stonehaven house. And you, young man?'

'McWhinny. Lingus McWhinny.'

'So she's right about the name. And the copulation?'

'I'm afraid this is a delicate matter.'

Sister Bariel sat on my knee, plucking at my crotch with chapped and swollen fingers.

'Hello there, big dick. D'you want me to stiffen it for you?'

'Not just at the moment, thanks all the same.'

'I saw you in a dream last night. Fucking. You and the lassie. You look a lot younger in the flesh than you did last night. Rejuvenated, eh? So that's what fucking does for a body? Well then, big dick, let me tell you, you can straighten my wrinkles any time. But hark! Do you ken you're getting a bairn?'

'Oh please, Sister,' said Mother Superior. 'If you insist on carrying on like a weird sister from the Scottish play I'm going to send for a translator.'

I turned my head away from the charnel-house breath of Sister Bariel, who was now grinding her bottom into my lap. She reached out a claw for my beer glass and I let her take it.

'No need, Sister Vincent. What she says is quite clear. She alleges that through congress with Mrs Razumski I have unwittingly gone half-shares in a baby. As I have said, this is a business of some delicacy, but her description of me – saving your presence, ma'am – as "big dick" leads me seriously to doubt her powers of clairvoyance. Time will test the matter. Sister Vincent, this woman, although undoubtedly holy, is profoundly disturbed. Will you remove her from my knee before she soaks my shirt with slaver?'

'Ay, as you soaked the spey of that pasty-faced quine wi' bairn-getting marrow.'

She spat the words in my face and I flinched from the heat and foul hogo of her breath. Sister Vincent gathered up her rosary. The crucifix on the end served as a whistle. She put it to her lips and blew, conjuring two nuns in the uniform of the Infirmary. Between them they unfolded a strait-jacket, looking towards their Mother Superior for confirmation. Sister Vincent said, not unkindly, 'I think Sister Bariel will benefit from a spell of peace and quiet in a darkened room. Keep her restrained, sprinkle her with Holy Water and place consecrated wafers over her eyes. Take her down.'

We sat in silence while Sister Bariel's cackling laughter

faded into the labyrinth below. Sister Vincent lit a small, black and pungent cigar. She passed it to me and lit another for herself.

'Now, young man, we were talking about Jude.'

C H A P T E R 11 ①

Close on four in the afternoon I left the Convent, no wiser about Jude's intentions than when I came in. But I knew she had something inside her now that belonged to me, and that changed things. Say what you like, fatherhood still counts for something in this world. Me and my dad are nothing to go by.

The next thing was to track Jude down and give her the good news. In the course of nature she might not know for a while.

I went out the side door. There were no vagrants or cripples about but a wayward vicar was standing on the pavement with his back to me. He had a large, brown, paper parcel under his arm and he was shouting for a pedishaw. I went up to him.

'If it's a cab you want, you stand more chance on the main road.'

He jumped like I'd jabbed him with a cattle prod. In the dusk I saw the white face of Reverend Bartleby. I put my hand on his arm and introduced myself in a friendly manner, to calm him down. I reminded him of where we'd met.

'Ah yes. But surely you were John Doe then?'

'Let's just say I discovered my true self. But who knows? John Doe may prove useful in the future. Do you always travel under your own name? In there, for instance?'

I jerked my thumb at the Convent door. I had a shrewd idea of what was in the parcel. The Reverend was silent. I said, 'Been to any naughty vestment parties recently?'

A palpable hit.

'I'd appreciate it if your discretion could be relied on in this matter.'

'Don't worry about me, Rev. I'm a fellow traveller.'

I pulled from my pocket the papal underpants, Father Michael's gift. I flourished them in front of his eyes. He looked nervously up the street, but when I pocketed the garment he relaxed and smiled.

'I'm so glad you're sympathetic. Sarah is a brick about my little foibles, as was her dear dead mother, although she does rag me about it from time to time. There's no real harm in it, but my congregation is very Low and it just wouldn't do for it to get about.'

'Especially with the new job, eh? That's why your chauffeur isn't here, right?'

'Partly, although Pocock is the least of my worries. He's a pious chap but the outward form of his religion is a matter of indifference to him. As long as it lays great stress, as a matter of course, on the irredeemable sinfulness of the abomination of the loathsome crime of buggery then he's quite content. Actually, he's gone with Sarah to the sales. Harrods has started stocking her samplers and she wants to see how they're doing. And to do a little shopping on her own account, naturally.'

'Naturally, which leaves you with the problem of getting a cab incognito. Ah, what a stroke of luck, there's one turning the corner now. Taxi!'

'I say, why don't you come back to Saint Sepulchre's and have tea with us? I'm sure Sarah would be delighted.'

'Are you? I'm not, but I'll come all the same. Sarah and I have a mutual friend whose whereabouts I wish to divine.'

The pedishaw cruised alongside and stopped. It was pedalled by a strong, muscular woman, past the flush of youth but with a handsome face under the grime of the road.

'Where to?'

'Saint Sepulchre's.'

'Is that Sepulchre's-in-the-Stews, or in-the-Mire?'

'In-the-Mire, without a doubt.'

'Hop in, your Reverence. You too, son.'

The jockey heaved herself up and leaned on the pedals, her weight bearing down on the driving chain. Her buttocks looked set to chew their way through her leather pants. I settled back in the wicker to enjoy the ride.

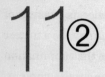

The Reverend Bartleby talked about Oxford most of the way home. He assumed I knew the place intimately. He talked of college, schools, gowns, hoods, silk, BAs, MAs, D.Lits,

Greats, Modern Greats, Firsts, Formal Firsts, Congratulatory Firsts, Jericho and Periclean Athens.

'When I entered the room, the Chief Examiner said, "Congratulations, Mister Bartleby." However, he kept his hat on and remained seated. As I understand it, strictly speaking, that is not a Congratulatory First.'

I grunted and kept my eyes on the jockey's buttocks.

Saint Sepulchre's was situated just off Trafalgar Square. We rode up Whitehall, past the Cenotaph then the statue of Charlie One, and into the Square. A chap with a camera was rubber-necking Nelson, much like the French sharpshooter must have done. Just before the turn to the Gallery, our pedishaw got stuck in a jam whose source seemed to be some drunken Yanks coming round the wrong way in a jeep. Our jockey bellowed along with the rest, standing up to get a good look round and maybe spot a way through. Nothing doing. A bobby came over to sort things out.

I was keeping an ear half-cocked to the Reverend Bartleby's monologue – he'd begun to tell me that Nelson was the greatest sailor the world had ever seen – and musing on the jockey's derrière, when I spied a young man in painter's overalls crossing the Square. He carried an aluminium stepladder in one hand and a bucket in the other. He had a sack on his back, with rolls of paper and brushes sticking out. He didn't look much like a painter to me, more like a philosophy student, with gold-rim specs and long hair flowing round his ears.

He stopped by a lion and set up his ladder. He climbed the ladder, carrying a roll of paper. He held the paper out at arm's length and let the roll drop. There was a strange device painted on the banner but I couldn't twig it. He showed it round the Square then hung it on the ladder. He lifted the bucket and poured whatever over his head. He took a fag from his pocket and a lighter and clicked, once, twice. He spoke to the crowd. Someone handed him a box of matches.

He struck a match, lit the cigarette and then he was burning from head to toe. He screamed and fell from the ladder and skittered about on his back, jackknifing and springing up like a Chinese cracker. The traffic cleared and we were off again, with the Reverend Bartleby talking of Oxford, oblivious. We made the church and I got down and paid the fare. The Reverend Bartleby said he'd go halves but found his pockets were empty.

'Oh dear, I seem to have spent all my money on frillies. Makepeace will reimburse you.'

The jockey handed me change and I gave her back a shekel, holding it out on the palm of my hand. As she took it she made a little circle with her finger in the middle of my palm. Her tongue flicked out from between her parched lips. I felt a lurching in my balls.

'Here, take this card,' she said, winking. 'If you ever need a cab, give us a call.'

The card read:

ErCabs
Percy's Cantina
Appine Way
Shanty Town
Booze Broads Dick Drugs
30207-902-47365

'I'll do that.'

I watched her buttocks heave away from the kerb.

'Or if tea isn't to your fancy,' said Bartleby, 'I have a superb fino that my venerable tutor Doctor Boggs introduced me to. I always drink it at home.'

Makepeace, aged family retainer, verger and church-warden, was at the vestry door to greet us. He was dry and shrivelled like a vanilla pod, with a strong scent of custard clinging to him. He bowed.

'Good afternoon, your Reverence. The kettle's on, and tea and crumpets will be ready presently. Will I lay an extra place for this young man?'

'Indeed, Makepeace. No, please leave the parcel, I shall carry it up myself.'

'As you wish, sir. Miss Sarah is already home, with an American gentleman. A poet, like old Sir John. Ah, there never was a poet to touch Sir John. He gave me a half-crown on Coronation Day – that's the old Queen's coronation, sir. I was "boots" at Brown's then, and I made sure Sir John's Oxfords had a lustrous sheen that day. Yes sir, I did. If I never shine another pair, I certainly shined those. Will I have the pleasure of laying a place for Mrs Bartleby, sir? Is she coming down today?'

'I very much doubt it, Makepeace. As I believe I must have told you, my dear wife, your quondam mistress, is dead.'

'Ah, so that's it. Dead.'

'Yes indeed, Makepeace. It explains rather a lot, wouldn't you say?'

'If you say so, sir.'

'Very well, let's go up.'

Makepeace stood aside to let the Reverend Bartleby go first. He put a finger to his temple and tapped, giving me a sly wink.

'Dead?' he whispered. 'I don't believe it.'

11 ③

We climbed the stairs and entered a stone-flagged corridor. At the end of the corridor the parlour door was ajar. Sarah was sitting by the fire with a sampler on her knee, stitching. Tatum Liotes sat opposite her with his hands outstretched towards the steep bank of glowing coals.

'Hello, Papa, who's that with you? Gosh, young Lingus. This is jolly. Look who I bumped into in Harrods. Mister Liotes was autographing copies of his wonderful book of poems, *Seven Ways to Peel a Banana*.'

'*Rainbow*,' said Tatum. '*Peel a Rainbow*.'

'Yes, and the punters were snapping them up, weren't they? And my samplers too. I've sent Pocock up to Arnie's in the Rolls to pick up another batch. It's all too jolly for words.'

'Makepeace,' said the Reverend Bartleby. 'Sherry for our guests, the Senior Common Room fino. And you may bring up the tea and crumpets.'

Makepeace poured sherry for Tatum and me. The Reverend Bartleby and Sarah declined sherry on the grounds of the sermon he had to write and the sampler she had to finish. We all ate buttered crumpets. I described the suicide I'd seen in the Square.

'Really?' said Sarah. 'We came that way in the Rolls. We must have just missed it. Did you find it terribly frightful, Papa?'

'To tell the truth, my dear, I saw nothing of the event our young friend describes. My mind was on Oxford.'

'What about you, Makepeace? See anything?' said Tatum.

'Afraid not, sir. I haven't set foot outside Saint Sepulchre's recently. Not since the wedding of the Duke – that's the King, now, sir, of course – that was my latest excursion, and I haven't cared to repeat the experience. I saw the way things were going and I was better off cleaving to the Mire.'

He looked sad, stirred by some melancholy memory. Then he brightened.

'I have taken the liberty, sir, of preparing a trough of hot custard against the inclement weather. Will yourselves and your guests taste it?'

'Good scout! I knew I could smell it, and this is just the weather for it. And to go with the unctuous yellow emulsion – first cousin to ambrosia, Liotes, wait till you taste it – perhaps a generous length of spotted dick, eh, Makepeace?'

Makepeace was puzzled.

'Oh no, sir. Just the custard. Mrs Bartleby always says my custard needs no adjunct.'

'Hear hear!' said Sarah. 'But perhaps you could bring in a few biscuits for those of us who aren't blessed with Mother's exquisite palate?'

Makepeace shuffled out and brought back the biscuit

barrel. He began ladling the custard. We arranged ourselves at the table.

'Hey, that's plenty for me!' said Tatum. 'Where is Mrs Bartleby anyhow?'

'My dear wife is no longer with us. That is her portrait over there, painted by Jeremiah Brandreth. It was his last work before the dreadful events of the Commune. My dear Emma was a Brandreth, you know. Jeremiah is Sarah's uncle.'

'Good old nuncs! Bags I the skin!'

Sarah draped the custard skin over a fork and lowered it into her gaping mouth.

'Say, this Brandreth guy? I'm scheduled to interview him on New Year's Eve. I hope he doesn't mind me hassling him the night before he takes off.'

'Oh no, Jeremiah is most mild-mannered and polite. Of course, the hospitality of the Tower may have jaundiced him somewhat, but I'm sure he'll do his best for you. It's in his own interest to co-operate with you for the historical record. I fancy he'll want to present Clio with his best profile, as it were. You will treat Jeremiah fairly?'

'Sure. I know I'm the Laureate and all, but I'm no stoolie. He'll get a fair shake. This Commune of yours, the way I see it, belongs to the whole nation, like . . . like the Beatles.'

We looked blankly at him.

'Listen, what I mean to say is the Commune was history as hands-on experience. The kind of history we all thought Britain was done with, since you lost those itty-bitty islands, what you call 'em?'

'The Malvinas?' I said.

'Yeah, wherever. Okay, here's the deal. You get your history bagged up in an epic poem, which is something no one has done since the Ancient Greeks and *The Iliad*, right? And what's more, you get it bagged up by a Greek, and the Greeks invented poetry.'

The Reverend Bartleby dunked a biscuit in his custard.

'Yes, I take your point, but I'm not so sure about no one attempting history in epic verse since the Ancient Greeks. There's Hardy for one, "The Dynasts".'

'Did this Hardy guy ever lie bare-assed all night on a hill with some evildoer trying to shoot his balls off? Me, I've seen action, I can relate to these people, the Brandreths, and even that guy Lingus says he saw torch himself down there. That's commitment. Sure, his ideas may be a crock, but if he believes in them enough to barbecue his dick, respect is due. Go for it!'

Tatum grabbed the sherry bottle — the label showed a tweedy don, glass in hand and pipe in mouth, sitting by an open fire in an oak-panelled and book-strewn room with a copy of Gibbon on his knee — and poured himself another glass. I followed suit. Reverend Bartleby said, 'Hang me and hang the sermon. It's Christmas. Fetch me a glass, Makepeace, and have one yourself. Sarah?'

'No, Papa. I was thinking of trying a drop or two of the Good Oil later. I'm not sure it agrees, on top of sherry.'

'Nonsense, my dear, I find they mix admirably. Sherry all round. Makepeace, open another bottle.'

We were spooning up the last of the custard. Makepeace dozed by the fire with a glass of sherry in his hand. Tatum talked some more about his epic.

'The Commune was like a family where two brothers are having a ruckus. Okay, they go outside and dust each other off with their mitts. Afterwards, they shake. Good buddies again, see?'

The smell of custard grew stronger. Makepeace, heavily impregnated, was baking fast in front of the fire and filling the room with fumes. Sarah pulled his chair away from the blaze. He woke up, drained his glass and said, 'Ah, you talk of poetry, but there was never a poet to touch Sir John. I remember when I was down on my luck and washing up at the Claremont. Sir John was in the dining-room and he asked for custard. They told him, "Custard's off." "Custard's off?" he said. "Yes", they said. Luckily I heard what was going on. I had a Thermos of custard handy for my own dinner, so I sent out to ask if he'd care to partake. "Would I?" he said. "Fetch the man himself that I might shake his hand." And so I was quickly spruced up and brought out to him, fetching the custard in the Thermos so he'd have the beauty of it hot. He shook my hand and gave me half a crown. He pronounced my custard the finest since Nanny Hodge's. I asked if he remembered me from Brown's, but unfortunately not. But a man in thrall to the muse can't be expected to remember everyone, can he?'

'I have problems in that line myself,' said Tatum.

Conversation came round again to Jeremiah Brandreth. The Reverend Bartleby said, 'Due to Jeremiah being family, and the Homeland Controller and myself in the same house at school, and together at the 'varsity . . . and him cox and me stroke in the college VIII, I have a special dispensation to claim the body for burial, which I intend to carry out in the crypt of Saint Sepulchre's, next to my dear Emma, so that she may lie with her brother at last, where I hope to lay my own weary bones one day. Jeremiah shall be embalmed. High John has offered to carry out the work himself. I wish High John had handled my Emma before . . . I mean when . . . she passed away.'

A sherry tear trickled down his cheek.

'But at least I have this fine portrait of her.'

Sarah put an arm round her father.

'There, there, Papa. I wonder, since Sir Lionel's dispensation only extends to our claiming the dead body of Jeremiah, and not to any last meeting and shriving of his living one, whether Mister Liotes might perform a small service for us?'

'Ah, my dear, I wish he might! It was my dearest wish to attend Jeremiah in the Tower and on the scaffold, but it was not to be. There are professional courtesies to be observed, and a certain jealousy involved. The Chaplain of the Tower guards his privilege with a fierce and scowling proprietorship. But if Liotes here . . .'

'Shoot, padre. You name it, I'll do it. Anything except springing him from jail or filleting his whang.'

'Filleting his . . . ? No, neither of those will be necessary, I assure you. I wouldn't dream of asking you to perform anything that would put you to any trouble. This is a spiritual matter. Sarah, do you have the Bible High John gave us?'

Sarah handed her father a tiny Bible, no bigger than a matchbox. Reverend Bartleby passed it to Tatum.

'Perhaps you could give him this and draw his attention to the verses marked on the flyleaf? They should prove a great comfort to him.'

Tatum flicked through the book.

'I sure hope Uncle Jeremiah has twenty-twenty vision. Say, who is this High John you all keep gabbing on about?'

'Who indeed?' said Reverend Bartleby. 'And what matter? He is inspired by God, a prophet. Sarah and I have recently begun taking instruction from him. His words of divine guidance supplement the daily bread of our faith and freshen up what through custom has become stale.'

'Kind of a vitamin E buzz for the soul, huh? Say, I had a guru once.'

'Oh my dear chap, if only you knew! He is a father to me, although in age we might be brothers.'

His eye lit on the brown paper parcel of vestments.

'He understands.'

Reverend Bartleby wept copious tears.

Sarah showed us out. I asked about Jude.

'It's such good news about Jude. Now that the time is nigh for High John to walk by day, Jude is chosen to walk with him. Do you know, I think I'm the teeniest bit jealous. So far, Papa and I have only heard High John's voice from behind a screen. I'm sure Jude must have been admitted to the full presence by now. Aren't you pleased for her?'

Before I could speak Makepeace rushed upon us, sparing me the embarrassment of an answer.

'Thank goodness you're still here. I've made up a Thermos of custard for Mister Jeremiah. He did so enjoy it last time he was here and I don't suppose they've been feeding him at all properly.'

'Thank you, Makepeace, but I don't think it will keep until New Year's Eve.'

I saw he was hurt.

'But I'll take it with me. I'm sure it will be fine in a Thermos.'

He beamed. Tatum joined us at the door.

'Cab along in two minutes. Here's your card.'

'Thanks,' I said.

We said our goodbyes and went out into the street.

Ah, here they were again! Those magnificent arse-cheeks fidgeting away, striking the rising blow, their leather cleft grinning. Pirate Jenny she called herself, after Brecht I suspected but she didn't say. She ranted and roared at anyone who got in her way while Tatum and I yelled at her to gee up. She rode like a charioteer in the Hippodrome. In Haymarket, Tatum leaned dangerously out of the wicker to conduct an altercation of his own with a dowager in a limousine. I grabbed his coat and yanked him in. Back home, I insisted I pay the fare. I gave Jenny two shekels extra this time. She grinned.

'I finish work at ten. Want me to drop by?'

'I want. Number ninety-nine.'

Tatum whooped. 'And I'll be tom-catting around, so you got a clear run.'

I took Jenny's hand and kissed it.

'Until tonight.'

CHAPTER 12

①

I opened the door of the flat and flicked the light switch.

'The bulb's gone,' said Tatum.

I stepped forward into the corridor and tripped headlong over a heavy object blocking the way.

'Jesus, what the . . .'

'Ah, sorry, man. Must be my butt of sack. They brought it up just as I was going out and I couldn't think where to stash it. Here, give me a hand. We'll set it up in the front room.'

Together we rolled the barrel down the corridor.

'Under the window. Yeah, fine.'

Tatum drew the bung and turned the tap. We filled a couple of bumpers and tossed them off in a toast to Charlie Two.

'One helluva groovy guy, best-hung King you Limeys ever had.'

We drank another toast, to Andy One this time.

'Andy One is a far-out cat,' said Tatum. 'Hey, it ain't his fault but I really had to hustle to get this Spanish ripple. No more than my due.'

'Better late than never.'

Tatum said he was going for a bath so I went to piss first.

I stood for a long while, waiting on my bladder. I looked at my face in the mirror. I was losing the healthy shine I'd put on with Orlando. Already? I nodded at myself: yep, sure was. My reflection smiled then winced. My head felt like a sickroom with the blinds down. What I needed was something to put me up where I was before. I buttoned my fly and went looking for the speed. Tatum was prowling around with a towel round his waist. He had a fistful of odd socks.

'If only I could get a pair.'

I found a partner for a lurid Argyle. Tatum went to run his bath. I chased a couple of blues down the hole with a sloosh of sack. I counted the blues left in the tub. Thirty-nine. Better just check. Thirty-eight, no, thirty-nine. I was aware of Tatum squinting at me round the door.

'No need to ration them; plenty left.'

Tatum splashed happily in the bath, crooning some drivel about a pony, a saddle, a trail, a buddy, another buddy, a buffalo and a pair of old chaps. I sat and smoked a cigarette, one of Tatum's 5/11s. I heard the rattle of the letter-box. I went out to look. There was an envelope lying on the carpet. No stamp, my name in block letters and a funny smell to the paper, like photographic chemicals but peppery. I took it into the living-room and looked out of the window to see if I could spy the messenger. A man in aviator's uniform was crossing the road to a Rolls-Royce. Pocock. I slit open the envelope.

Dear Lingus

First off, let me say I'm happier now than I've ever been. I feel I've come home. And you have to take at least some of the credit for my happiness. I think I may have gone on for ever, a wretched castaway clinging to the wreckage of my marriage, if you hadn't turned up. Taking you in when you were down and out, seeing you come back from the dead, seeing you blossom, helped me wake up to the premature burial of life with Wence. And to realise that things don't have to go on this way for ever, that change can come if our will is strong.

Thank you, dear Lingus. I hope you will always think kindly of me. I'm sure you will have lots of other girls before you settle down, but you won't forget me in a hurry, will you? Does that sound vain?

You won't tell anyone about, you know, my Christmas present? I've sworn Sarah to secrecy. She's a brick and I'm sure I can rely on you. Things are a bit delicate here, you see, and I'd rather it didn't get about. High John, or Daddy as he likes me to call him, is rather keen on the fact that I'm technically – well, you know – 'pure', sort of. And I am chaste really, in a married way, except for just the once with you. What Wence used to do doesn't count, because of never getting to Condition 3, as I explained before. And it was him I was – technically – married to, not you.

Anyway, I've already written to the Pope asking for an annulment on the grounds of non-consummation. Father Michael helped me write it – because it has to be in Latin (I thought they'd abolished it?) – and he says consider it as good as done because of the two thousand shekels I put in the envelope, with five hundred on top for Father Michael.

Which leads me to my main point, my big, big news! I'm married again. Yes, really, so soon. Isn't it wonderful how things turn out? And to the most marvellous man: High John, my very own 'Daddy'. We were married this morning. He sent for me last night – just like that, so masterful! – and I had a bodyguard of the Sons of Onan to bring me into Shanty Town. It was the arrival of the Queen of Sheba all over again (without her hairy legs – I'd had a wax).

I don't have time to go into all the details – the bridal ritual of the Shanty Town women last night, the marriage ceremony this morning – because I'm scribbling these few lines while Pocock sorts out another batch of samplers from Arnie, and I thought I'd just snatch the opportunity to let you know the good news, and Sarah too, of course. I think even she'll be surprised how quickly it's all happened, although she knew something was in the wind and didn't tell me, naughty girl, but that was Daddy's orders, I suppose, and I must say it's all been a wonderful surprise.

There's a wonderful surprise coming later tonight, too. Daddy's out arranging it now. Apparently he knows some people – he would, of course – who can smuggle us out of the country to an undisclosed honeymoon destination, though

Arnie says it's most likely Tirana, as apparently Shanty Town is building up quite an export trade to there (black economy, naturally, if you'll excuse the expression). We'll travel by submarine, says Arnie. I'm sure I'll love it. As long as I'm snug as a bug in the rug of Daddy's arms, I don't mind where I am. Oh dear, am I making you jealous? I don't mean to, honestly. (I say, I just remembered the time when you were barmy and thought 'Daddy' was your 'daddy', if you see what I mean. What a lark if he really was!)

By the time you get this, I'll be en route for Tirana. Wish me luck. If you see Sarah, tell her pip-pip and chin up – she's a super girl, we're really close now, like sisters, and if Daddy wanted her for a concubine I'd be so proud, but he says he has other plans for her (don't breathe a word – whatever it is, Daddy wants it to be a surprise).

Bye bye and lots of love,

Jude

PS – Daddy conducted the ceremony himself. Maybe we'll get a chance to meet when we come back from honeymoon and I'll tell you all about it.

PPS – Regards to Tatum. Arnie gave me a copy (pirated of course) of *Seven Ways to Peel a Banana* as a wedding present. I haven't read it yet, but I'll take it with me to read on the submarine.

Cheerio for now!

12②

Tatum was dressing to go out. He stood in front of the mirror and tweaked his hairpiece into shape.

'There's a box under the bed. There should be a couple of tapes and a disc or two. Have a listen and write down anything you think I can use. No rush. Meantime, roll me a spliff the size of a donkey's cock.'

I don't know much about donkeys, but I assume they're well-hung. I built a whopper, packing it with dynamite hish-hash.

'Going anywhere special?'

'I got a date with a Lifeguard, cavalry trooper, very smart. You think he'll notice this?'

Tatum patted his scalp. I lit up and took a good long draw. Tatum got a looking-glass and shimmied until he could see the back of his head. I blew smoke out through my nose.

'If it bothers you, maybe you should get a transplant or a weave or whatever the fuck, you know?'

I handed the joint to Tatum. He hunkered down, holding it between his pinkie and ring finger. He cupped his hands and pressed them to his face, sucking hard, taking in a lot of air. The joint burned sparky and fast. Tatum rocked back on his heels and grinned. We passed the number between us until we hit cardboard. Tatum got up and drained off another couple of bumpers of sack.

'This stuff looks like piss. Good though. The guy I'm seeing tonight, he's a vet.'

'What, like a horse doctor?'

'Vet as in veteran. Saw action against the Commune. Says he's the scion of a noble house but he enlisted as a trooper for the rough trade. A gentleman ranker out on a spree, doomed from here to eternity, right?'

'If you say so.'

We sat in silence, side by side, impassive like a couple of Buddhas.

'Maybe she won't show,' I said.

'Mata Hari? She'll show.'

Tatum stood up and wandered about like a man trying to find his way out of a maze. He opened the drawer and took out the blues. He swallowed a couple and pocketed some more.

'Help yourself. I got some crystal meth due soon, if you feel like taking some real drugs. Coming in from Hawaii, the Crystal Island.'

'A little taste never hurt anyone.'

I skinned up a second spliff – the size of a budgie's dick, not wanting to look greedy. Tatum frowned at the mirror and fingered his 'hair'.

'My date tonight says he can give me elocution lessons.'

Tatum finally got his hair where he wanted it. He whistled.

'Pretty tasty. What do you say?'

'Yeah, like Michelangelo's *David*, but real old.'

Tatum gathered up his keys, a pack of 5/11s and a bottle of rum.

'Treat the place like it's your own. When Catherine the Great arrives, use the bed if you need a bed for what you got to do. Here, just a bite . . .'

He kissed the budgie's dick goodbye. After he'd gone I sat and smoked another, the size of King Kong's prong. I watched the furniture come alive and stroll about. The room shimmered like a mirage. I dug out the box from under the bed, fitted a tape in the machine and sat with my pencil poised on paper. After a clatter of mike noise we were off. Tatum started off okay: name of informant, date of recording, venue . . . a bar somewhere on the fringe of Shanty Town. In a storm of slurping and shouting, an old man drooled into a glass and moaned about his shitty, pathetic life. Tatum goaded him on with the prospect of another drink, not a sound tactic, and after a bit the brain damage began to show, wet rot in the attic. Out of the mumble came a surprisingly lucid sequence about drinking in the latter days of the Commune.

TATUM: Oh yeah? What did you gargle after that?

OLD MAN: We was down to Purple Haze — that's meths, see? Some of the petrol bombers used to get fed up waiting for a tank to come and they'd think 'fuck it', you know, and just drink the petrol, but I could never fathom that. It don't do nothing for you, much. But meths, yeah, that's okay, you know . . . er . . . if you follow the right . . . er . . . the right . . . What's the word?

TATUM: Don't ask me, man. I never sunk so low. Sounds like a heavy chemical overload.

OLD MAN: Oh well, why should we worry? It was a case of *Moritori te salutant*.

TATUM [astonished]: Huh?

OLD MAN: We didn't give two fucks.

TATUM: Oh right, chug-a-lug, yeah.

OLD MAN: We had a system, see. We got rid of the purple
dye by straining it through a piece of bread. Mind
you, we were so hungry, most of the time we ended
up eating the bread anyway. Some days I could've
eaten a donkey's plonker fried in tar. I'm not so sure
I didn't, come to that . . .

And so on. This was advancing the cause of epic poetry not
one whit that I could see. I made a few notes anyway, just
in case Tatum's muse fed on garbage and passed on. Next
up, Tatum was in a honky-tonk where a band were busy
cursing and tuning their guitars. The drummer kicked the
bass tub a few times, eager to be off and running. An
E-string slipped and was cranked back up to pitch. I felt a
twinge of lust for the salty taste of rock and roll. I heard
Tatum shout abuse, very drunk. Up on stage someone said,
'Old English number, right? Kick it.'

The band hit a groove. A guitar screamed high and hot,
threatening meltdown, and the mortar-bomb vocal lobbed
through the air.

Auntie Maggie in the bathroom, brushing of her teethy-pegs,
Big pile of rubble, Uncle Harvey underneath he begs.
Hello! Is there anyone to hear me pray?
Now the bomb's gone off, please come and take the bodies
  away.

A barrage of bottles hit the stage. The singer threatened to
smash sundry skulls with the mike stand. A table splintered

and there was a rebel yell, Tatum probably. More screaming and breaking glass. The rest was silence.

I switched off and checked the clock. Half past nine. Time for a bath. In the tub, I anointed and flattered my body. Geordie breached the water like a periscope.

I was sprinkling talc between my toes when the doorbell rang. Jenny. I hung a towel over Geordie and crabbed it to the door. She was hot from the saddle and her tan-coloured leathers were streaked with oil. Her face was dirty and pitted with grit.

'I brought this.'

She held up a bottle of Johnny-Jump-Up. She had a duffle bag in the other hand. I brought her inside and closed the door. I kissed her, letting the towel fall.

'Hey, let me wash up first.'

I showed her my bogus vaccine certificate and then the bathroom. She stripped off and climbed into the water I'd just left. I took the soap and began lathering her. She grabbed my wrist and pushed my hand between her legs. Then she took the soap and washed her face. I handed her a towel. Geordie craned towards her like a plant to the sun. I leaned over the bath with my hands on the wall while she took me in her mouth. Her mouth was hot, a tropical forest, and her tongue fluttered like a humming bird. I tried to flee but her gums held me fast. Her fingers were splayed along my pelvic bone and her thumbs were tucked under my stones. And then I came, writhing like an eel in a creel. She swallowed, pushed me away and stood up. A trace of cuckoo-spit flecked the corners of her mouth. She gave me a tidal-wave kiss and I tasted my own saltiness, riding sly and subtle in the undertow, a phantom surfer. She sank into the bath and creamed her thighs with lather.

'Fetch me a drink. Got any beer? We'll save the Johnny for later.'

While Jenny splashed in the water, humming a tune from an opera I couldn't place, I prowled naked around the flat, fast and jerky like an overwound clockwork toy. I checked my eyes in the mirror. Flying saucers. I was spitting cotton again. I flew in the kitchen and popped the tabs on a brace of cans. I drank one straight off and took the other through to Jenny, along with a ready-rolled. She smoked and drank while I soaped her broad shoulders.

'Tell me about yourself.'

I gave her a story-so-far routine, leaving Dad and Jude out of the picture.

'You have many girls?'

'A few. One at a time.'

She pulled the plug and stood up. I rubbed her down with a towel. She spread her legs to let me dry her quim.

'I got precautions to take. Go to bed and wait for me.'

She bent down and nibbled Geordie. A fresh charge of lightning mustered in my stones.

12③

I lay on the bed and gazed round the room. Say what you like about speed; it does wonders for the look of a place.

Sharp outlines, singing colours. All in all, I felt better than I'd ever felt in my life, Joshua's trumpet about to blow. I sat up and clocked the picture above the bed. Everyone in it was on the move, like ants, rhythmic, powerful, organised. I switched on the bedside light and turned off the bare bulb overhead. I looked down at my groin. My shrink-wrapped balls had vanished inside. More like no-balls. Geordie Cyclops wobbled in small circles, a drunken umpire checking the state of play.

Jenny came in, her nipples standing proud, a light-blue-touch-paper-stand-clear number. I stood to greet her and, for the first time in my life to anyone at all, I told her I loved her, blah blah. I switched to gibberish, sucking her teats and moaning. I dropped on my knees and nuzzled her belly. I bowed my head and licked the stiff hairs inside her thighs. She massaged my scalp like she was kneading dough. We toppled over on the bed, with Jenny sitting on my face. She was luscious and soft, a ripe and bursting fruit. Her lips closed round Geordie Shafto and her tongue probed my glans, lapping up the marrow. I licked. She sucked, tugging me into her throat while her haunches gripped my temples and her buttocks ground my face to pulp.

Clogged with sweat and juice and jissom, we rolled over for some face time, to kiss and taste the ghost of our genitals in each other's mouths. I sighed and Geordie sagged, folding against Jenny's thigh. She slid down my belly to lick him clean and stand him up, a mare with her birthed foal.

Jenny squatted above me and screwed herself on to my shaft, an inch, two inches, all the way down, until I was thrusting up underneath her belly, a blind fish in the ocean trench, squirming in Creation's cleft, pickled in the briny, oozy weeds twisted about my gills.

Then it was over. We lay together, hot and cooling, newborn planet and moon. I pulled the eiderdown across and we crouched in each other's arms, breathing our sweet-sour honey and ammonia. At times like this, so they say, lovers swoon. But with three drinamyl ticking away inside me, giving off a plutonium buzz, I felt like I was wired into the Grid. Jenny had no trouble dropping off. She lay with her head in the crook of my arm and began to snore. I guessed she was well on the far side of forty. Jude was a long way back in my mind, a smudge of light in an overexposed snapshot. I got out of bed and wrapped myself in Tatum's Chinese dressing-gown. I went through to the living-room and switched on the television. I caught the start of a show. Star-spangled chorus girls came high-kicking across a rickety set while the band played some post-diluvian slime, heavy on brass and reeds, with trombones bawling stops and saxes snorting through the changes. The girls shuffled off and a tea chest in a tartan tux popped up like Punch and began to spiel. After a bit I took him for a comic and immediately warmed to him. I started a letter to him, telling him how he made the world a brighter place. I was laughing, high and jagged like a hyena, through clenched and grinding teeth, when Jenny wandered into the room, rubbing sleep from her eyes. She looked about to spit.

'You like this shit?'

'Eh?'

'For God's sake, switch it off and let's talk. How about a drink?'

I poured a couple of brimming beakers of Johnny-Jump-Up, keeping my eyes on the screen, grinning like a skull.

'Hey, that's enough, not on the carpet.'

Jenny bustled across to the set and pulled the plug. I felt a quick jolt of rage and then relaxed. Jenny sat beside me. With finger and thumb she spread my eyes wide open. She peered inside. My gormless phiz leered back.

'Ho hum, I thought so. You got any more of that?'

I cackled and fingered the drawer. She got the dooby-doobs and for a moment I was afraid she was going to flush them down the pan.

'Three for me. One more for you?'

I took two. Jenny started talking, telling me her life story in no particular order, scavenging among the years. But when she held them up to the light they sparkled with myriad reflections of complication and consequence, resonance and meaning, meeting and correspondence, time, strength, cash and patience. She paid heed to history, took it personally like she was a figure woven into the tapestry of the epoch. But history never made sense to me, no more than the nightmare you wake from to find you're in another nightmare. She had a high opinion of herself — why not? — and she babbled of destiny and greatness. She was vague about the coming shape. I tried to draw her out but she gave me a sideways glance and clammed it. I asked how come she took up cabbying.

'I was married to a kinky git. It was shit. Now I haul ass. I heave the wicker, hump the lump, whatever. Most pedal jockeys ride for a syndicate — Dublin Frank over in Kensal Green, Grandma Moses on the southside, Billy the Kid up

Highbury way. Then you got two other stables, besides Old Black Hack — Fifth Commandment and the Zoo Boys, the ZeeBees, right? Ever see *Ben Hur*? Young blade gets a capture, so maybe he's looking at two to five in the Hulks. If he's got legs, and bungs the bench, he can join the ZeeBees. Kind of a tax-deductible charity organisation — the guvment loves it — reformation through work, oh yeah? The boys are chained to the frame and wear open-crotch drawers so they can piss and dung where they go — the Shiteing ZeeBees. The Yanks love 'em , do big business there. Hey!'

Jenny dragged me to the floor and rammed my head between her legs. I licked but my mouth was dry. No matter, she was wet enough for both of us. I drank greedy for five minutes or so while she wailed and bucked, arching her back and pounding my hurdies with her heels. By now hot-dog Geordie was a straining greyhound in the slips. Jenny flung me up and around until goo-gam Geordie was gooming her tonsils. Jenny was a sucking tornado, turning me inside out. I stuck my finger full-length in her arsehole and nearly had a stroke when she bit me, but it did the trick. We came together, rolling over, and I thumped my head on the wall. Jenny spat out Geordie like he was gristle she'd found in a pie. I peeled my face off her quim and sat up on her belly, facing her, but I couldn't see as my eyelids were stuck together with vaginal sludge. I blinked into the light — diver surfacing — and watched poor wee Geordie dump a few smears of egg white flecked with blood in Jenny's belly button. She lifted her head and demanded a drink, then she was flat out on the carpet, nostrils flaring like a steeple-chaser. I asked if she wanted another bath and she said what did I think she was, a whore? Her head nodded from side to side. I began licking her clean, sucking the slime off her hair and her clit and lapping up the lather as she came again, jabbering away in a heathen tongue like she'd been zapped by the Paraclete.

I lit the gas fire. Pressure was low. I fetched a couple of beers and switched out the light. We smoked and gabbled for an hour and Jenny told me her story again from a zillion angles, and I prated about the last time I got pilled up, which by now was, uh, let me see, yesterday morning when Tatum came home. The doobs in between didn't count somehow. They just put me up where I was before.

We took it in turn to spiel at first, like a conversation, sort of, each pretending to listen to the other, each locked in a furious and frantic silence, waiting for a break in the rhythm, a pause for breath, to snatch the baton and run, gabbling our routines while the other fidgeted, nodding empathetically and all the time watching and listening for a chance to dismiss the legion of monologues crowding the echoing brain. The more we shouted, the more we found to shout about, each thought the parent of a thousand, and at last we didn't even bother to keep silence for each other but gabbled together in parallel. Oddly enough, this made it easier to concentrate on what the other was saying. Our proper routines played out without effort, like canned music.

At last Jenny told me to get dressed, she was taking me out on the town.

'Better open a window before we go. This place smells like a spunk hospital.'

We got outside to her pedishaw and I mounted the wicker

while she straddled the saddle. On Edgware Road we hung left and scooted towards Marble Arch. Just past midnight in the catatonia between Christmas and New Year, and few people about. Over in Hyde Park a brazier was burning where soldiers stood guard at the gibbet, where the trio of frosted stiffs had hung since Boxing Day. A wagon pulled up, unloading coffins. Dressed in prison-blue, dark as midnight, the London hanged were candied plums. We stopped for a gander.

Jenny pedalled on, shouting her story over her shoulder, while I sat silent in the wicker, swigging on the bottle. I was feeling high and mighty and nicely stoned, with the speed cutting through the hash like the sun through haze and the barbiturate in the blues taking the edge off the speed; the smoothest ride going, nothing like it.

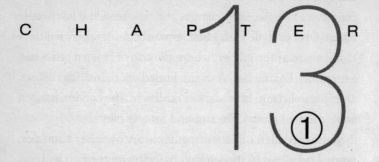

CHAPTER 13 ①

I lay on the hard-packed mud floor of a Shanty Town cantina and made an inventory of my bits. My tongue ranged over my teeth. No fresh gaps. I opened my eyes carefully. I flexed my limbs. Fingers and toes present and correct. All in all, in fair shape, except for my prick garrotted in the elastic of Father Michael's underpants and my bladder screaming for a piss.

I staggered up, a gangling shambles of protein jury-rigged into humanity by some primeval joker. Rain played bongos on the tin roof, thunder rolled and skybursts of blue fire raked the walls.

Scattered about me were the companions of my debauch, slaveys in Satan's kitchen, lying in a welter of beer and piss and dog-ends. Over by the stove sat a young man, a long thin cigar smoking on the table beside him and a guitar in his lap. His stubby brown fingers plucked a soft minor sequence.

'PeeJay's gone to hump the lump. She told me to tell you she's knocking off early because of New Year. For PeeJay to knock off early any time, let alone New Year's Eve, it must be love, little brother. Said she'll see you here tonight when you get through with Jeremiah Brandreth. If you can go the distance after the last three nights in the K-hole, that is. You and your uncle sure shift some stuff.'

I saw Tatum on his back and snoring, his head against a beer crate. A youth lay at his side, fast asleep, his arm thrown over Tatum's face. He didn't look much like a Lifeguard. My nose picked up the hum of the latrine. I picked my way through the bodies and went outside to the yard. A morose three-legged Alsatian squatted to defecate beside a lean-to of zinc and rotting timber. I kicked open the door. While I teetered on the brink of the earthen pit I studied the tag-wrack scrawled on a sheet of cracked plasterboard: 'I lick Yankee a/holes . . . When you think no one is thinking of you your mother is . . . Sunz uv Onan R loyal . . . Lingus4Jenny', and a poem, signed TL – 'If it smarts/Go to Barts/Think on this/When you piss' – evidence that the Laureate's muse followed him even here.

I buttoned and hurried inside the cantina, out of the cold and stink and rain. I sat down on a keg by the stove and fanned my hands over the heat.

'Smoke?'

I swallowed a mouthful of bile, coughed up a knotty wad and took the cigar.

'Yes indeed, little brother, it's been a mighty shindig these past nights. I can see by your eyes your memory is wiped. I'm Jolly Roger, yes? The guy you been playing congas with eight hours at a stretch, when you're not upstairs with PeeJay.'

I looked up at the tin roof.

'Upstairs?'

'Well, the roof is what I mean. The cold don't seem to bother you two, but you like your privacy. Your uncle, on the other hand, ain't so fussy. Percy had to have words about that. He's got a strictly-no-fucking-on-the-dance-floor policy. Now then, Lingus my man, are you in need of a song to serenade your Pirate Jenny? I'll write you one as a trade for anything you get off Jeremiah about his deeds and stuff – the real McCoy, mind. I want to make it to Hyde Park tomorrow with the ballad of Jeremiah Brandreth, but it's got to be the ace and deuce of *last goodnights*, see? Too many chancers on the ground as it is, so you have to stand out with the genuine jimson. When you get through visiting the grand-daddy of all insurrectionists, get your ditty-box back here.'

He brushed a chord and growled, *'The night before Larry was stretched / The boys they all paid him a visit.'*

He broke off and laughed.

'Don't forget, if you want a love song for PeeJay, look no further.'

I felt an itch in the crook of my arm. I rolled my sleeve to scratch. Three red puncture marks tracked a vein: methamphetamine stigmata.

'Oh that's bad business. Daddy oughtn't to let you play on the Crystal Island, dear me no. Where'd he get it? No, don't tell me.'

Jolly Roger worked his guitar, beating out a fandango. A few souls sat up, got on their creaky knees and began to crawl towards the bar, a macabre ballet choreographed by Ezekiel in his valley of dry bones. The music was wide and luminous, Spanish colour, Moorish intonation. Flamenco, Tango, Rembetika, Blues, home-grown Shanty Town Jive. Jolly Roger sang the refrain over and over, his melodic line swinging like a lariat.

'Ahoy caballero, Rio de Janeiro, poor Sons of Onan are loyal.'

From the floor an harmonica began to blow the changes. The song was an anthem. The skeletons mumbled it on their way to the bar. The storm had passed over now and grey daylight covered us like ash. Behind the bar an old man with a broken Roman nose and a head of tight white curls was hosing out beer on draught. Tatum joined me at the bar. The white-haired man was Percy, owner of Percy's Cantina.

'You two boys coming tonight? Big dog-roast up on the Midden.'

He indicated a poster. I nodded.

'If Jenny's here, I'm here, but me and Tatum got some business first.'

'Bonfire and fireworks too,' said Percy. 'What say you to that, Yankee Doodle?'

'Ah, count me in.'

We drank beer with Percy until close on noon. The meth was all gone and the ketamine too. Tatum produce a big bag of dexies.

'Have to be these from now on. Remember, they got no barbiturate in them, not like the blues, so you got to liquor up a little bit more.'

We got on to the subject of the referendum, and the good fist the Government was making of things these days, doing right by people, said Percy, you know, *asking them what they want for fuck's sake*.

'Face it,' said Percy. 'We'd have no judicial hanging other-wise.'

He mimed a noose stretching his neck.

'Referendum?' said Tatum. 'Sounds a mighty teejus way of doing things to me. In the States we used to elect a guy and he gave the orders. You mean you like the guvment calling you out of the can every five minutes to give your opinion on a donkey's fart? They fix it anyway for sure.'

Like it? Percy thought it was beezer. He saw himself as the ex officio mayor round here. He'd acquired extra voting rights over the past few years, buying the registration of desperate and broken drinkers. Percy was much taken by the vigilante spin on criminal justice.

'Hang 'em high, I say. Let 'em swing. The way I see it, what would really put Shanty Town on the map would be if we could get a municipal gallows up there on the Midden. A gibbet would be a kind of focal point for the community – twenty feet high, I reckon, floodlit by night and covered in bitumen, creosote and shit, real weatherproof. It's in the Shanty Town community development plan, and I got a peti-tion to King Andy, God bless him. Here, care to sign? There you go, stick your moniker on there.'

I signed my name and passed the sheet to Tatum. He held it up between his finger and thumb like it was a pus-stained bandage.

'You guys already got a penal code the envy of Nero.'

'What I say is, thou shalt not kill. If the stable is full of shit, you got to muck it out.'

Tatum sighed and scribbled his name with a chewed stump of eyebrow pencil.

'That's kind of a classical-type allusion, to Hercules, yeah? He was a Greek like me. Say Percy, did you know the Greeks invented poetry?'

Of course Percy knew; he stood Tatum, umpteen generations removed from Parnassus, a drink on the strength of it. Tatum chose the speciality of the house, a Green Howard cocktail: half a pint of Johnny-Jump-Up with a crème de menthe float. The petition lay on the bar. I picked it up to save it from getting soaked and flicked through the names. A few weeks back a clutch stood out. They were Yankee names, ranks and numbers. Among them was one I recognised from somewhere – oh yeah, Private First Class Belusski, currently residing in a grave outside Saffron Walden, according to Manley Stanley. I shipped out in a trance and saw his round fat face, the colour of lint, and thick specs over the pale discs of his eyes. But something was weird. I didn't get any buried-alive-in-mouldering-earth vibration off his image, more a lost-in-space-where-the-fuck-am-I kind of buzz. I asked Percy if he remembered him.

'Remember him? I sold him a tricycle. He was in here one night – was this Belusski a mate of yours? No? – and this busker come by, looked like Robin Hood, if you know what I mean, spotty-looking article with a green hat and a bow, and arrows in a quiver. He done all sorts, juggling, dice, card tricks. Played the congas with Jolly Roger for a bit too, like yourself. Then he done the rope trick. Got it up stiff as a poker, pardon my French. Then he grabbed Benito the cantina moggy and sent him up the rope. Poof! Gone just like that. Your mate Belusski took umbrage and he says, "You're a fucking fraud," so Robin Hood says, "If you're so clever, you climb up and tell us what you see." Up he goes and . . . Poof! Big flash and he's gone. 'Course he must have been in on the act, sort of a stooge, see? I asked Robin Hood if he wanted to sign but he said he couldn't write. That's his X right there. Never saw the Yank from that day to this. Funny though, 'cos he'd already paid me and the trike's still outside.'

C H A P T E R 14

①

Through the rear window of an armoured limousine I watched the moon rise above Big Ben. We drove east along the Embankment. Out on the river a police launch butted into the current, its searchlight scouring the southern shore. Across the water the campfires of the dossers began to burn.

'Over there, I believe, is where the last barricade of the Commune was defended.'

The civil servant who spoke waved into the night. He perched opposite us in the dicky-seat. His suit was black with a faint chalk-stripe. A pregnant swelling under his armpit betrayed his holstered pistol. He patted it fondly.

'I'm afraid my tailor didn't foresee me bearing arms. I shall have it rectified at my next fitting.'

He smiled. Tatum and I sat together in the ample plush and chain-smoked Black Death, a Shanty Town brand that Percy was eager to push. Our smoke spewed through the ventilator into the atmosphere. Mister Sweet made small talk to calm his nerves. He spoke of Oxford and his salad days beneath the dreaming spires. He talked of himself very much as someone else, as if fondly remembering an amiable and eccentric relative now dead. His youth, he said, had been without shape or purpose, vague and blurred like a snapshot taken with an unsteady hand. Now, under the tutelage of a stern and caring government, he was strong, a well-wrought tool. He had always, in his heart, known it would be so and was glad.

We drew up at the cordon around the Tower. Mister Sweet dealt a hand of passes through the window. We drove on, over the moat, through the portcullis and stopped. A yeoman warder opened the door and saluted.

'We have to walk from here,' said Mister Sweet. 'It's only a short hop.'

We were conveyed towards Tower Green. He pointed out the Queen's House.

'And over there is the chapel of Saint Peter ad Vincula, where they buried Anne Boleyn beneath the altar, coffined in an arrow chest. Nineteenth of May, fifteen-thirty-six. Just a little way now.'

We were shown up a winding stair to a solid oak door. Another yeoman was standing guard. He checked our passes. He rapped on the door and a cheerful voice bid us enter.

'Your distinguished visitors, Governor Frank-Afraid-of-Horses.'

A red-faced old man, dressed in Native American costume with a magnificent head-dress of Grey Eagle feathers, rose up from behind a desk.

'Welcome, most welcome to my Lodge. But where in the name of the Great Spirit is Colonel Mawby? Really, things are getting so lax around here. Security's just a joke. Colonel Mawby should have shown you up.'

The yeoman warder withdrew and the Governor came forward to shake hands. He exchanged pleasantries with Tatum about South Dakota and the reintroduction of the buffalo while I looked round. The walls were hung with Navajo blankets and pictures of kings and queens and various Native American chiefs. The floor was covered with buffalo-skin rugs. On a bookcase of polished walnut, under a glass bell, a sleek-feathered bird looked down with baleful eye.

'That's Moses,' said the Governor. 'The very last raven in the Tower. Manley Stanley's chaps held the Tower during the Commune, and when we got back in we found that the ravens were all dead. They'd been eaten, feathers and all, except for Moses here. I must say, whoever it was made a good job of him.'

We murmured our appreciation of Moses and the unknown taxidermist. The Governor opened the drinks cabinet.

'I don't want to waste your time, Mister Liotes, but perhaps a glass of fire-water? Brandreth will wait, I'm sure. Sweet, be an angel and pour.'

We polished off a bottle of Final Tutorial. The label showed a gowned don and an undergraduate drinking each other's health, while an elderly 'scout' toasted muffins on a prong over an open fire.

'Sweet, do open another bottle; Mister Liotes is thirsty. I must say, Liotes, the whole tribe awaits your forthcoming epic with bated breath. Just the sort of thing we need to help us all pull together again. Like the silver voice of the cox echoing over the Isis. Or – to change the metaphor if I may

– the body politic is in convalescence after heroic surgery, and the patient is, as it were, lying down in a darkened room with cucumber slices on his eyes. We need a ray of sunshine, to kindle hope and encourage the patient to assist in his own healing. Your epic will be that ray of sunshine; it will be the chant of the medicine man . . . and more . . .'

'Quite so, Governor,' said Mister Sweet. 'And now we really must get on and beard the decrepit lion in his den.'

'Just say the word, Sweet. By the way, I'm told a man of the cloth, the chap's brother-in-law, is to have the body after decease. Usually I would be in charge right to the end, but Sir Lionel says this clerical chappie . . .'

He tweaked a card from his head-dress and peered at it.

'. . . the Reverend Bartleby, is to be given every assistance. Quite agreeable to me. I looked him up in Crockford's. He's an Oxford man, like Sweet and myself. It's rather put my chaplain's nose out of joint. He's a Cambridge man, you see. But still, it can't be helped and he must learn to live with his disappointment.'

'Quite so, Governor,' said Mister Sweet. 'He wishes to inter Brandreth in the crypt of Saint Sepulchre's. As long as his bones do not become an object of veneration or Saint Sepulchre's a site of pilgrimage we see no objection.'

'I shouldn't think that's very likely. I am sure that once we snuff his vital spark any live embers of disaffection will dampen down. And now, gentlemen, I raise my glass, not for the first time tonight, and give you a toast. To the future. To the return of the buffalo. To . . .'

He scanned the ceiling, silently moving his lips.

'And let us not forget the nine worthies, the nine muses,

our immortal Laureate Bard Liotes, the tepees of our ancestors . . . and . . . and . . . God Save the King!'

'Yeah, Andy, here's looking at you, kid,' said Tatum, raising
his glass in the direction of Buckingham Palace.

14②

The air grew cold and damp, and I felt we were burrowing
beneath the river. The narrow passage opened out into a
wide dungeon, green with moss. Torches burned on the
walls. Two yeomen stood guard outside a nail-studded door.
We showed our passes and one of them put his fingers to
his lips and whistled. Some distance away, we heard the
rattle of keys; then, in the farthest gloom of the gallery, we
saw a lantern bobbing from a pole. It threw a halo of fuzzy
green light around the head of the jailer. His uniform was
immaculately pressed and his black sealskin hat gleamed
slick. His white beard spilled over his ruff.

'Welcome, sirs, welcome. I was expecting you earlier, but
never mind. You'll have been to see Governor Frank-Afraid-
of-Horses. He likes a bit of company, he does, and a very
generous man he is. Now, the prisoner Brandreth awaits you
so we'd best delay no further.'

He twirled the lock and opened the door. There was no
light in the cell, except for what spilled in with us.
Brandreth's tatters were stained with mildew and ordure,
criss-crossed by the shining slime trails of slugs and snails.

Around his waist was a metal girdle, and with this he was bound by links of chain to three iron hoops set in the wall. He looked up with piteous eyes, beseeching us in a voice that was faint with weariness and trembling with fear.

'For the love of the risen Christ, feed me, I beg you, feed me.'

The jailer put his arms under Brandreth's shoulders and lifted him into a sitting position against the wall. He stroked Brandreth's head.

'All in good time. You just get used to the crowd in here first. Pretty soon you won't need feeding any more, not where you're going. You must think on these last things, you must, for the sake of your immortal soul.'

The prisoner sat silent, eyes closed against the light. The jailer licked a finger and wiped away the dirt from Brandreth's eyelids.

'I don't know. It's one thing to scrag a chap, but it isn't right to send him aloft dressed worse than a chimney-sweep and trembling with cold for lack of something warm in his belly. Every man likes to make a good show of dying; if it comes to it, there's nothing to do but die. But the Homeland Controller doesn't want that, and that is cruel and unusual punishment. Don't you think, sirs, it's a pity that this chap, who fought so brave and draws and paints like an angel – I've seen his work, sir, in the National, and he scratched on the stones here until they cut off his light – should be denied the chance to cut a fine figure at the last?'

Sweet scowled.

'Penal policy is none of your concern, jailer.'

'Shame on you for those words, sir. See, I've brought this

poor fellow my snap, which is bread and lard and a slice off the pork pie the Governor gave me and the wife for Christmas, and a tot of grog – that's rum and water, sir. And he'll eat and drink, sir, as I'm a believer in the Great Spirit in the Sky, and with the permission of our brave Governor, Frank-Afraid-of-Horses, despite all your Homeland Controller's rules and regulations.'

I stepped forward.

'And I have a Thermos of hot custard here in this duffle bag. It was made a few days ago, but it's been in the fridge and seems to have remarkable staying power. I heated it up to a safe temperature before I came out.'

'Bless you all,' said Brandreth.

'Listen,' said Tatum. 'It's pretty morbid in here. Take a few of these with a slug of fire-water and pretty soon you'll be dancing on the roof.'

He handed Brandreth a palmful of dexies. Sweet was livid.

'This is too much!'

Tatum fitted the heel of his hand snugly under Sweet's breastbone and pushed him against the wall.

'Aw, button it, tight-ass, 'less you want a fat lip.'

'And there's this,' I said, 'which your kin hope will be of comfort to you.'

I gave him the tiny Bible. Brandreth's eyes filled with tears as he lifted it to his lips and kissed it. Then he set about the food and drink, first off swallowing the dexies with a good draft of grog. When he had finished licking the last streaks of custard from the Thermos cup he asked me to remember him to Makepeace.

'He could never tell me apart from Sir John Betjeman,

but if they have anything as fine as this emulsion in Paradise I shall rest content through all eternity.'

Sweet and the jailer stood on either side of the door while Tatum and I squatted on our haunches before Brandreth. I set up the disc recorder.

Brandreth was silent for a while, listening inside himself, and then he grinned and – whether it was the dexies in him or, more likely, the dexies in me, I don't know – began to shine, like a vision in a grotto. He coughed and then stretched out his manacled hands.

'Good evening, if it is evening . . . and welcome to my death cell.'

14③

Rather than tell Brandreth's story of the Commune, I might as well tell it my way. But a condemned man should be allowed a few words of his own so, before I spiel, here they are:

'In the quiet watches of the night, in the last days of the Commune, Manley Stanley had me paint his portrait in oils. His head made me think of a turnip, or an onion. Yes, an onion – dense and layered, hard and mysterious, permeated with a consciousness whose formation has been slow and subject to intense pressure, almost geologic. You see the train of ideas? That's when I hit on it. After all, I couldn't paint him as a sly and subtle vegetable. He wouldn't have liked that at all. In the light of a hurricane lamp it was easy to see his head in terms of a desert landscape. Eyes like dried-up water-holes and a cactus nose, with a mouth like the sepulchre of a long-dead tribe. I chose ochre and a sandy palette and worked his head against a backlight of shadow, like an Arizona bluff in the last rays of sun before nightfall.'

Jeremiah focused his eyes on me and smiled beatifically. 'This young man can vouch for what I say. He was there.'

CHAPTER 15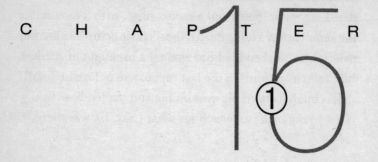

I'd sat quietly in the corner of the harness-room of the Tower during those latter days of the ousted Government, when the besieging rebels were turning the final screw on the Coalition of Saints and their ill-fated Commune, and I had watched Jeremiah Brandreth make Manley Stanley's portrait. Manley was not a good sitter — too fidgety — and, given Jeremiah's controlling metaphor of geologic time, this was a difficulty. Yet Jeremiah himself was calm and unhurried, distilling out what he saw as the essence of the poltroon before him, flensing off the sour reek of fear, the jagged, startled movements when a jeep backfired, the constant licking of his upper lip, the dive under the table when one of Cockeye's squibs exploded by mishap two hundred metres away. Jeremiah inclined his head; he measured his subject; he picked up the paint from his palette and flicked it deftly on to the canvas. Then he worked it.

The head and shoulders of Manley Stanley emerged with more reality on the painted canvas than they did rising from his fleshy torso. But the reality was an illusion, at least from where I was watching. To me, Manley Stanley was nothing so geologic and massive as an Arizona bluff. I thought Jeremiah had it right the first time: Manley was a sly and subtle vegetable. Although I had to give way to Jeremiah on one count at least. When you got up close to Manley his mouth certainly smelled like the sepulchre of a long-dead tribe.

15②

I hadn't stuck around to see the finishing touches to the portrait. Dad had reminded me, with a lick of the cat-o'-nine, that there was work to be done, and anyway I'd wearied of Manley's stench. Just because you're facing the last days of your attempt to retake the State from the *force majeure* of a *coup d'état*; just because you're thinking that maybe in a couple of days you'll be lying in the ground as a cold, dead thing, and that when the end comes it will be excruciatingly painful and you've never been good at managing pain: these aren't reasons to become a soap-dodger, to cease all sluicing. Sure, the rebels besieging the Tower cut off the mains water. But it rained constantly during the latter days of the Commune, and we collected as much water as we could in buckets and barrels, and in tarpaulins. Then there was old Father Thames, shuffling back and forth at Traitor's Gate. No excuse.

The strange thing to me, though, was that Manley still seemed able to pull. He had a harem of dutiful concubines, and every now and then one would come to the harness-room and Jeremiah and I would go outside and smoke while Manley drove whatever demons were afflicting him out through the end of his prick. He was the fastest exorcist I've ever met, and we barely had time to snatch a Rizla, snag a pinch of tobacco, roll it up and lick it, light it and burn it down to our fingers before the concubine came out, often sobbing for some reason or other I couldn't fathom (maybe she'd been pushed rather than pulled), and Manley appeared in the doorway, hitching up his lilac pants.

15 ③

Dad didn't approve of me smoking. At this time I was in my thirteenth year (unlucky for some), so he had a point, blah blah, but I carried on anyway. The world was turned into such a mire that worrying about my health seemed pointless. Of course I see now he was right, but this was then.

Anyway, there was work to do and Dad kept me busy. Among other tasks, I learned how to ply a needle and thread and I spent some time patching up the robes of the soldiers of the Flagellant Faction. Most had suffered some sort of mishap — anything from snagging their hem in a bicycle chain to taking a high velocity bullet in the chest, or in the head (making a slit for a third eye in the hood). The stains needed washing out before they could be patched and given to one of the new recruits, and new recruits kept coming, sneaking through the rebel lines and finding their way in through the old sewers or swimming up the river at night. I was short of washing powder. But with the robes being dark brown, the stains didn't show after I'd given them a good scrub with the pumice stone that Dad, in more peaceful times, applied to his calloused, horny feet.

But I was in the maelstrom of puberty – my voice was breaking, a certain part of me had started leaking – and I began to figure that this was women's work, not fitted to a mannish boy.

I turned my duties over to a ten-year-old urchin I quickly trained up, and went off to help Cockeye.

15④

Had he lived, Cockeye the Cockney Einstein would be a national treasure. Who knows where his mechanical ingenuity might have led?

Cockeye's talent was weaponry – everything from improvised, home-made small arms and ammunition through booby-traps to weapons of mass destruction. He'd armed a 'don't try this at home' atomic mine and wanted to send it downriver to Tilbury, where, now that the United States Government had declared for the rebels, the First Infantry

Division ('The Big Red 1') were coming ashore on their way back from the Equator. But Manley Stanley vetoed the proposal.

Dad was all for it. At the Council of War he argued strongly the Apocalypse Brief. He dressed in his smartest brown robes, the hood starched and rising to a stiff peak like a meringue made of shit, and as he spoke through the mouth-slit, in his cadenced screech, he beat time with his left hand, wielding his discipline with gusto and smacking his back with the nine-tails knotted with ball-bearings.

He spoke of the star called Wormwood falling from the sky, as foretold in Revelation, which will make bitter the waters. (Smack.) He said the atomic mine was Wormwood, the fulfilment of Revelation. (Smack.) He said we must seal a Covenant of Fire and Blood. (Smack.) He didn't say who with. (Smack.) And so on. But his pitch didn't go down too well. The women of the Cunt Coven, sitting opposite with their banner draped with symbols of the magical power of menstrual blood, were singularly un-impressed.

'If it's covenanted blood you want, love, have some of ours,' shouted a Covenanter, throwing a used feminine hygiene product in Dad's direction.

The meeting broke up in disorder, and Manley's veto stood.

15 ⑤

I left the meeting with Cockeye.

'Shame about that,' he said. 'That's been our trouble all along. Not ruthless enough. Come on, I'll show you how to booby-trap a packet of Trojan condoms.'

So he showed me that particular trick, just to ease me in. To this day, as far as I know, I've never blown the knob off anyone.

Cockeye took me up to the top of the Bloody Tower, where, in a crenellated nook, he'd set up on a swivel a sniper rifle with a telescopic sight.

'Take a look. Go on, it doesn't bite.'

I fixed my eye on the scope and traversed quickly, making everything a blur.

'Go slow and steady,' said Cockeye.

So I went slow and steady. I settled on a line of soldiers – we'd stopped calling them rebels, we were the rebels now – passing sandbags one to the other in the rain, building a sand and canvas blanket round what looked like some kind of rapid-fire cannon. Six barrels. How many did the first Gatling gun have, I wondered?

'Got a target?' said Cockeye.

'Not really. Just some guys piling up sandbags.'

'Okay. Want to take a shot?'

I was squinting at a youth a few years older than me. His face was sallow and his combat fatigues were stained with sweat. The cross-hairs of the sight located his nose. You can't shoot someone in the nose, for pity's sake. The day was growing dimmer.

'No thanks,' I said. 'Booby-trapping a prophylactic is one thing, shooting a guy in the snitch is another.'

What was really on my mind was that there had been no shooting for the last two days, from either side. This seemed good to me — you know, no one shooting at you. Not having to shoot someone else. What I didn't know at this time was that surrender terms had been sent in. There was no formal truce. People just seemed to stop.

But not Cockeye. He eased me away from the rifle and got into position, bracing his legs one in front of the other. Then he cocked, aimed and flicked the trigger in one smooth movement.

The usual crack, smoke and stink. I felt numb. But no one fired back from their side, no one even stirred from our side that I could tell. Cockeye pulled the rifle in. It was coming on dusk. Too much twilight for a killer shot, I said under my breath, but I knew I was kidding myself. Cockeye squealed.

'Shit, fucking bats,' said Cockeye. 'Bastard bit me on the ear.'

We went below.

15 ⑥

I grabbed a bite to eat – a thin stew made from the carcase of the last-but-one raven of the Tower – and then it was my turn for the Infirmary.

We had the worst of the sick and wounded down in a low vaulted space that might have been a wine store back in the days of King John – or Julius Caesar for all I know – and they were in pretty bad shape. You didn't get down here unless you were ready to do the mortal-coil shuffle. Everyone knew this, so to be carried down here – to the orlop deck as it were – was no boost to patient morale.

Dad did what he could in the Infirmary, togged in civvies, which showed some dress sense for a change. I mean, if you're about to nip your turd, do you really need to see some guy in brown penitent's robes and a big pointy hood talking to you through a slit? At first he took a bit of persuading – like he was being asked to go naked – but Rasp, a trans-gendered nurse and associate member of the Cunt Coven, took him aside and put him straight. Dad was unusually meek about it; he must have spooled back from Revelations to the Sermon on the Mount, thinking maybe there was still a chance the meek would inherit the earth.

One level up, we had a side-vault for an operating theatre; this was where most of the heroic surgery went on. Amputations stood some chance of success. Other casualties, after being mangled by well-intentioned hands, were taken down the slimy stone steps to the orlop and allowed a fatal veinful of pethidine. When the pethidine ran out, Dad or some other ministering angel would suffocate them. After a while the pillow they used got tacky with spit and blood and snot, so I tactfully suggested that maybe they could look around for something else, or try the Beefeaters' laundry baskets for a new pillowcase. Or wrap the instrument of deliverance in one of our spare hoods.

Apart from this example of healthcare consultancy in the realm of patient comfort, what I mostly did is best described as sanitary work. And let's leave it there.

15⑦

Word got round that Manley Stanley and Errol Sachs were nowhere to be found. The sewers had all been blocked off by now, so it was difficult to see how they could have got out that way. The Royal Navy was in the river, keeping its distance on the other side of Tower Bridge, and although crazy swimmers still occasionally made it through to us, from upstream and downstream, neither of our political leaders could swim the way you'd need to swim to make it out.

The radio told us that Hampstead was subdued, and that the fighting in Carshalton was now in the mopping-up phase. There was one barricade still being defended, down on the South Bank, where all offers of surrender terms had been thrown back and the Communards had declared their intention to rename their stockade – apparently without irony – the Alamo, and to die with their boots on, facing the Texas Rangers and the Big Red 1.

Then a crazy cackling, crackling message came bursting out of the radio in a blur of manic blips and a continuous whine, urging us to hold on because the Albanian Liberation Force was about to set out from Tirana as soon as the coaches arrived. They said they'd already sent a submarine. What little I knew of the Albanian Navy suggested that it may have been some ancient Italian rust-bucket of a submersible, if it was coming at all.

We held a Council of War – a very subdued affair, with even Dad saying little. Behind his hood I guessed he was scowling, if he still had the energy to scowl after his extended shifts in the Infirmary.

The surrender terms were read out. We were asked to give up to save bloodshed in a hopeless cause, to let our wounded get proper medical help, and to preserve the fabric of the Nation's Heritage (the Tower). Hostages on both sides would be exchanged, we would leave our arms piled behind us, we'd be searched by the soldiers and then allowed to march out, under our own discipline, to demobilise and return to our homes. No recriminations.

Manley Stanley and Errol Sachs were not mentioned in the surrender terms.

Cockeye gave a passionate speech, caustically berating our vanished leaders and their social democracy, their lack of ruthlessness on coming to power, their lack of ruthlessness in the prosecution of the fight, and offering a shrewd

177

critique of social democracy in general. He quoted Lenin and Trotsky, which received a slew of heads nodding approval, then Stalin, who set fewer nobs a-bobbin', and then lost it for me by suggesting we end it all by joining hands around the atomic mine, singing 'Auld Lang Syne', pressing the plunger and going up in glory.

This last suggestion seemed a bit nihilistic to me, the trouble with such gestures being that you're not around to see how things pan out afterwards. It being granted that we all check out before Earth's final curtain, I like to feel I'm getting something back in the way of entertainment and curiosity satisfied — no more than my due for what I've endured.

Then Jeremiah Brandreth spoke. He urged us to transform our armed resistance into something symbolic, something ineffable, which would be a seed-bed for future progress and reform.

'If we are to have a revolution in future, let it be a revolution for fun. Let our resistance from now on be ludic, playful, teasing and seductive.'

But, so many days into the siege, we weren't inclined to party or act all coquettish. So the upshot was that our diverse band of brothers and sisters, freaks, saints and dull political animals from the straight world took the view that, all things considered, the terms offered were worth taking. We'd gone past the first flush of martyrdom. The barricade on the South Bank, the Alamo, was defended by a more homogenous group — the Little Sisters of the Circumcision — and that was presumably why they had the bottle, the discipline, to die fighting. We were tired and wanted to go home, to wash, to make tea, to argue with the neighbours over playing loud music or the lighting of autumnal bonfires – or, in the case of the Flagellant Faction, to patiently take complaints about the odd thwacking sounds, accompanied by mournful chanting, that came day and night from our respective domiciles.

15 ⑧

We were due to march out next morning. Cockeye's ear began to play up. He complained of itching and then a stabbing pain. His mood began to swing down towards depression and paranoia.

'This amnesty, it's a trick. They'll get us out of here and then you'll see what happens.'

He didn't sleep that night. He was pacing around, restless, talking fast and incoherent, constantly pulling at his ear and smacking himself on the side of the head. After I'd been woken a second time by his ravings I stayed up with him. In his current mood there was no telling what he might do. I asked Jeremiah to make sure the atomic mine was safely locked away.

'Already done. Maybe you should get your old man to take a look at him.'

Cockeye was sitting on the flagstones, hugging himself and rocking backwards and forwards. He was grinding his teeth and swearing in a low monotone, cursing Manley

Stanley, Errol Sachs and all degenerate social democrats, making sweeping prophecies of the treachery and terror to come.

I found Dad in the Governor's office, without his hood, putting the finishing touch to Moses, the last raven in the Tower. The table was strewn with sawdust, and the innards of Moses were leaking red and brown through a newspaper parcel. The window was closed and a pungent chemical miasma lay brooding in the room. Dad popped in the glass eyes and settled the noble bird on his perch, covering him over with a glass bell.

I gave Dad a quick run-down of Cockeye's condition. He nodded.

'Bitten by a bat, you say? Then I'm afraid it looks very much to me like comrade Cockeye has contracted rabies. Make sure he doesn't bite or scratch you.'

Dad was about to give me a full account of the natural history of European Bat Lyssaviruses 1 and 2, genotypes 5 and 6, but I asked him could he just come and take a look.

'No point. He's most likely been bitten by a rabid Daubenton's, or possibly a Serotine. The kindest thing to do is to put him out of his misery. It's too late now to vaccinate, even if we had the vaccine, which we don't.'

I got angry, but Dad put his stained hands on my shoulders and looked steadily into my eyes. He carefully explained what the likely and all-too-hideous course of Cockeye's disease would be, once he was in the second stage of 'furious' rabies.

'I'll come down and euthanase him shortly. Just give me a few minutes to clear up here.'

I opened the window to let in fresh air. Down in the court-yard the hostages had been brought up from the dungeons. They huddled together, looking nervous. Jeremiah Brandreth spoke reassuringly to them. His soft voice drifted up. He apologised for what they had endured. He reminded them that the rapist had been severely punished. He said they'd be free in the morning. He made no effort to justify our cause.

Dad and I went to find Cockeye. He was crouching in a corner, waving his hands rapidly in front of his face. He screamed and began brushing furiously at his arms.

'Get them off. Get them off.'

'Oh dear,' said Dad. 'He can see "the wee men".' He called for Rasp and together they managed to skin-pop a syringe of phenobarbitone into Cockeye's rump, just enough to calm him down and make it easier for us to hold him still while Dad brought the fatal pillow over his face.

15 ⑨

Next morning was bright sunshine. The Communards marched out of the Tower in column, under our own disci-pline as agreed in the surrender terms. The women of the Cunt Coven led the rout, holding their jam-rag banner proud and high.

Weary soldiers and police flanked us. They stared with sullen and silent contempt. We'd not come far when three

Special Branch men pushed in and grabbed Jeremiah Brandreth. He protested that he had safe conduct but they slapped him about, handcuffed him and hauled him off. They threw him in the back of a Scorpion. Brandreth's secretary, who'd been walking beside him, broke away now and ran over to the Brigadier commanding the troops. The Brigadier stepped back quickly, snapped his heels and saluted.

Undaunted, the Flagellant Faction marched along bearing the new colours Manley Stanley had given us a few days before. We sang 'Hail to the Flail', with our cats swinging away nicely to the beat of my side-drum. The Brigadier ordered us to halt while the Special Branch men looked us over. They lifted our hoods and peered into our gaunt faces. Then they relaxed and laughed and waved us on. Dad lifted his voice and his crew chanted the Flagellant Anthem one last time.

At Tower Gateway, which was the agreed demobilisation point, the Flagellants stood at ease in their ranks while Dad gave each man a token flick of the cat and received a ceremonial stroke in return. There was a peculiar tenderness in these strokes. We took off our robes, shook hands and embraced. A few sentimentalists swapped hoods. I gathered up Dad's robes and my own Junior Flagellant's outfit, wrapped them in a polka-dot curtain and tied them in a bundle on a stick. I set the bundle on my shoulder and trailed behind Dad, towards Cheapside and the westward road.

A news photographer suddenly ran between me and Dad, crouched down and let off a volley of flash-shots in my face.

I ducked my head sideways and gave him a V-sign. That picture of me and my polka-dot bundle, a bedraggled urchin ducking and flashing his fingers like an Agincourt archer, went around the world. Maybe you've seen it as a still in one of the unbroken chain of television documentaries which binds us to all our yesterdays.

I recovered, remembered I was my father's son, stood straight and smiled for another flash. I shouldered my bundle again and then me and Dad were stepping westward, just as Bow Bells, behind us in the east, pealed out for noon.

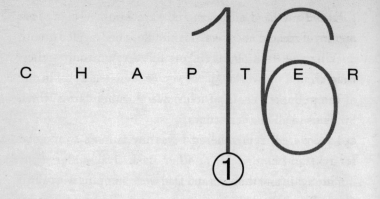

C H A P T E R 16

①

We finished recording Jeremiah Brandreth's reminiscences and said our last goodnights. Tatum was on the cusp of breaking down, most unusual, and he began to liquor up kamikaze-style to help him cope. Me, I gave a mental shrug and moved on.

Mister Sweet dropped us on the outskirts of Shanty Town an hour before midnight. He didn't wish us Happy New Year. Tatum was too drunk to care. I stuck two fingers up to the vanishing rear window. A sturdy urchin with a wheelbarrow was lurking at the crossroads. He whistled us.

'Taxi?'

Together we dumped Tatum in the wheelbarrow and trudged towards the lights of Percy's cantina. Tatum began to moan tuneless dirges of his infancy, miming guitar and shouting, 'Tequila!'

We stopped for a minute to let the Poet Laureate vomit over a drain. The urchin peered close at Tatum's effusion, for reasons best known to himself.

The cantina was empty, apart from the bartender and an aged crone sitting by the stove with a mug of mulled Johnny-Jump-Up.

'Howdy,' said the barkeep. 'Ain't nobody here 'cept me and my monkey. They're all up the Midden.'

'What about it, Tatum? Think you can handle a dog-roast?'

Tatum wiped his puke-stained face on his sleeve.

'I sure as hell ain't spending New Year with a couple of specimens. What do you say, sturdy urchin? Are you game for another heave?'

'Sure thing, but first buy me a beer. I'm parched. Got a smoke?'

We took three schooners of foam to freshen up with. I offered the kid a Black Death but he held out for a 5/11. Tatum sprinkled salt on a pickled egg and swallowed it whole. Then we dropped some dexies for *auld lang syne*, to keep continuity between the old year and the new. The kid saw the dooby-doobs and began to hop.

'Sir, if you want stuff, I can get it cheap. Special price and top-hole gear. You want acid?'

'What do you think we are,' said Tatum, 'a couple of nuts? Acid my ass.'

'You want ass, sir? I can get ass for you.'

'Jesus, don't tell me it's your sister.'

'No sir, our sister is dead from the plague. But mother would be only too happy to oblige a gentleman like yourself. Or maybe you'd like a boy?'

He ran his thumb down the inside of Tatum's pants and simpered.

'I can turn a trick for you now, sir, and make it a real happy New Year!'

'Listen, kid, I don't make it with minors. Do I look like

a pervert, that I should get my rocks off shafting a kid? Jesus, what's the world coming to?'

I put the empty glasses on the bar.

'Listen. We want you for one thing. You push the big white hunter here up the Midden. We pay you handsomely. After that, the rest of the year's your own. And how old are you anyway?'

'Don't know, sir. Maybe twelve. Strong as an ox, sir.'

We unchained the wheelbarrow from the hitching-rail. Tatum climbed in and we headed up the Midden. The kid grunted a bit but we made it to the top. Up on the heights we were among the shining faces of the crowd milling around the barbecue pits. The bonfire spat sparks into the midnight sky and music and laughter chased after them. We paid off the boy. I walked over to a liquor stand, expecting Tatum to follow me, but a surge of dancers doing the conga came between us and when I looked round he was lost in the crowd. No worries; I had some dexies in my pocket. Catch up with him later.

I bought a quart of Johnny and mooched about, looking for Pirate Jenny. Feeling I ought to eat, just to put something in my gut, and with the dexies poking me towards adventure, I stood in the barbecue line for my first-ever dog-meat sandwich. I strolled about, munching. A tattoo artist I knew from way back shouted me from his booth. I waved hello and walked by. Still no sign of Jenny.

An air-horn farted a warning and a line of heraldic trumpeters appeared. They blew a fanfare. Towards the bonfire came a painted cart, like a gipsy wagon, pulled by a pair of steady-stepping, stoical donkeys. A guard of honour kept pace. The Sons of Onan slow-marched to the beat of a bass drum. They were naked from the waist up, and their torsos, which were greased against the cold, glistened in the fire-light. They chanted a low and mournful dirge, singing the old year to sleep. On the cart was a monstrous structure of twisted withies, woven into the semblance of a gaunt tree that sprouted jagged branches. Captured birds and rodents dangled in wicker cages. The creatures squawked and squealed, spinning in the draught of the fire.

The Sons of Onan halted before the bonfire and made ready for the sacrifice. The donkeys were unhitched and led away. Arnie shouted the order and his pandemonic crew, in a drug-induced ecstasy and careless of the fierce heat, braced their shoulders against the wheels and tailgate of the cart. They heaved the cart – and its living, screaming cargo – slowly and steadily into the fire. I held my gaze as the cages burned, as the victims shrieked and the crowd shouted in exultation.

16②

I found Jenny in the cantina, drinking at the bar with a short elderly man in a trilby. I sent the urchin back up to the Midden to find Tatum and crossed over to join them. Jenny gave me a hug.

'Happy New Year, lover. Sorry I missed you earlier, but a twenty-carat job came up and I made some mega-shekels.

May I introduce my godfather, Josh Rumbold.'

'Pleased to meet you, young man. Jenny's told me all about you. What will you have?'

I asked for a Green Howard. I took a sip and said, 'Excuse me, haven't I . . .'

'Seen me somewhere before? Most probably, lad.'

He handed me his card. In raised Gothic type it read: 'Josh Rumbold. Master Barber and Public Hangman. By appointment to Sir Lionel Dingwallace.' The address was a working-class district butting on to the gasworks on the other side of Shanty Town. I'd seen him, sure enough, turning off the notorious child-killer known as the Clerkenwell Bluebeard, one cold November morning a couple of years ago. Rumbold should have been the most popular man in London that day, when you consider the widespread prejudice against the torture and killing of young children, but the mob pelted both him and the malefactor, throwing turds and rotten fruit. Boos were mixed with cheers. Early in the proceedings a clique of hardcore Bluebeard fans had even attempted an attack on the parents of the victims, who were in the grandstand to see justice done. Rumbold trod the boards, indifferent to it all. With nods of his head and snapping fingers he directed to their allotted places his assistant, the chaplain and the deserving victim. Rumbold was the complete Master of Ceremonies. Even the condemned man seemed to appreciate his unruffled, unassuming and, above all, professional demeanour. He thrust his own head into the noose, anxious to please. Rumbold climbed the ladder and adjusted the rope, clapping the man on the back — friendly and considerate but not too familiar.

Now he began to speak of barbering.

'When you start shaving, lad, perhaps you'll come to me. As for a haircut, which you're sorely in need of, I can give you a decent scalping – a one-inch Brutal, or a full Magwitch if you like, to keep the lice down. Half price, since you're a friend of my Jenny.'

'Thanks very much. I'll be glad to come to you.'

'Not all my customers can say that.'

He winked at me over his pale ale. Jenny said, 'Josh has had a disappointment.'

'Oh, it's nothing really. Just a job I had lined up for tomorrow. I shan't be needed now. The Good Lord has seen fit to gather him to his bosom without my offices.'

I guessed he wasn't talking any more about the haircut side of his business.

'Still, anyone is bound to feel cheated of the opportunity to practise his craft. Not that I'm questioning God's right to dispose of us how he will.'

He looked up and smiled, making the best of things.

'I was hoping to catch our Percy here tonight. Usually, before I perform, I like a good night's rest, following a tumble in the nest with Mrs Rumbold and a nice hot milky drink. But with tomorrow being cancelled I thought I'd nip over. Percy sent word he'd like my advice on the municipal gibbet he's setting up. It's only in the early stages but it's never too soon to take professional advice. Take my tip, lad: in everything you do, be professional.'

His eyes grew misty.

'When it comes to gallows protocol, there's not much I don't know. But I don't claim to know it all. No man can know the whole of the gallows and its work. There is a residual mystery. Like what they think about as the trap drops. If they get a drop, of course.'

'I've always thought you were a bit like a priest,' said Jenny.

'What's that, Jenny? A priest?'

'A guardian of mysteries. Yes, a priest, and do you know, I think it's high time women were ordained to your priesthood.'

Rumbold nodded his head.

'I expect it will come in time, a woman officiating on the scaffold. She'd have to start the usual way, of course, as an assistant. But if she was any good, and studied hard, she could make her way in the craft. Especially if she loved her gallows work as I do.'

We had another round of drinks and a pickled egg each. Mister Rumbold stuck his thumbs through his braces and tugged.

'The day I got my licence from Sir Lionel was the happiest day of my life bar none. After all those wilderness years of abolition, when I honed my skills on a sandbag in the stairwell . . . And evenings spent with my dear wife, the two of us pasting choice items into a scrapbook, snippets about the great craftsmen of the past — Pierrepoint, Carr of Doncaster, Calcroft and of course my own great-grandfather, Henry Rumbold, who hanged Joe Gann in Bootle jail . . . I had an opportunity to qualify and practise abroad but I always felt an Englishman should officiate at home or not at all. After we bought the house next door I was able to move to the full set-up — trap, lever and beam in the front bedroom, with the front parlour beneath as a pit. I began scouring the clothes shops for old dummies. If you weight them up and thicken the necks accordingly, you've got a variety of body types to work with. Because it's the variety of people that make this job so interesting.'

He took a sip of pale ale and smacked his lips.

'I have to say, it took us all by surprise, hanging coming back so sudden. There was a time during the Terror when all it seemed to be was shooting, from dawn to dusk. Messy and noisy, complaints all round, and they even tried bayonets for a while but you can imagine, can't you, how unsatisfactory that method proved to be?

'When the referendum got the principle of capital punishment established in peacetime, all that was needed was a satisfactory modus operandi. It stood to reason it had to be hanging, which is something we Englishmen shine at — we do it in our sleep almost, with centuries of heritage and traditional know-how behind us. I'll always remember something old Calcroft wrote in his memoirs: "In the ravelled hank of history's yarn, through it all, the hangman's rope binds and twists like a golden thread." He had a way with words, old Calcroft.

'We've had other methods through the ages, of course. Drowning pits — popular with the Anglo-Saxons, they were. Burning at the stake, but that's too cruel in my opinion. Then there's boiling to death. Boiling was for poisoners, and in bygone days, before refrigeration, many an unfortunate cook went that way. I've never found out if they started out cold and heated them up, or dropped them straight into a cauldron of boiling water . . .'

'Like lobsters,' said Jenny.

'And then there's beheading — a classic method, and as reliable as you can get. If you cut someone's head off, that's it: goodnight Vienna, no argument. But hanging is so versatile and clean — as long as you give the nervous ones leather drawers.

'You can easily do yourself in with hanging, even in a bungalow. Doing it in public was a big surprise, but it's what folk want — and now we've got the telly coming in. I'll have to make sure no Johnny-come-lately celebrities cash in. Perhaps I'd better employ an image consultant. And I'll need an agent, at least for the international market.'

'Mister Rumbold,' I said. 'Tell me — and I hope this is not impertinence — have you ever hanged an innocent man?'

Josh Rumbold pursed his lips and stared up at the ceiling. Then he looked down and sideways, avoiding my eye.

'How would I know? Some of them have said they were innocent at the last, but that's none of my business. I am an officer and instrument of the State. There may be mistakes, but that's a tricky area and I don't want to get into it. Our bodies have always been at the disposal of the State, in war and peace. You lease your body from the State. It's a contract, unwritten and implicit, and understood imperfectly perhaps by the average citizen until they meet me. And then, as Calcroft used to say, "Innocent or guilty, in the face of the gallows each must stand in awe." Anyway, I'm a religious man. It stands to reason that there must be something there, where you go afterwards. After you've been hanged. I'd hate to think I was annihilating anyone, know what I mean?'

'You could annihilate my "ex" for all I care.'

'Oh dear, Jenny, it still rankles after all these years, does it? Well, if it comes to that, several of my clients have been personal acquaintances, so you never know.'

Percy popped up grinning from behind Rumbold's shoulder.

'Great to see you, Josh. I thought you were working tomorrow?'

'I'm afraid not. I was just saying to Jenny and her young chap, I was up the Tower earlier to get a last look at Brandreth. He'd lost a lot of weight and, because he was being allowed a drop, on account of being an Oxford man, I thought I'd best check my calculations. It was likely I'd have to give him an extra foot or so, see, being careful not to overdo it.'

Percy nodded vigorously.

'Too right, you can't be too careful. You don't want his head coming off.'

Josh winced.

'You'd be surprised what I've been asked to arrange by the powers that be. You have to know where to draw the line. That's professionalism, see, like I was telling this young man earlier.

'Anyway, when I got up there, the Governor met me at the gate and told me my services were no longer required. It seems the poor fellow was mad from hunger and had snuffed it in a moment. The poor chap's wits were addled and he'd tried to eat a miniature Bible someone gave him. And this was despite a slice of pork pie from the yeoman warder and a good dollop of custard. Seems he choked on Holy Writ. The doctor has certified him dead and his brother-in-law is coming to fetch the cadaver.'

Percy whistled.

'Well, I'll be buggery-whipped. So Brandreth's cheated the gallows?'

Rumbold took a large handkerchief from his pocket and blew his nose.

'Man proposes, God disposes.'

Someone was tugging my trousers. It was my sturdy urchin.

'Sir, sir! They've taken him. Out of my barrow, coming down the hill. They've tied him up and taken him away. They said to give you these.'

He handed me Tatum's wallet and a note written in green ink. I read the note out loud.

> The Poet Laureate we have taken away
> And a ransom you must pay.
> The go-between, Lingus must be,
> Between Sir Lionel Dingwallace and we.
> So ring him up without delay
> And make sure he will pay.
> Otherwise, Liotes meets his dying day.
> Ten million shekels we demand,
> To free our native land.
> We'll call you, you can't call us,
> You're either on or off the bus.
> Happy New Year when it comes.

'Oh dear,' said Jenny. 'It doesn't scan very well. Lingus, darling, you've gone all white.'

Percy took us into his parlour to discuss the matter.

Rumbold came too. I said, 'Have you a phone? We must contact Sir Lionel. His number is here in Tatum's wallet.'

'Yes indeed,' said Percy proudly. 'The cantina is on the phone. We need it for the cabs, see?'

'Pardon me,' said Rumbold. 'But I think Sir Lionel will be at the Tower by now, tearing a strip off the Governor. Do you want me to try? I've got my password, so we'll be through to the boss in a jiffy. He likes to call me out now and again, in a private capacity. For a haircut or shave, I mean. He knows me very well indeed.'

He took the phone and dialled, while Percy cranked the generator, and in a short time he was through. He told us to cover our ears while he gave the password to the switchboard operator. He spoke at some length and then put the phone down.

'He'll call us back. They're alerting him now.'

He smiled pleasantly, pleased to demonstrate his power. We sat in silence and waited for the call. Rumbold gave me a chilling smile. I had a funny feeling he was trying to guess my weight.

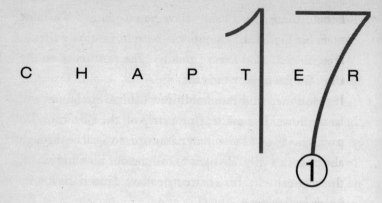

C H A P T E R 17 ①

Dear Lingus

I expect you're surprised to get this letter. I do hope
you're somewhere private, now you're reading it,
because I don't think it would do your case much good
if you were caught with it. It's a bit naughty of me to
send it at all. Do you think I'm terribly irresponsible?
Daddy tells me off sometimes about security. It's my
chief weakness, though goodness knows I have others,
as Wence was fond of reminding me. Still, with the
help of Daddy I will become a better person. As
for sending this letter, sometimes you just know
something will be all right, don't you?

Well, now for some news. Daddy will soon be a
'daddy' for real. I'm seven months pregnant. It must
have happened on honeymoon in Tirana — how
romantic, and by the way, what a delightful town. I
met Manley Stanley — a real charmer and not at all
the psychopath some have made him out to be.
Prime Minister Sachs was indisposed. We were only
there for a couple of days but it was a welcome

196

break. We were back soon after New Year.

Talking of New Year, Tatum Liotes sends his regards. I must say we're all a bit disappointed about the ransom. You'd think they'd pay up, wouldn't you? It just shows what they really think about the importance of the Arts. Mister Liotes says that perhaps they thought you and he were 'in cahoots' about it and that's why you're inside. Is that what the authorities think? Whatever the reason it must be thoroughly dreadful, I'm sure.

By the way, did you find this note under your pillow (you do have pillows, don't you, poor things?) or was it pressed into your hand at some frightful below-decks mealtime scrum? I imagine things can get pretty squirmy at 'chow-down'.

Mister Liotes is being treated well and is quite comfortable, although of necessity several of his appetites have been curbed. No drugs or drink, but he does have perverted sex with one of the guards. Daddy doesn't know about that, and I think he'd have a fit if he did. So would P——k. You know what he's like about the 'the loathsome crime of buggery', as he calls it. Or is it just doing it with animals that he objects to? I really can't fathom him. Indeed, this whole sex business is beyond me at the moment, although naturally enough I still submit to Daddy as a good wife should.

Anyway, Mister Liotes seems glad of the opportunity to rest and recuperate and is working furiously at some sort of poem. Whoever sits with him gets treated to an earful. I'm no judge, I must say, because visual and plastic arts and dance are more my line as you know, but some of it doesn't seem too bad at all. There's one chap here, a poet himself – no names, no pack-drill, as Pocock says – who goes green about the gills with jealousy and wants him stopped, no more paper and ink etc. But Daddy won't hear of it. The fact is, we thought Mr Liotes was a charlatan before, but he seems to have turned into a genuine poet – or maybe he was one all along; it's so difficult to tell, isn't it? Well, it is for me, but not for infallible Daddy ('In-falli-daddy' as I call him when he's having sex). He thinks we should encourage Mr Liotes because the Arts will be very important after the Liberation. Daddy has hinted that Errol Sachs has hinted that Manley Stanley has hinted that the Arts portfolio might be mine when the Government of Democratic Saints (GODS) is finally established. It's good for Mister Liotes' morale too, to have something to keep him occupied.

Mister Liotes feels guilty about getting himself kidnapped like that, and he thinks that if he'd stayed sober none of this would have happened. He's very fond of you and is very sad the way things have turned out. He thinks, and I agree, that it was very enterprising of you to escape. (Was it from the Tower, like they say? I hear that someone called Colonel Mawby was sacked earlier this year. Why don't you write your thrilling story? Can you write? Properly, I mean.)

He also thinks, and I agree, that it was rather silly of you, after you escaped from the Tower, to go to the Refuge and expect Wence to help you, no matter what he has said in the past about 'one big family' (yawn!) and coming to him when you're in trouble. B———t! says Mister Liotes and I must say I'm inclined to agree. I was 'married' to him, so I should know. Obviously it suited him to turn you in. We can only think drugs and pain clouded your judgement. You were so horribly tortured, we heard. How is life with only one testicle? And how did you find time to 'score' when you were 'on the lam'? I heard from Orlando that when you got to the Refuge you were 'high as a kite', that you couldn't walk and they had to carry you indoors. Mister Liotes says, though, that 'speed' can really get a hold on you and you'd crawl naked over broken glass to 'score'. I think it's terrible what people do to themselves with drugs. Why, why, why? After the Liberation, drugs will be abolished and anyone pushing them or taking them will be executed. That will stop innocent boys like you being manipulated by the Masters of Death.

I'd better close now. But you know you're not forgotten, and you have some idea of the Power of the Underground. The very fact you got this letter must prove something and buck up your morale. When the Liberation comes, we'll make it up to you.

Lots of love,
Mrs Daddy

17 ②

I'm often awake before the others. A sudden drop into consciousness, like I've not been asleep at all but have just had my memory edited overnight by whoever is producing this farce. If I believed in God I'd be an atheist by now. I can't help feeling there's a personal spite in all this, a malicious familiar down there among the DNA spinning it out. Or the way I usually think of it, some demiurge is paying out a long rope of shit and coiling it into this painted apology for a world. Scratch everything and the gilt comes off; yes, it's shit, the universal Play-Doh.

That's when I'm sorry for myself. Other times I wake up and it's blind chance brought me to this stink-can. I see the indifference in the wheels of the world, as they shunt my bogey here and there, and I cast a cold eye on life, on death, as the man said you should.

The heat in the dormitory is wet and heavy. It's a relief to get on deck, where August is baking September brown and gold. Across the estuary the woods are already dyed with streaks of henna red, where the creek flows down to the river and the sea.

Working in line across the decks on our hands and knees, studying the next few inches to be scoured, sometimes the squawk of a gull will make us look up to see the sails of yachts and dinghies, red, yellow and blue, arcing out from the creek, billowing in the westerly gusts that the other lads say smell of home. The overseer's boots squeal as he turns on his heels, grinding rubber scorch-marks into the deck where you've just been working. He stares at the water, where the sun burnishes a surface as pure and revealing as Achilles' shield, but he just sees the glare. The days go by.

I lie naked in my bunk and watch the sleepers, stacked like catacombed martyrs. Some are as still as death, while others heave and groan, mimicking the labour that brought them into the world. I think of my unknown mother, limbs wound around me, holding me tight in bed, wiry hair curled and creeping like the tendrils of a vine towards the thin lips of stocking-tops.

Down here there are no portholes. We're below the water-line. The neon night-light, dimmed to quarter power, shines feebly above the door. In a minute the klaxon will sound reveille, and I clamber down from my top bunk to be first through the door in the rush for the heads. The night-soil bucket, a big two-berth commode on castors, stinks in the corner. New boys get the bunks nearest to it but we take it in turns, in pairs, to empty it.

My partner is an Irish boy, 'Silent' O'Moyle. He's a member of the Red Hand of Ulster and he's in for something to do with explosives. He's escaped the gallows on account of his youth, being fifteen. At seventeen and a half, I'm getting too old for this kip. When I turn eighteen I'll be sent to the Humber, and then each birthday farther north until I'm cooking the waste. If they find Tatum I might get parole. Under torture I told them all I knew, but no one was impressed. Absolute drivel, a preposterous story, said Mister Sweet, selecting a thicker cane as I hung upside down, naked, with my legs apart. An obvious cover story. Have you ever had training in an Albanian terrorist camp? Or are you just greedy and depraved, willing to sell your master to Manley Stanley for thirty pieces of silver and a handful of drugs?

Now I languish here until I cough up Tatum. So says Mister Sweet, and he should know. I scratch my one remaining ball and sigh.

The klaxon klaxeth and the screw unlocks the door from the other side. He ticks my name off and I'm allowed to pass, unescorted, to the heads. It's been a point of honour with me so far never to use the night-soil bucket. Lucky I've never had the squits. Silent is close behind me in the race for the heads. The cubicles have no doors but we leave each other in peace. No practical jokes. This is the nearest we get to a religious experience.

Silent speaks reverently of his mother. His breathing quickens and in the next cubicle I can sense an infinity of pleasure compressing into two minutes. Silent's mother is the only woman he has ever truly known and she's here with him now when he needs her. Silent is delivered with a sigh.

Palmer the trusty comes to tell us we're over our time and there's a line backing up outside. He has a good mind to revoke our privileges. Later, at breakfast – one deck up and still no daylight – Silent talks to a new boy. We fell asleep last night through his sobs. Silent takes a firm line.

The drill sergeant is sick with something – galloping knob-rot says the grapevine, but most likely the squits. No one else has the energy to take us for PE so it's a double period of holystone and sand. The scabby sun, vicious after his nightly keel-hauling, puts himself on the payroll of torture, burning furiously at noon. Two boys collapse from dehydration. The overseer knows without a water-break he may have a death on his hands. We work on. At one o'clock we grovel at the trough, where translucent shapes swim in the water.

I'm on kitchen fatigues this week, so early afternoon I flay the skins from potatoes that look like Sir Walter's original samples. My thumbs gouge out eyes and burst pussy abscesses. After fatigues I get half an hour's recreation, which I spend in the lee of an old rope-locker. All I have to read is a few Catholic Truth Society pamphlets I got off the visiting RC chaplain, but they pass the time. The one on the catechism is my favourite: 'Who made you? God made me. Why did God make you? How the fuck should I know?' Silent says 'Catholic Truth' is a good one. I tell him it's an oxymoron. He says only a poxy moron would fall for it.

Tonight there's 'privileges'. Once a month there's a tombola session, run by the Anglican chaplain. 'Biblical Bingo' he calls it. He's had cards printed, with pictures of stories from Holy Scripture and numbers superimposed. He calls the numbers, adding little tags to each in the manner of bingo callers everywhere. A game might go like this:

'All the twos, King of the Jews, twenty-two.'

Yes, a good start. I've got that, to the left of the woman going to the well for water.

'Ninety-nine, the Gadarene swine!'

No luck . . . wait a sec, yes, there by the Pharisees.

'Thirty-three, Calvary Tree!'

Bullseye!

'Twenty-one, the virgin mum.'

Holy Mary, I'm nearly there!

'All the eights, Pearly Gates! What shall I do?'

And the congregation replies, 'Shake the bag!'

Shake it, shake me a hundred, a hundred.

'One and two blanks, the leper who gave thanks!'

'Bingo! Bloody bingoooooooooo!'

Two days in the hole and a week's loss of privileges for swearing in front of the padre.

Tonight Silent gets lucky in a full-house game and trots up to the pulpit to get his prize: a modern French edition of Montaigne, with the bookmark set at the essay on cruelty, and a box of two hundred Black Death. The Shanty Town economy must be on the up, with a contract to supply the prison fleet.

Before we go the padre gives us his talk, reminding us to be good boys and keep ourselves pure for Jesus. He wants a smart turnout for church parade on Sunday. A Very Important Parson is coming to conduct the service – the Inspector of Chaplains in His Majesty's Hulks.

Come Sunday we're mustered on deck. These days I stand with the little group of RCs. So does Silent, though he's an Ulster Protestant. We stand rigidly at ease until the bosun's pipe calls us to attention. A bubble of conversation floats from the hatch and then the platform party appears, led by our own chaplain. No mistaking the Reverend Bartleby, blinking into the light, and there's Sarah just behind. She wears a white cotton pleated skirt. Her hair is in plaits. Her face is in shadow under a wide-brimmed straw hat but there's a hint of tan on her smooth bare legs.

Mrs Galopede, the Governor's wife, bustles about the platform. She serves lemon squash to the guests. Sarah wraps her long slender fingers round her glass and sits with one leg crossed over the other. Our chaplain is talking now but I'm not listening, and I don't think anyone else is either. We all watch Sarah and the fluttering of her skirt in the breeze. I'm falling into a swoon, going on a long, vertiginous journey up Sarah's legs.

The hymn-book monitors are among us now, one book between two. The fat cook's concertina wheezes an intro, key of C, and we're off.

Rock of Ages, cleft for me
Let me hide myself in Thee.

Amen! Reverend Bartleby steps forward.

'Let us pray.'

We bow our heads and clasp our hands over our concave bellies.

'Oh Heavenly Father, who ordained the motion of the heavenly spheres! Look down on this stationary portion of the sublunary world and grant, we beseech you, your Divine grace and mercy to those whose lives are arrested here, frozen in the ice-bound stream of time. Warm them with the radiance of your heavenly love and melt their hearts, that they may know what brought them here, better to understand themselves and the origin of sin, through Jesus Christ Our Lord, Amen.'

The service wears on. More singing, more prayers. Then a sermon from Reverend Bartleby that threatens to be a filibuster. Taking a liturgically unseasonable theme, he speaks on the Resurrection. But then, as he shows, the Resurrection is perennial. The freshening breeze lifts Sarah's skirt and she lets it blow, until a look from Mrs Galopede prompts her to tuck it down.

Reverend Bartleby talks on, about our green age and the force that through the green fuse et cetera, the greening of grace and the grace of the risen Lord. He talks of our salad days, when we are green in judgement. He talks of the Fall, of Redemption, the blood of the Lamb. Christ died for us. Beyond his death is the Resurrection. His death alone redeemed us, but his Resurrection lifts us on high with seraphim and cherubim. And yet Satan is abroad in the world. Champions of righteousness are yet needed if he is to be thwarted. Once in a millennium such a supreme champion appears, and we must all be ready to buckle on our armour and gird our loins to follow his Crusade. A Crusade which amplifies the centuries-old resonance of the rolling stone and the empty tomb.

Well, I'm listening anyway. Our chaplain seems lost. He scratches his head and squints at the sun, and then at Reverend Bartleby. He scratches his head again. What on earth is he talking about? And who?

Shucks, I've got a fair idea who he's talking about.

The Governor seems to have nodded off. Mrs Galopede digs him in the ribs. He wakes up and mops his forehead with a large blue polka-dot handkerchief. Mrs Galopede smiles gamely and nods, screwing her currant eyes against the currant bun. Sarah presumes to pour herself a glass of lemon squash. She lifts it to her pout and I hear the clink of ice cubes.

Suddenly I'm aware of Silent, at ease with his hands on

his hips and transported to some transcendent realm. I know he's not wafted there on the wings of Reverend Bartleby's eloquence. His Adam's apple bobs and he licks his lips. A faint rumble like a litany reaches me. There's a passion animating his face that you sometimes see arrested in the marble faces of saints. Under his shorts, straining upright towards the thin elastic cordon dividing modesty from shame, 'Mickey' is intent on taking the air. With subtle, almost imperceptible rotations of the pelvis, 'Mickey' glides to and fro against the navy-blue canvas shorts. I can only wonder at Silent's daring, at the fierce hunger he must feel and the awesome compulsion of the demon he must propitiate. I usually think of Silent as a two-minute man, but today he plays himself like a big-game fisherman with the catch of a lifetime.

At last I feel something fly out of him, winging overhead like a migrating soul. But it's his third, or maybe even fourth, this morning, so there isn't much to show for it, just a stain the size of a shekel which quickly dries white in the sun.

Reverend Bartleby is into his peroration now, speaking once more of the empty tomb and the risen Christ. In time, when time shall be no more; when the Son of Man shall come to judge the living and the dead; when pilgrim species Man stands at the bar of Heaven, accused; then, on that day, will graves gape open and the sea give up its dead. The ashes of the cremated, scattered in wind and flood, rolled round the oozy ocean floor, sedimented in the tide laving the sandy fringes of foreign shores, will coalesce, each grain seeking its fellows by spiritual gravity, binding one with the others like clay beneath the potter's hands, infused with the breath of eternal life.

'The Resurrection of the Body! Oh my sons, a terrible beauty is born! How will it fare with you on that far-off day whose coming, once the veil of death is drawn across your face, will be swifter than the larkrise?'

He lifts his arm and points to the sun, as if the Son of Man is even now descending in a chariot of fire. He lowers his arm, swift as a semaphore, and with one bony finger pointing from a bunched fist sweeps across our pink, sweaty faces.

'How will it fare with you?'

His voice is husky. His head is suddenly bowed and he staggers back as if struck. He takes his seat with the assistance of Mrs Galopede and Sarah, who passes him a glass of lemon squash. Our own chaplain rises to conclude the service with a short prayer, then a longer speech of thanks, slightly puzzled, to his superior and then the final hymn. The fat cook muffs the intro, starts again, and we're off with 'We Plough the Fields and Scatter'.

Early Sunday evening we have 'association' for an hour. We have 'liberty' on deck. We can smoke. Silent and I lean on the rail and gaze at the purple evening spreading like a bruise across the wooded shore. We smoke Black Death, lighting each fresh cigarette from the butt of the last. Palmer sidles up to us and bums a fag. Silent waits for him to go then says, 'Did you hear the buzz?'

There's usually a rumour going round and Silent always hears it before me.

'It's to do with the Holy Joe that was mouthing off this

morning. Him with the ice-cream daughter. Aaah!'

'Don't start, please, just tell me.'

'Eugene was waiting-on down in the wardroom where they were taking the post-sermonal dram. He heard the chief sky pilot say there's to be an amnesty, because of the Coronation. Not everyone, mind, and certainly not me, unless the King is minded to reassert his claim to the throne of Ulster. But you may be in with a chance. Eugene swears he heard your name on the lips of the virgin vision and her pappy.'

I shake my head and spit into the water.

'I very much doubt it. It looks like six months of this and then a trip north to the hot-box.'

'Ach, McWhinny, you're a dour sort. Do you never look on the bright side?'

The whistle blows. We nip our fags and get in line. The boys from Raleigh dorm file past. Then Blake, Rodney and Nelson. We're in Drake, and we're top dogs this week — kit inspection, fatigues, drill et cetera. We stay on deck an extra two minutes while the others swarm below. I take a last look at the evening and wonder about the chances of making a dive and swimming ashore. Silent's bound to try it some day. In the dormitory, locked in for the night, we have five minutes before the light goes dim. There's a line of lads waiting to perch on the commode. Looks like the squits. I bury my nose in the sheet and try to sleep.

It's a troubled night. More groaning than usual and yelps of pain. I try to ignore it, drifting in and out of sleep. But at last I have to sit up. It's pandemonium in here. Silent sits on the bottom bunk with his hand on the brow of a comrade.

Despite the heat, the boy's lying with the sheet gripped tight to his chin. His teeth are chattering. His body goes into spasm.

'McWhinny, see if you can't get the screw to open up. I think it's cholera.'

There's a couple of lads already at the door, pleading to be let out or at least for the doctor to be called.

'Can't do it, lads. You know the rules. And the doctor's ashore for the night at a Masonic. Anyway, what's the night bucket for, eh?'

Perched on the commode is the fattest boy in the dorm, his face a rictus of agony. Next to him, sharing a hole made for one, are two lads, white-faced and shivering, clinging to each other so tightly they look like Siamese twins. Round about, in the gangways, others are squatting rigid, too agonised to move. They clutch the iron uprights of bunks and their breath is short and tight. Pools of shit, loose and yellow, lie festering. About half the dorm is suffering. Palmer sleeps through it.

Suddenly panic sparks the air, arcing from boy to boy. I run to the door, push the others aside and, in my best mimic of an Oxford University voice, I talk very deliberate and slow to the screw. The silence beamed back tells me I'm winning. The bolts are drawn back and the screw peeps round the door. Everything is smothered in green neon quarter-light. I take his arm and guide him into the dorm, showing it off like a prize. He claps his hand over his nose.

Together we go for the Governor.

17 ③

Silent takes the shoulders this time and I take the feet. My turn to look into the boy's eyes and mutter banalities. The boy is too far gone to pay heed. He stares through me with slitted eyes, spitting fever. He's watching something far away, a castaway scanning some indoor horizon.

It's difficult to make the twists and turns that lead up to the deck. His body is rigid and won't bend, like rigor mortis has already set in. But his blowtorch breath comes fast. His ankles are slippy with his sweat and my sweat and I'm scared of dropping him.

At last we get him into the air. The shadowless blue of early dawn colours everything flat, a one-eyed perspective. The doctor, still in evening dress, his bow-tie askew, moves among the boys. He carries a pencil torch. He peers into eyes burning with pale fire and presses the tom-tom pulse.

We lay the boy down and wait for the doctor. Silent wants a smoke but he thinks it wouldn't be right. The doctor comes over and shines his light. He listens to his chest.

'Starboard side with this one, lads.'

We pick him up and bring him to the dead. He's the fifth. There's still nothing to cover the bodies with but I can't bear the sight of his eyes, wide open and staring at the sky. I take off my vest and lay it on his face. I can't touch his eyelids. Silent crosses to the rail and spits. There's a whistle from the hatchway.

We're needed below again.

Seven o' clock we're relieved by a pair from Raleigh and we're allowed aft, away from the sick. There's hot, sweet tea and we can smoke. Word comes that another two are dead and the doctor's sent for help. The sun is dogged by a pelt of cloud in an otherwise clear sky. From the north comes what Silent calls the 'batty-churgle' of a helicopter, a Yankee flag on its belly. It looks like it's going to land on the helicopter pad but it hovers and drops a rope ladder. Two figures in orange climb down. One is a woman, and she's in charge.

By noon there are twelve dead. Silent and I bag them up in the rubber shrouds the Yanks have brought and we take them below. We take them to a cold store. We stack them up.

The illness starts with the squits and convulsions, then proceeds by degrees of fever to paralysis. No one knows what it is. It isn't cholera. The Yankee doctor, Erica Levine, radios a colleague who's seen service in the Tropics. There's talk of parrots, monkeys, liver fluke, yellow jack and colonic catalepsy. Silent says if he ever gets out of here he's going to study medicine.

Silent falls in love with Doctor Levine.

Mr and Mrs Galopede go ashore for the sake of their health. The overseers go crazy. Anyone not sick and not on sick-duty is sent doubling round the decks carrying sand-bags, 'to sweat it out of them'. Doctor Levine has a row with the Deputy Governor and the lunacy stops.

Too late for some. Worn out by 'exercise', more boys succumb to fever. By nightfall thirty-one are dead. Silent and I make more trips to the cold store.

Doctor Levine says we two are honorary corpsmen for the duration. She takes us out of the orbit of trusty and overseer.

Later that night, Silent and I snatch some rest in a linen store. Silent lights another Black Death and says, 'The way I see it, they have to take the bodies ashore sometime. My guess is they'll wait till the epidemic dies down and then do it in one hop. They'll take them out in bags or maybe box them up. If I can lose one of the stiffs, I take his place. I'd swim for it, but that squad of militia on the shore looks a pretty effective quarantine. What do you think?'

I shrug.

Seven days on and Silent slips his cable. He lies naked on a pallet, under an awning of flour sacks. The white-hot sun burns through, cooking him in his own waste. The sick are not allowed below. When they die we shroud them in rubber and take them down. Levine asks why we can't take Silent somewhere below but the new Governor, close-cropped hair and magenta sunglasses, asserts his command. The overseers and trusties, infused with fresh bile, swagger in their pride, eager to tighten ship.

The breeze fails. Doctor Levine wipes Silent's face with a cloth while I fan him with a Catholic Truth Society pamphlet on consanguinity. Silent is the last of the sick. The others are in recovery or are beyond help. About two in the afternoon his paralysed frame gives a jerk. His eyes swivel and focus on Doctor Levine. He says, in a soft voice of terror, 'Mother', then he dies. Doctor Levine closes his eyes.

Together we box him up in cardboard. Today is the day they've come to take the bodies away. The last body bags are emptied, the last cardboard coffins filled. A Yankee quarter-master has arrived to make sure no Government property goes to the incinerator. He counts the body bags.

Silent is just in time for the wagons, drawn up on the shore. Across the water we hear the stamp and whinny of blinkered horses.

Cardboard coffins are a bad idea. The frozen stiffs are beginning to melt in the heat. The seams of some boxes are already leaking, staining the deck. An overseer struts and tut-tuts over the mess, measuring the hours of holystoning to come. We begin hoisting the coffins over the side and into the tender. Halfway through, the derrick jams, with a coffin swinging out over the water. We can't lower it and we can't bring it back. The trusties get in each other's way, trying to clear the line. A brown stain spreads quickly along the bottom of the box and it begins to sag. Suddenly it bursts and the body, naked except for blue canvas shorts, lurches and rolls and plunges into the river just ahead of the tender. A circus of gulls swoops, skittering and screaming through the splash. The crew of the tender rake the water with boathooks but there's no sign of the body. We clear the line and once more begin swinging them overboard.

Silent is the last to go. Doctor Levine lifts the lid and stethoscopes his chest, just to make sure. Together with another lad we carry him to the hoist and watch him ascend. The pulley creaks and down he goes.

As the evening shades come down a helicopter skims the trees on the far shore and crosses the estuary. This time it risks a landing. I glance up from the brown stain I'm scrubbing out and see Doctor Levine and her crewman making ready to board. There's no one from the ship to say goodbye and thanks. They climb inside and the hatch closes. As the rotor spins and the machine lifts off our own doctor comes running. He squats by the rail and waves as the bird rocks gently into the darkening air.

Last task of the night is to finish sluicing the body bags, dirtying the deck once again. We turn them inside out to dry. The Yankee quartermaster checks them against a tally on his clipboard.

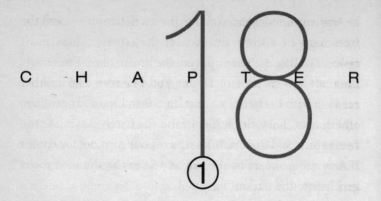

CHAPTER 18

①

I was scraping flabby carrots when Palmer came along and told me I was down for Governor's interview.

'When you're finished here, wash up, get into Number One kit and wait for me in the dorm. I'll take you along to Governor Pargiter.'

Number One kit was the same as any other, except the shirt and shorts were embroidered with the ship's badge and you wore a pair of socks. I dressed and sat on my bunk in the empty dorm, waiting for Palmer. He came to the door and beckoned me to follow.

Governor Pargiter was dictating into a machine. He switched off and waved Palmer out.

'At ease, McWhinny.'

He picked up a thick vellum scroll and unrolled it, fixing each end with paperweight skulls.

'No mistaking the King's seal, is there, McWhinny? You're a fortunate young man.'

'Is it the amnesty, sir? For me, sir?'

'Yes and no. Tatum Liotes sends his regards and says to tell you he's finished his epic. He escaped from the hovel he was confined in, as soon as the work was done, and the first thing he did when he was free was assert your innocence. Sir D'Arcy Peever was behind the kidnap. These Poet Laureates can be rather jealous types, I believe, and it rather rankled with him that he'd lost his job to Liotes. There were others too, political malcontents who took advantage of Peever's . . . well, peevishness, I suppose. Unfortunately, Sir D'Arcy slipped on a bar of soap at Mister Sweet's emporium and banged his head and died before he could name his accomplices. Rather a feeble sort of chap, so I've heard. Most of us slip on a bar of soap and come to little harm, as you know yourself. Bit of a poof, this Peever chappie, if you want my honest opinion.

'Strictly speaking, McWhinny, you've been cleared of involvement – provisionally, at any rate. By seven tomorrow morning you'll be off this ship and out of my custody. But, despite Mister Liotes' good opinion of you, we remain suspicious, so you're being paroled into the guardianship of the Reverend Bartleby. You are to become a lay missionary in his Mission to Repatriated Hulkers. Here, read this and sign it, to say you understand the instrument of parole and abide by its terms.'

He passed me a form laid out with a labyrinth of clauses and sub-clauses, among which I guaranteed not to write any autobiography or fictional work, or make any film, or assist in such, et cetera, pertaining to my experience as a trainee in His Majesty's Hulks.

'Fair enough.'

I signed.

'Remember, McWhinny. This is parole. You can be

bounced back here at any time. Now, cut along to have your medical papers signed and then get your civvy-street togs. I shall see you in the morning before you go.'

'Oh dear me, laddie,' said the doctor. 'Out into the world with only one testicle, eh? Still, it shouldn't give you any trouble – the remaining one, I mean – and it's still perfectly possible to father healthy children. Nature has a way of compensating us for these shortcomings. You came to us from Mister Sweet, didn't you?'

'Yes, sir. The last time I saw him I was hanging upside down having my buttocks and scrotum lashed with a cane.'

'I think you mean you last saw him when you slipped on a bar of soap and hurt your "sit-upon", don't you? Yes, I've heard he can be a little over-zealous when it comes to hygiene. Soap isn't to be sniffed at, though. We wouldn't get much done without soap, now, would we?'

'Indeed not, sir.'

18②

I stood on the main deck of *Vindictive* and waited for the tender to cast loose from the jetty and bob across the water. On the road by the jetty, parked a little way back among the dunes, was a long black limousine. Pocock, in aviator's uniform and peaked cap, sat on the bonnet rolling a cigarette. Bruiser and Sham climbed out of the car and waved to me. I waved back. I was sorry not to see Sarah with them. She'd come stickily to me in the guise of a succubus the night before.

I shook hands with the Governor and climbed over the side and down the ladder. The tender headed for the shore.

'Well met, *compadre*,' said Shamela.

'Good to have you back,' said Bruiser.

We sat in the back of the limousine and drank Coronation Ale and smoked 5/11 King Size, while Pocock drove us towards the Refuge. Out in the eastern fields the harvest was nearly gathered in. A copper sun climbed steadily towards its zenith.

'Saint Sepulchre's is closed for renovation,' said Sham. 'So the Mission to Repatriated Hulkers has set up in the west wing for the time being. I've been painting a mural for the refectory, to help establish the proper moral tone for you wayward boys.'

'It's all about smiting the Philistines,' said Bruiser. 'I've been modelling Goliath.'

'Now you're back,' said Sham, 'I can start on David. By the way, Reverend Bartleby sends his apologies for not coming to pick you up in person, but him and his snow-queen daughter are preparing a welcome-home surprise for you.'

'I can think of a surprise for her,' said Bruiser. 'There's nothing wrong with her that nine smokin' inches wouldn't cure.'

'You poor deluded *boy*. She's out of your league, you fool,' said Sham.

We talked about Tatum and Wence.

'Wence is sorry he turned you in,' said Bruiser. 'But he really thought you'd sold Tatum down the river. He hopes there's no hard feelings. He wants you back in the bosom of the family.'

'Why should there be hard feelings,' I said, 'when that which does not kill me makes me stronger? In some ways he's done me a favour, giving me a chance to detox like that. From now on my gig is strictly legal; it's lashings of alcohol and tobacco for me and nothing else.'

Pocock steered with his elbows while he rolled a fresh cigarette. Bruiser offered him a beer but he turned it down. Up from the horizon came a flight of American warplanes, barrelling in close formation.

Pocock spat his extinct cigarette into our slipstream and screwed a fresh roll-up between his lips.

'Spawn of Satan, guv,' he said cheerfully.

The ale hit me hard after so long an abstinence, and I slept uneasily with my head on Sham's breast. In delirium I saw Sarah Bartleby, in full snow-queen regalia, furiously sewing a sampler. She gabbled as she sewed. 'Spawn of Satan, yes. Demons from the bottomless pit, who wander through the world for the ruin of souls, who make our country a vassal state, just like King John tried with the Saracens. But he didn't get away with it. Men were men in those days. Now what have we got? Milksops who cravenly quake before the hydra-headed, jack-booted octopus, the eight-legged ball of perversion perpetrating any and every atrocity to ensure that usurious capitalism survives. I know I'm a fine one to talk, with my sampler business going so well, but after the Liberation I'm going to set it up as a workers' co-operative.'

I woke up with wee wicked Geordie beckoning through my pants.

18③

We scooted over the causeway where the Victorian bulk of the Refuge peeked through the trees on the shoulder of the lake. Towards the river a dusty, sunlit haze rose from resumed digging on the canal. Pocock slowed to let me take a look.

'Wence got the money to finish the job,' said Sham. 'A grant from the Coronation Celebration Fund.'

I smelled the dust and sweat, and heard the grinding of machinery and the rattling of chains as buckets of clay were lifted from the diggings and dumped into waiting trucks. A high, ululating Shanty Town voice called out the line of a work-song. Somewhere in the dust the rest of the gang came down on 'Unh!'

Wence was at the door to greet us.

'Forgiven?' he said to me.

'La vertu se perfectionne par les combats,' I replied with a grin.

'I'll take that as sincerity,' said Wence. 'Tatum wants a word. He's in the billiard room. When you're through with him I guess you'd better scut on over to the west wing and report to the padre.'

'I'll go and tell him we've arrived,' said Sham.

'Okay,' said Wence. 'Bruiser, my chemically dependent, mentally impaired *boy*, see how healthy Lingus is looking since his prolonged convalescence. Go see Chef and tell him to defrost the fatted calf. Maybe we'll have a little party and celebrate the one lost sheep who returned to the fold.'

Wence shook his head.

'Jesus, listen to me, the way I'm going with the biblical iconography. Bartleby's inane chatter is finally getting through. I'm going to go clear my head with a canter through *The Tibetan Book of the Dead*. Bruiser, you need some exercise, you're running to flab. Go help the pioneers digging out the canal. Work up a lather, lose some pounds.'

'Give me a break,' said Bruiser. 'Since when has this job involved me working like a navvy? It'll kill me, the state I'm in.'

'I guess it will, or make you stronger, like Lingus says.'

Bruiser shot me a sour look.

'Steady on, B,' I said, putting my hand on his shoulder. 'Don't blame me, blame Freddy N, the syphilitic sage; those are his words.'

Bruiser looked blank.

'He's talking about Nietzsche,' said Sham.

'Oh, right. Of course. I knew that. See you later.'

Sham and Bruiser went their separate ways, Bruiser a little slower. I crossed the hall and went downstairs to the billiard room. Through the green baize door came the sound of balls being racked up.

I went straight in.

'Lingus, good to see you,' said Tatum Liotes. 'Fancy a game? At last I got a proper pool table in here. Listen to the word: "pool". Can you hear it?'

'I'm not sure I'm with you,' I said. 'How about giving me a clue?'

'Pool. It's a simple word. It's a simple game. Pure and cool. Pool.'

'Tatum, I was given to understand that captivity gave you the chance to go cold turkey and get yourself clean. You sound as if you've been tucking into the 'shrooms.'

'No such thing. Going straight has sensitised me to the subtleties of the American language. Fancy a game?'

'I don't know how to play.'

'It's easy. Catch.'

He threw me a cue. He was right, it was easy. We played three games and I won them all.

'Best of five?'

'I think you mean best of seven. But no. Come on, let's have a snifter and catch up.'

We went to the canteen. The bar was closed so we settled for hot green tea.

'Blow on it,' said Tatum, 'or you'll get cancer.'

We settled into a comfortable old sofa and put our feet

up on a low table. A slattern came by and flicked a duster at our feet. We said sorry and put our feet on the floor.

Tatum told me how he was kidnapped — it wouldn't have happened if he hadn't been so upset over Jeremiah Brandreth and gotten paralytic drunk; how he was imprisoned — it wasn't so bad, and it gave him a chance to finally shack up with his Muse and show commitment after years of fannying around; how he escaped — it was easy, he just pulled the window bars away from the crumbling frame and climbed down a drainpipe on the wall of some nondescript slum in Clerkenwell; how the milipols had gone to the slum and found an unwashed Sir D'Arcy Peever on the nod before a cold one-bar electric fire, without a shekel for the meter, but with evidence of other occupation scattered around; how they'd hauled Peever away to Sweet's emporium to renew his acquaintance with 'soap' and then staked out the place but no one came; how Tatum was sorry for Peever — they'd had a mutual masturbation thing going for a while but could never take it any further. There were no other clues to offer — beyond hearing low voices at dead of night, chanting some melancholy gibberish, and a thwacking sound like a wet fish being slapped down on a marble slab. The important thing now was where the muse would take him next — into a dramatic multimedia piece which Wence was scoping and planning. Hence the canal.

'Yeah, the canal will allow King Andy to get from the river to the lake on his royal barge. The show is a celebration of Anglo-American unity and "can-do", and the theme, as always, is reconciliation. We've got so much to celebrate.'

'And much to be reconciled to. Come on, Tatum, I'm not

questioning the lovey-dovey thing you've got going with Miss Muse, but I figured you had a more cynical streak.'

'When it comes to Wence, let's say I'm learning cynicism fast. But it's a Barnum and Bailey world out there. I've got no axe to grind.'

Tatum went on to explain the show. The one book he'd had 'inside' was a dog-eared copy of *A Masque Presented at Ludlow Castle, 1634*, otherwise known as *Comus*, which Peever had lying around. The only other reading materials were an old copy of *Taxidermy Today* and *This is Norway, 1954*.

'Yeah, and I found out since that Little Johnny Milton was really called Big John Milton, and he wasn't an Oxford man, he went to CamTech. That's Hollywood for you: they changed the guy's name. And his school. Anyway, Big John's masque is the way to go, sort of Dionysian, like a carnival, with riot and misrule and stuff leading to the restoration of the natural order, so it fits in with what Wence is doing already. Except this has got to be fit for a King. Say, I haven't told you about the Coronation yet.'

'Don't bother, I'll wait for it to come round on the newsreels. Tell me some more about the show.'

18④

The west wing was a dilapidated part of the Refuge, not much used until now except for storing stage flats and such, but with Sham as straw boss and a crew of slaveys under her it was beginning to look ship-shape and fulfil its charitable function as a halfway house for repatriated Hulkers. The walls of the refectory were washed and primed and freshly painted in neutral tones. On the wall above High Table the mural was taking shape, opposite a high arched window. It was mostly figures in outline but the huge bulk of Goliath was fully fleshed. If I hadn't been told that Bruiser was the model for the Philistine giant I might have had trouble working it out. Bruiser's habitual and characteristic expression, of dopey bewilderment and resentment mixed with the cunning of a shithouse rat, was absent. In its place was a manic and purposeful stare, emerging from a style of Stakhanovite social realism which suggested that the 'big fella' was busting his drawers to get on with whacking Israelites on the bonce and upping his quota. In his huge paw he hefted a lurid neon, nail-studded baseball bat. Sham and I stood below the mural and squinted at Goliath through the clear north light. I made a sucking noise with my teeth.

'I know, I know,' said Sham, 'the baseball bat isn't strictly biblical, but Sarah Bartleby thinks it gives a kind of street-credible Shanty Town vibe. She who pays the piper . . .'

'When do you want me to sit for David? And will I have a slingshot, or something more in keeping with the Shanty Town vibe, like a rocket-launcher?'

'It's funny you should say that,' said Sham. 'Sarah came back from Arnie's the other day with an RPG — no, don't get worried, a decommissioned RPG — and she said I should paint you aiming it at Goliath's crotch. And sit when you like, this is hardly the most pressing job around here. I reckon it's another three months' work.'

'I'm not going to interfere, but don't you think the rocket-propelled grenade will miss the point of the original story – you know, unequal contest, the slingshot and all that?'

'I made the point to Sarah, but she said no one but a halfwit would tackle a champion of the State with a slingshot in this day and age.'

'So what else have we got planned in this hotchpotch of a picture – no offence, Sham.'

'None taken, I'm sure. We've got Little Jack Cornwell VC, the boy hero of the Battle of Jutland, who stuck to his gun quite literally. And, continuing the naval theme, Reverend Bartleby wants the death of Nelson, with Nelson modelled on himself, and Jeremiah Brandreth as Captain Hardy.'

'You'll have to work from a photograph of Brandreth. Or maybe a self-portrait.'

'Bizarrely, no. Sarah will show you later. They've had Brandreth embalmed. Now, down to the right, see, where I've had trouble blocking the lines? That panel represents the Marriage Feast at Cana, loosely interpreted.'

'Naturally. But with Wence as a bald Jesus?'

'Yes, but I won't paint the wrinkles and I'll double the length of his beard to hide his gut. And the bridegroom, that's you again. They obviously think you have the right fresh-faced look for these young parts. Now, the bride . . .'

'Cooee! Lingus!'

Sarah came running up.

'Oh you poor, darling boy, at last you're free!' She threw her arms about me and jigged me around.

'Don't mind me,' said Sham, flashing her metal teeth in a humourless smile.

'Please don't be huffy,' said Sarah. 'Arnie's just driven up with more paint. Go and pay him.'

'Right you are, Your Majesty, your obedient servant I'm sure.'

'Just get on and deal with it, please, and belay the sarcasm.'

Sham folded her arms and fixed Sarah with a scornful look. But she said nothing to her, turning to me with a quick 'Catch you later.'

'Missing you already,' said Sarah to her back. 'Come on Lingus, I'll show you the Chapel and the first of our surprises.'

18⑤

Sarah scraped a match and lit a tall orange candle.

'There, that's better. Over here.'

Our shadows billowed across the vaulted roof as we crossed the cellar of the west wing, now converted into a makeshift chapel. On a dais was a wooden bier, and on the bier a glass casket. Fresh flowers were strewn around. A portable air-conditioning unit hummed in B flat. We stepped up and peered through the lid. The casket was lit from within, with a faint radiance like the luminosity of moss. The candle flickered over Jeremiah Brandreth's face, animating it with a restless and enigmatic expression. His hands were folded across his chest. He held a revolver and a decorator's paintbrush.

'We've had him stuffed and mounted by the best in the business,' said Sarah. 'As soon as the restoration work on Seppie's is finished we'll take Jeremiah back to the Crypt and put him on public display.'

'He's looking better than the last time I saw him.'

'Yes, High John really did Jeremiah proud. He came back by submarine from Albania especially to do it. He's away again, of course. Jude the Holy Mother is expecting the new Messiah very soon. It's a shame the embalming was necessary at all. If we'd got him back to Seppie's in time, High John assures us the antidote would have snatched him from the brink of death. The timing was always the sticky element in the plan, but at least he was spared the attentions of Rumbold the demon barber.'

'You said antidote?'

'Yes. Lingus, you have the glory of being the comrade who brought deliverance to Jeremiah. The pages of the Bible you carried to him were impregnated with a powerful hypnotic, a cold infusion of a root procured in Illyria by Manley Stanley himself, and which has been used through the ages by Albanian *banditti* to counterfeit death. Jeremiah, fore-warned, knew the Bible's significance as soon as he saw it. But I'm afraid there was a bit of a slip-up, and Makepeace put a double dose of hypnotic in his custard, thinking it was vanilla essence. The aroma is much the same. What with the impregnated Bible and the custard on top, it all proved too much for Jeremiah, he was so weak.'

'You said this was just the first of your surprises. Not that I'm greedy, or dismissive of this display, but I'm curious to know what else you may have in mind.'

'Lingus, we're both of marriageable age. We're going to be married.'

'Who to?'

'Each other, you silly.'

'Shouldn't one of us propose to the other, traditionally me to you? Unless this is a leap year.'

'I don't think it is. And anyway, this is an arranged marriage.'

'Arranged by who?'

'By High John, your father, the Daddy of us all — and Papa too, of course. Lingus darling, I'm so sorry I doubted you before, when you said High John was your father.'

'That's okay, you're forgiven. I hope Dad's not expecting an invitation to the wedding, although it would be nice to see Jude again. But what's brought about your change of heart towards me?'

'Now I know you're High John's first-born, everything is changed utterly. One might say a terrible beauty is born. I thought of you before as fairly bright, although intolerably low-class. However, you being the son of a demigod and the half-brother of the new Messiah does rather push you up the hierarchy a bit — well, quite a bit, actually: two rungs down from the top. High John (may peace dog him all his days) won't be at the ceremony; he's too busy drafting a New Manifesto.'

'Can I have time to think about it?'

'What is there to think about? You've been celibate for months. That chap Bruiser says you must be gagging for it by now. And I'm a virgin, which is exciting for you, and I promise I'll stay still while you rectify that state of affairs on our wedding night. And afterwards you can do it every night if you like, I shan't say no.'

'I believe many a marriage has started on worse terms. All right, it's a bargain. But it's a shame my mother can't be at the wedding.'

'It's a shame that my poor dead mother can't be there too, but I know she will be looking down from heaven and blessing our nuptials. As for *your* mother, we're all agreed your father did the right thing in taking you away from her and changing your name. It seems she was little better than a prostitute. Come to think of it, she *was* a prostitute.'

'If we're going to get on together through the course of our married life, we may need to find some other sobriquet for my mother. Anyway, even if she was a prostitute woman, which I doubt, didn't Jesus himself defend Mary Magdalene?'

'That was under the New Law, which replaced the Old Law. Now we have a new New Law, closer to the old Old Law. I believe it's a product of the dialectical process. Papa will explain it to you in detail later when you're taking instruction, but for now . . .'

'I'm afraid I have to insist on remaining an agnostic on this one, so no instruction, please, especially in dialectics. Your faith should be mature enough to cope with what I believe is termed a "mixed marriage". Where is Pops anyhow?'

'He's gone to the Wivenhoe International Water Sports Facility today for his final scuba-diving lesson. He gets his certificate today. I'm already qualified. If you were qualified we could go somewhere hot for our honeymoon, with lots of lovely sand and clear water.'

231

'Like the Albanian Riviera, perhaps. I think before we get round to that you have a few English bedroom ceilings to get acquainted with first.'

'Oh, Lingus, you sound so masterful when you speak masterfully to me in that masterful way. I can't wait to become Mrs McWhinny.'

'Yes, now you come to mention it, I'm getting quite agitated myself. And let's hope you have better luck with the name McWhinny than my mother the prostitute did.'

18⑥

I spent what was left of the afternoon settling into my new quarters. I was the only occupant of a six-bed dormitory and the other beds weren't even made up. There was a 'No Smoking' sign above the wash-basin but I ignored it. I opened the window though, and leaned out to smoke. There was a pleasing view over the croquet lawn. The sun glinted off Sham's teeth as she battered a helpless croquet ball round and round in a solo display.

I lay on my bed for a while, with my hands behind my head, enjoying the trace of a languid nicotine buzz. I thought of bringing my hands down and pleasuring myself, then thought of pleasures to come which would be sweeter for the mastery of abstinence just now. I was feeling quite smug. There was a knock at the door. I shouted, 'Come,' and Sham appeared, croquet mallet over her shoulder.

'What's this about you getting married . . . to *her*?'

Right away I felt uneasy. Sham's flashing teeth didn't help.

'Married? Who to?'

'Who to? You're winding me up. It's all over the Refuge. You know she's a religious maniac?'

'She's Church of England, if that's what you mean.'

'Don't be smart. Look, I know you've been umpteen months without any ring-dang-doo . . .'

'Such a quaint expression.'

'I said don't be smart. You don't have to *marry* to go ugly-bumping, you know.'

'I do if I want to make love to Sarah.'

'*Make love*, he says. Spare me.'

Sham was a good mimic. She had my mincing tone off pat.

'Okay then, call it class vengeance.'

'From simpering lover to cynical tough guy in a heart-beat. Lingus, you are seriously, seriously in the wrong.'

I felt a shiver of rage but it passed.

'Just be happy for me.'

'I bet if we fucked right now you'd forget all about marrying little Miss Frigidaire. A good despunking is what you need.'

I was tempted, despite the teeth. But I spat in the Devil's eye.

'Sham, please, just be happy for me. And close the door on your way out.'

Sham didn't make any more fuss. She said, 'Guess I'll bundle and go.'

She left the door open.

18 ⑦

One of the 'Silent Night' choirboys, voice now broken, stopped by to tell me I was summoned to Wence's office. Leah Dingwallace was there, lying on a chaise longue with her hands clasped across her swollen belly.

'When's it due?' I said to Wence.

'The kid will arrive in his own good time. Unless we induce. This is a joyful but also a stressful time for us. Leah hasn't been very well this last month.'

'It's nothing,' said Leah. 'Mostly just the usual stuff, the swollen ankles and the chronic fatigue. But there was a bit of spotting. Daddy has asked if the King's physician can see me. I'm a little overdue.'

'Pocock is driving us up to Harley Street tomorrow morning.'

'Sincerely, I hope everything will be fine.'

'Thank you,' said Wence. 'Now, to cut to the chase, I've been talking to Tatum about the masque we're promoting. This is a big thing for us, you know, with the King coming and all, and we need help. I'm producing, Tatum is writer-director, and we want you as first assistant director.'

'But I haven't been to theatre school.'

'Go to the library. There's a shelf of books on "how to", mostly film but what's the difference? Bone up and then deal with it, according to your usual principle of "if it ain't gonna kill me", et cetera.'

'There's just one problem – apart from my inexperience.

I'm supposed to be a lay missionary in the Reverend Bartleby's Mission to Repatriated Hulkers. How will I find the time?'

'Bullshit. Can you see any repatriated hulkers round here? No. That's because they're still in the hulks — where they belong, I might add, present company provisionally excepted. The Reverend Bartleby is full of shit. I'm sorry I ever encouraged him. Have you seen that stiff he's got downstairs?'

'Oh Wence, darling, don't be so harsh. Don't forget that Obadiah is an old school and varsity chum of Daddy's. The friendship and alliance of the houses of Bartleby and Dingwallace go back to the accession of Jimmy One-Six in sixteen-oh-one.'

'Okay, okay, he's harmless enough for a crazy guy, and Saint Sepulchre's will be finished early in the new year, so after that he can go and evangelise the pigeons in Trafalgar Square. And take the family corpse with him. Lingus, that's all. See you later.'

'Wence, darling,' said Leah. 'We haven't congratulated Lingus on his engagement to Sarah.'

'What's to congratulate? Young people, I think I don't understand them any more.'

'Oh Wence, darling, did you ever? You're so sweet. I'm sure when you were a toddler you walked around scowling, with lines on your forehead already and a big beard to mumble into.'

'The scowling I'll admit to.'

'When Junior appears I think you'll find your tune changing.'

Leah held out her hand to me. I took it.

'I know Wence will make a wonderful father. And so will you, Lingus, one day.'

I kissed her hand with a show of gallantry.

'I'm looking forward to it. Very much.'

18⑧

One thing – okay, several, but one thing in particular – was bothering me round about now, and that was Jude. Or, more specifically, my child that she was carrying.

Her last letter to me showed how committed she was to the whole mad idea that Dad had impregnated her – couldn't she count? – and the latest news from Sarah wasn't particularly reassuring. Did I want my kid being brought up to believe he was the new Messiah? That sort of thing could seriously warp his brain and impair his ability to form normal relationships. Quite likely he'd end up 'New Messiah No-Mates'. True, I hadn't had many friends while growing up – any friends, to be frank – and, although I came to no harm, I didn't want it for my kid. At the back of my mind was the idea that maybe things could have worked out a bit better for me – and that's what we all want for our kid, right? The chance for him to have what we never had, to do what we never did, and to avoid . . .

No, this wasn't working. He'd have to avoid being born of

our line in the first place, of the House of McWhinny, as Leah Dingwallace would surely say.

18⑨

A couple of days later the telephone lines were down again. There were rumours of sabotage by disgruntled communication workers, but it was more likely just everything running down and wearing out. I needed to speak to Sister Vincent, to hear if there was any news of Jude. I fibbed to Tatum that I was going off to talk to a guy who'd done the music for a revival of *Comus* at the University of Debden Broadway, back in the ancient days of Good Queen Bess Two.

'An excellent idea. We don't want rockabilly as the default option.'

'I think we're talking ethereal but earthy too, kind of a mixture of the sublunary and the music of the spheres.'

'Just what I was thinking. Let me know how you get on.'

So I took a furlough for the rest of the day and headed south on a rickety tricycle for the Convent of the Ever-Open Wounds of Christ the King Crucified, taking a risk in violating the terms of my parole, but Sham had a good sideline in snide papers which stood up to anything but the hardest scrutiny. The checkpoint at Southwark Bridge was pretty lax, now the worry of the Coronation was over, and they just waved me through with a cursory glance at my ID.

It was nearly time for the noontide Angelus when I arrived at the Convent and hitched my trike to the railing. The queue for the cocoa and the bread and marge was longer than the last time I saw it, with fewer absolute derelicts and more of the shabby-genteel huddled in line. They were pasty-faced and thin, clutching threadbare collars turned up against the chilly wind. I heard a tubercular cough. Palmerston Street too was looking more down at heel, with whiffy rubbish strewn about. A broken water main gurgled feebly under low pressure.

I jumped the queue and headed straight for the door, ignoring the polite whines of protest behind me. No one answered my ring. I tugged the bell-pull again. The door opened a crack and Sister Joseph stuck her nose out.

'Cocoa's not till twelve, so scram.'

A beady eye looked me up and down.

'Oh, it's you. Come in.'

Sister Joseph opened the door wide and let me through. She faced the mob.

'The rest of you can wait until after the Angelus. Patience is a virtue, gluttony a sin.'

She shut the door.

'There, that's told them.'

She looked me up and down, nodding approval.

'I must say, you're looking so much better than the last time I saw you. Where have you been on holiday to get that tan? Now, if it's Mother Superior you want, she was on a pretty energetic sleepover round at Archbishop Cyril's last night, so she's having a lie-down. She won't want to miss the Angelus though. Go and wait in the Limbo Room. You know the way.'

I heard a distant music, which grew louder as I climbed the marble stairs. It was a quintet of recorders playing something courtly and stately. Soprano, two altos, tenor and bass. The Angelus bell began to toll.

'Long time no see,' said Sister Vincent. She took the crucifix from her rosary and flicked the cap off a bottle of Coronation Ale.

'Fancy a snort?'

'I came by trike, so no. I can do without being breath-alysed.'

'Suit yourself. Don't mind me.'

She took a long steady pull, gasped and wiped her mouth on her sleeve.

'Sorry about the racket,' she said, jerking her thumb at the door. 'It's Archbishop Cyril's installation next Sunday so they're rehearsing night and day. Now, you want to know about Jude. I can't imagine you've come for anything else.'

Sister Vincent delved into her robe and brought out a dirty and crumpled postcard.

'This is all we've heard. It came last week.'

The picture in lurid colour showed an Albanian dockside scene, with jolly Albanian Jacky Tars doing the hornpipe to an accordion and bagpipe. I turned it over. It was franked from Tirana and bore an Albanian stamp — a new issue showing the head of Manley Stanley, his face disfigured by cheap plastic surgery, and the bilingual legend: 'International

Hero of Labour, Second Class'. The date was unreadable, just a smudge.

'Yes, I know,' said Sister Vincent, noticing my frown. 'It's a puzzle. You'd think they'd be generous enough to make Mr Stanley an international hero of the first class, wouldn't you?'

The handwriting was small and neat, recognisably Jude's. It said, 'Weather dull and cloudy, and humid. Wettest summer in living memory. Coming home soon to have baby. Too risky here, not very hygienic. No one washes hands after lavatory.'

And that was all. 'I wonder if it's true about the hand-washing,' said Sister Vincent. 'I don't think it can be, do you? But she says she's coming home. Wherever that might be.'

'They say it's the place where, when you have to go there, they have to take you in,' I said. 'Wherever that might be, as you say.'

'I'd better make the Infirmary ready, just in case, and get the parish midwife scrubbed up and on stand-by,' said Sister Vincent. She burped and her hand flew to her mouth.

'Better out than in,' I said.

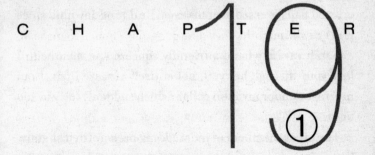

C H A P T E R 19 ①

Reverend Bartleby said he didn't believe in long engagements. Sarah said neither did she, so I cast around for my groomsman. Tatum turned me down; so did Bruiser. They didn't want to upset Sham any more than she was already.

'Look,' said Tatum. 'I'd be glad to, but it'll make too many waves. How about Pocock?'

'I think he's already one of the witnesses.'

'Makepeace?'

'Likewise.'

So Orlando it was.

19 ②

Orlando led the way down the staircase of the west wing and into the chapel. Sarah was already at the ramshackle altar. I stepped up beside her. Due to the dignity of the occasion, Pocock was now five minutes without a cigarette. He was lathered in sweat, eyes bulging and teeth clenched. Makepeace huddled nearby, moaning, fingers with custard-crusted nails pressed over his eyes. He'd gone downhill since last I saw him.

Sarah gave my hand a friendly squeeze and mouthed, 'I love you,' through her veil, not entirely sincere I felt. I ran my finger under my Eton collar, which suddenly felt way too tight.

The other members of the wedding party retired slightly, leaving the bride and groom standing at the head of the congregation. The chapel was silent except for a mouse scratching among the orange-box pews, the ticking of death-watch beetle and the unsteady B-flat drone of the portable air-conditioning unit.

Jeremiah Brandreth's mossy luminescence added to the lustre of the occasion.

Behind me I heard the door open and the footsteps of the Reverend Bartleby start up the aisle. He hurried along and stood to face us. He began to intone, 'Man that is born of woman hath but a short time to live . . . No, that's not it. Dearly beloved, we are gathered here together . . .'

When he got to 'Who gives this woman?' there was a moment of confusion. 'Oh dear, I suppose that's me,' he said, but Sarah said not to worry, she was giving herself.

The service went on according to the Book of Common Prayer, 1662. Sarah promised to obey and I promised to worship her with my body – no hardship on my part after eight months in the hulks. Then it was over. Man and wife. 'Licensed for embracement,' as Makepeace said glumly in a lucid moment.

19 ③

We had some trouble smoothing things over with Makepeace, who seemed distressed by the whole business. But Pocock rolled him his first ever cigarette and the subsequent fit of coughing and retching took his mind off everything else for the time being. Sarah and I said our goodnights and went up to bed. Her room, now our room, was heavy with incense.

'Everything's ready. Gosh, I'm so excited.'

A small night-light burned before a Tirana photo-booth snap of Jude and dear old Dad. Sarah lit a candle, cupping her hand round the flame.

'Isn't this jolly? Jolly romantic, I mean.'

I was already halfway out of my trousers. My foot caught in the bell-bottoms and I fell, cracking my head against the wardrobe mirror and fracturing it from top to bottom.

'Oh dear! Seven years' bad luck! Come here, silly-billy.'

There was a trickle of blood from my forehead. Sarah licked it off. Then she pulled my shirt over my head. She tweaked my nipples with her teeth.

'Ouch! Ouch!'

'Don't be such a baby! Just think what I've got to go through tonight. Gosh, are you really going to stick all of that inside me?'

'Most of it.'

'Now let's see if we can't get it even bigger. In for a penny . . .'

She knelt down and parted her lips. Her tongue lolled forward. She giggled.

'I say, I've just thought of something funny. This is just like my first communion. Well, come on, don't stand there looking concussed.'

Gingerly I laid the staff of life on her tongue.

I woke up not knowing where I was. I sat up in panic and saw Sarah, already up and dressed, brushing her hair in front of a looking-glass. Sunshine from the skylight lit the room. She spoke to my reflection in the glass.

'Last night doesn't really count. Erection, penetration, ejaculation. All three conditions are necessary for consummation, as you very well know. You missed out the second, so you'll have to try again later.'

'I'm sorry, but it's been so long. I think I was a little bit, you know, overwound.'

'Is that what you call it? It took me ages to get it out of my hair, and there was no more hot water. It all went in your bath. Honestly, what a night! My mother always said it would be a night to remember. Up to the ears in freezing cold water with Makepeace rattling the doorknob, calling me Penelope and demanding his conjugal rights. Goodness knows who he thinks he is. Anyway, I didn't open the door. I thought, despite everything, I might as well save myself for you, romantic fool that I am. And when I got back here you were sprawled across the bed, snoring fit to bust, and to top it all I fell asleep with wet hair and it's gone all funny down one side. Look!'

She presented a pouting profile to me. Her hair ballooned out in tangles over her left ear.

'Keep brushing. It will come right eventually.'

She turned back. Our eyes met in the glass. She said, 'God, what a fright you look. I'm beginning to think I've made a terrible mistake.'

The candle had burned down in a mess of greasy tallow and was now extinct. I didn't exactly feel like the conquering hero, but I was most annoyed about breaking the mirror. It didn't augur well.

Still, I told myself, we've only just begun.

19④

The schedule for the show was tight, with no slack anywhere, so a honeymoon was out of the question. There was barely time for breakfast.

We joined a crowded table in the canteen, where Tatum was holding court. Sham saw us coming, pushed aside her coffee, got up and walked away.

Bruiser leered at Sarah.

'Sleep well?'

'Hardly a wink. But it's not what you think.'

She pouted. Bruiser gave me a mocking look and said to Sarah, 'Did you not get enough action last night? Is that the grief?'

'I suspect it is, actually. It was a bit of a disappointment, to tell the truth. That's probably why I'm so crotchety this morning. And he's only got one thingy.'

'Well I'll be dipped in dogshit,' said Tatum. 'How many did you think he'd have?'

'Not the big thingy that stands up, you silly; the little thingies that hang down. It's a worry in so many ways. Deuteronomy says that a man who is wounded in the stones or has his privy member cut off shall not enter the congregation of the Lord.'

'Is that right?' said Tatum. 'And how does Satan feel about it?'

'Satan will take anyone,' I said.

I excused myself and went to find Sham.

'Script conference in twenty minutes: be there or it's your ass,' said Tatum.

19⑤

Sham was up a ladder, putting the finishing touch to the death of Nelson. I whistled to let her know I was there. She turned and acknowledged me with a wave of her brush then went back to work. I climbed up the ladder behind her and put my arms round her waist and pressed my face into her smock, savouring the sour reek of sweat and paint, linseed oil and dust. I felt her stiffen and then relax. But her voice had a sarcastic edge.

'You should be with your *bride*, your high-class piece of *cunt*, you low-class piece of *shit*.'

But she finished with a laugh, so I couldn't take offence. I murmured, 'I don't think it's working out.'

'Rather early to say, isn't it?'

'Sometimes you just know.'

She wiped her brush and said, 'Let me get down.'

We faced each other at the bottom of the ladder.

'I'll tell you now, rather than wait. I've had enough of painting images of our nation's mighty sea power and Bible crazies. As soon as this show is finished I'm leaving for Salamanca. I can get on a crew out there doing fresco restoration. I'll leave you my address before I go.'

She grinned, and this time the teeth didn't intimidate me at all. Sham looked down at my crotch, pointed at the High Table draped in paint-spattered sheets and said, 'Under there. Now.'

'I can't, I'm a married man.'

But I did.

19⑥

I was late for the script conference. Tatum and the Reverend Bartleby — who had been drafted in as continuity-checker — were sitting round a low table, sifting papers.

Tatum looked up, shook his head and sighed.

'We're up against a tight deadline here, Lingus, so if you can do us the courtesy of showing up on time when there's a call, we'll be mighty obliged. Okay, let's go through the scenario.'

Tatum turned to my father-in-law and said slowly and clearly, 'Padre, it's good of you to offer to help out. There's a lot of co-ordination involved here, so we can be ready for the King's visitation.'

'I'm only too pleased to assist,' said Bartleby. 'As you know, my Mission has been slow in getting started, so I'm pleased to have the time to spare you for such a worthy cause. It quite takes me back to happier days at Eton and the varsity.'

Tatum lit a cigar and we went through the programme, beginning with the opening of the causeway at ten in the morning and the admittance of punters to the grounds, where a medieval fayre would be set out, with booths and stalls, buskers and street theatre — the usual sanitised version of the times. For example, no lepers.

'Lepers are a downer,' said Tatum.

'I beg to disagree,' said Bartleby. 'Surely there's a place in our fayre for the leper?'

He spun us a riff about Jesus curing ten lepers and how only one came back to give thanks, and shouldn't we represent that one leper?

'And nine didn't?' said Tatum.

'I'm afraid not.'

'That's lepers for you,' said Tatum. 'But, you know, I think lepers are a distraction, padre, so if we could just move on?'

'I'm so sorry.'

'No, that's fine, we value your creative contribution; we just don't need it, that's all. Your job is to make sure everything runs to time and that what's in the scenario gets acted out in the right place, according to schedule. It's a logistical role.'

'I do apologise. I had no intention of usurping your creative function.'

'That's okay, padre, just so long as we understand each other.'

After the fayre had raked shekels from the crowd and a cavalcade of floats, representing key scenes from recent history, had finished circling the lake, the next phase in the entertainment would come: a sylvan tableaux version of Milton's *Comus*, freely adapted by Tatum and now more suited for a modern age and audience. Tatum planned to set up the tableaux along a semicircular trail, beginning in the sycamore grove, then going up the hill through the wood and finally back down to the lake. Punters on the trail could gawp at the marvels on display then assemble by the lake as night began to fall, ready to witness Andy One's arrival by royal barge and the spectacular firework climax.

Tatum summarised the revised plot of *Comus*.

'So he's Komus with a "K", see? We're lucky to have Orlando to play him. He has the right kind of kooky feel.'

'It comes natural to him,' I said.

'The outline is this: Komus is the enchanter guy who lives in the wood with his crew of drug addicts, misfits and malcontents. So there we have the old regime of Sachs and Stanley in a nutshell. Degenerate and out of touch – in the wood, not the 'hood, see? And Komus hits on this young virgin who's lost in the wood – she represents the elec-torate – and he tries to seduce her with his charming-rod, to get her all jiggy and loved-up and intoxicated – that's the bullshit social-democratic reform-type dreck Sachs and Stanley were peddling – and at first she falls under his spell – that's the General Election. But along comes Sir Lionel Dingwallace, a valiant knight of merry England, and he cuts off Komus' head and sticks it on a pole. With the assistance of the Attendant Spirit, of course: Sir Lionel couldn't get it up on his own. Milton calls the spirit Thyrsis, but I think we don't need a name, just some geek acting the part of a trooper from the Big Red 1. What do you think so far?'

'A very succinct representation and allegory of our recent political strife,' said Bartleby.

'I've tried to preserve the complexities of the situation,' said Tatum, 'while keeping the storyline clear. I'm a bit worried about the head-on-a-pole thing though. It might come across as triumphalist. Remember, this show is part of the healing process, to help people draw a line and move on.'

'But there *were* heads on poles during the Second Terror,' I said. 'So you're being truthful. And while the truth may be painful at first, there's no healing worth a damn without it. I say keep the head, keep the pole. Wence's choirboys can sing a madrigal. Something like "Watch 'em roll, stick 'em on a pole". And we can use a recorder quintet I met recently. Not live, but a piped recording. Bruiser can take care of business in the studio now the canal is finished.'

'Yeah, the canal, that's good news. Those chain-gang labourers the Homeland Controller drafted in really made the difference.'

'They're excellent workers. The chains don't seem to hamper them at all,' I said.

'So, at this point, with night coming in, we get to the heart of the show. The hoi polloi are all round the lake and we give them flags to wave.'

'But which flag?' said Bartleby.

'Arnie is handling those. Expect a delivery some time this afternoon. I don't much care what flag it is, so long as the stiffs wave it. And here we bring on Sabrina the river goddess and the water nymphs.'

'My daughter Sarah is so happy to be playing Sabrina. Of course, were she not willing, I could play Sabrina myself. I made the role my own at Eton in the Oppidans' presentation of the masque. "Gentle swain, at thy request I am here." '

'Like I say, padre, it's good of you to help.'

'Hang on,' I said. 'Since when was this decided? Sarah plays nothing without my permission. She made a solemn promise to obey, and if she plays Sabrina it's only with my say-so.'

'Lingus,' said Tatum, 'don't be a jerk.'

'I trust, Lingus, your permission will be forthcoming?' said Bartleby.

'That's fine, as long as my position as head of our household is recognised.'

Tatum described the climax of the show: the King's barge sailing through the canal and into the lake to the anchor point by the newly built pier; Sabrina on tippy-toes to the end of the pier and the water nymphs paddling out from the shore to welcome their sovereign deity; the choir of hosannas and hallelujahs; the firework display, the drums, trumpets, pomp and circumstance.

'Then it's the after-show party. No need to draft a scenario for that. I guess we know roughly how it's going to go.'

'I hear Wence has laid in a hundred casks of Johnny-Jump-Up for the groundlings and serfs,' I said. 'And a thousand packets of Trojan. So we know precisely how it's going to go.'

19⑦

Arnie stopped by with the flags. A white field with a red ball in the middle.

'They're Japanese,' he said. 'I got a discount.'

'They'll do,' I said. 'Tatum tells me the Sons are coming over to join Orlando – sorry, Komus – and his crew.'

'Correct,' said Arnie. 'Wence made a suitable donation to our Lodge. And we like this sort of work. This is one of our easier jobs, just masking up and taking the Good Oil. And raking in the shekels.'

'Tatum's really pleased you managed to get in touch with the Cunt Coven. I didn't think playing water nymphs in a show like this would have been their thing, somehow.'

'Times change. We're all going mainstream. There's talk of the Cunt Coven rebranding as Front Bottom. Adore the rising sun, like High John says; may peace dog him all his days.'

'Have you seen him recently?'

'Only by night. He doesn't walk by day for fear of Saracens. Although surely the time will come when he will. He's back from Tirana and living in his hutch in our compound.'

'That's nice. And Jude, is she with him, in his hutch?'

'No. She proved to be a whore like all the rest. High John had to chastise her and send her away. If he hadn't then the demons who suspirate from the Bottomless Pit would be swarming all over us by now, with legs above their feet.'

'Since the demons aren't swarming all over us right now, we can only assume he's done the right thing.'

'No need to assume. He can do no other.'

C H A P T E R 20 ①

After a hard half-hour of cranking the telephone generator
I managed to get through to Sister Vincent.

'No, we haven't seen her. What you say is very worrying.
There's not much we can do here except pray for her and
wait, but I'll get the Papal Nuncio to have a word with the
Albanian Red Crescent.'

I said adios and rang off. I told Arnie's news to Sarah.

'But that's great,' she said. 'He's back.'

'Yes, but what about Jude?'

'I feel sorry for her, obviously, of course I do; she's been
like a big sister to me. But equally obviously, if High John
has cast her aside into the outer darkness then there's
nothing much to be done.'

'But not so long ago you told me she was going to bear
the new Messiah.'

'Self-evidently that can't be the case, can it? But there
will be a new Messiah, of that there's no doubt. It's been
prophesied. And there will be a Holy Mother to bear the
child in High John's line. Jude has proved herself unworthy
in that role. So I think you'd better come upstairs with me

now and consummate our marriage. I've been meaning to speak to you about it since this morning. I know we've all been frantically busy, but I've been the tiniest bit suspicious you've been trying to avoid me.'

'No, not really. It was the humiliation of our wedding night.'

'If at first you don't succeed, says High John (may peace dog him all his days), then try, try and try again. Come on, I think it's just the right time of the month for us to hit the jackpot.'

So upstairs we went and, despite what my pitiful ghost of a conscience was whispering to me, the foul old Adam laid down in my bones roused my blood and there was nothing I could do to gainsay him or his familiar, wee wicked Geordie. So Adam and me and Geordie got on with what a bridegroom has to do, and Sarah, true to her word, stayed perfectly still as I shuddered to orgasm deep inside. Sarah gave a sigh, but it was a token of achievement rather than satisfaction.

'That's better. Now we're properly married. I feel sorry for Jude, of course, and the mistake she made. But it's an ill wind that blows no good to anyone.'

'Yes, dear,' I said listlessly.

20 ②

I went back to the west-wing dormitory to collect a few things. I opened the door and jumped with fright. There was a young man lying there on my bed with his face turned to the wall. I coughed.

He turned round to me. I kept my gaze fixed on him, willing myself not to look away in disgust. His face had been terribly burned and rough skin grafts had done little to restore whatever looks he had before. One tuft of hair grew from the crown of his head. His hands looked like ragged claws. A loose-fitting smock came down below his knees.

'Sorry,' he said. 'I didn't realise there was anyone here.'

He spoke slowly and painfully. He'd bitten off part of his tongue in whatever agony he'd been through and I had to concentrate hard on what he was saying.

His name was Andrew. He'd suffered a turbulent time during his early teenage years, with repeated episodes of self-harming, mostly razor cuts and cigarette burns. His family had vanished by the end of the Second Terror. No home, no job, he was living rough until he was taken in by the Meek, sharing a squat in a community of squats round Shoreditch. This was an area and a community I knew for a time.

'I met a chap, he was working casual in Canning Town,' said Andrew. 'Not much older than me. He told me it wasn't just my family, God was dead too. Then he told me about Martyr's Torch. Shortly after that I saw one Torcher go up in the Mile End Road and I thought, fuck it, why not? Might as well. What have I got to live for? So I got in touch and they scripted it. What I hadn't bargained for was some inter-fering sod throwing a bucket of sand over me. Then I was very ill, down in East Grinstead. They did what they could, which you can see isn't much. And then it was the hulks, *Retribution*, off Felixstowe.'

'I was in *Vindictive*.'

'So you know the score. Anyway, thanks to the Coronation Amnesty, I got paroled here. They've got some part in a show for me. Sort of a freak show. I've got to sit dumb on a pole with my scars on display and be driven round a lake on a float. But what could I say anyway? Please can I have my face back? An American bloke called Wence explained it all to me. He said I was part of his family now. I don't know about that. It would be nice to think he means what he says, but I can't see it somehow. Still, it's better than holystoning the deck from sun-up to sundown.'

We swapped a few hulker anecdotes, old lags' tales of scores settled and privileges lost. I offered to roll him a snout but he said no, his lips and lungs were too fucked to smoke. I gathered my clothes and sandals, my drumsticks and practice pad, said a hurried goodbye and left him alone.

20 ③

I spent time with Bruiser and the sound crew, sorting out the amplification for *Komus*, running cables from the studio out to the various tableaux sites and bracketing speakers on the trees, using tarpaulin covers in case of rain. The electricity was even more shaky these days, but Wence fixed it so there were generators around to take the strain in case the Grid shut down. We mostly chose off-the-shelf library recordings to pipe out — lutes and theorbos, virginals, cornetts and sackbuts. But I hired the Convent's recorder quintet to come in and record Adson's *Courtly Masquing Ayres*. They were a fine bunch of nuns, with excellent breath control. Before they went home I asked about Jude, but still no news.

Despite the build-up to the show Sarah kept me at it, discharging my marital duty to impregnate her with the new Messiah.

'I've read in my magazine,' she said, 'that if you dangle your sack in a mug of ice-cold water before we have intercourse you'll raise your sperm count. And substantially improve our chances of conception. As you're dealing from a half-deck to start with, I'd seriously like you to consider it.'

Anything to oblige. So now, last thing at night, I crouched in the bathroom with my 'balls' in a gaudy painted mug — a souvenir of the recent Coronation — and an expression of vicious agony on my phiz, in sharp contrast to the benign and regal grin of Andy One. Then I came to my bride, flourishing my engorged charming-rod. After the usual 1-2-3 I withdrew immediately, as Sarah told me to.

'I'll just lie here with my legs up,' she said, 'while you go and get some more ice.'

'Yes, dear,' I said, listless as ever after orgasm.

Luckily she hadn't yet read about the deleterious effect of smoking on the motility of spermatozoa. I did find a reference to it in the parenting magazine she subscribed to, but

I carefully sliced the page out with a razor blade before she had a chance to open it.

20 ④

The pace stepped up, and Wence was in a foul humour most of the time – Leah was still in hospital, with the baby boy in intensive care – but, fair play to him, when it came to resources he shelled out without question. Whatever we wanted, we got.

'Lingus, this show is the most important of my life. We've got a good scenario and we've got the greatest cause to serve. Two mighty nations to be yoked in amity: Britannia, old and haughty, proud in arms, with a fine history of exercising her puissant sea power in the service of her empire and commerce; and Uncle Sam, the biggest shit-kicking, maggot-crushing, nation-breaking war machine the world has ever seen. Truly, this union will be an empire on which the sun never sets. And if Old Sol dares, we'll blast him out of the firmament.'

'Wence, you're truly cosmic.'

'Yeah, I know. Tatum has really got me turned on to this Milton guy. He got hold of an old movie. Turns out John Milton was an early American colonist, but he came back home to start your Civil War, which you had to have, so you could live in peace and harmony again under Charlie Two. So you see how it all fits with the Commune and Andy One.'

'Yes, I see. Perhaps we really are approaching the end of history after all. How's Leah and the baby? Coming home soon?'

'They leave hospital tomorrow. It's been a hard few weeks but Sir Lionel made sure they got the best of care. I tell you, Lingus, that was the most magical moment of my life. To see your own child born, sprung from the loins of two mighty nations, is truly awesome.'

'Have you got a name yet?'

'We're calling him Lionel, after his grandfather.'

'Nice. Can't wait to see the little prince. Now, Wence, what I need for the next phase . . .'

20⑤

What I needed was to get Komus and his crew into shape. Arnie brought the Sons over in a lorry and Orlando and I put them on parade and gave them their induction. There were special dietary requirements, of course, but they'd brought a pack of Alsatians with them and said they'd sort themselves out with food, so that was a big help.

'Just try to butcher them out of public view,' I said. They were sensitive about the need for discretion, so we dug a slaughter pit up in the woods, along with a propane gas-fired grill so they could barbecue without having to chop the trees down. We agreed the Sons could camp out in the wood. It was what they wanted, and accommodation in the Refuge was getting tight.

Next up was a difficult situation, liaising with the royal security team, a mixture of thugs from both sides of the Atlantic led by a stunted beast with the eyes of Caligula. Reverend Bartleby showed himself an effective negotiator. He offered a path through the maze of niggling points they raised.

'The scenario and script are finalised, and signed off by Sir Lionel Dingwallace himself. Every detail has been thoroughly checked for continuity, so I will make a copy for each of you. Then you can check that everything is going to plan according to the script. Will that be satisfactory?'

'Great idea, your holiness,' said Caligula, cleaning his fingernails with the tip of a bayonet.

I crossed another task off my clipboard.

20⑥

Then it was the morning of the show, and also the anniversary of the Battle of Trafalgar, as I discovered when I checked the times of sunrise and sunset in the Arts Council diary. 07.36 and 17.51, with a full moon rising early.

Wence had procured a full set of radio headpieces so that we could keep in touch with central control in the Refuge gallery. I parlayed with Bruiser over last-minute arrangements for the music and then switched to Tatum.

'Break a leg, Lingus,' said Tatum. '"England expects", and all that.'

It was nine o'clock in the morning, and the women of the Cunt Coven chose this moment to sit down and get into a political discussion over whether or not they should change their name to Front Bottom.

I pleaded with them that euphemism was hardly the most important issue right now, and could they just pick up their charming-rods and get on with the final arrangements for water-nymphing.

'Fuck off,' said Rasp, the transgendered nurse, no longer an associate and now accepted as a full Covenanter or Bottomite, whichever. 'You're a man. Your opinion doesn't count, so leave us to it.'

Just then Sarah happened along and lounged beside them, turning all of her considerable charm on the Covenanters and their problem. She persuaded them to defer the decision until after the show. They went off happily enough.

'There, that's sorted. We've already billed them in the programme as Front Bottom, but they don't seem to have noticed. By the way, I've got two lots of good news and one lot of bad news. Which do you want first?'

'Let's try the bad.'

'Well, I'm afraid I won't be able to play Sabrina after all.'

I screamed, hopping up and down and cursing.

'No, this can't be true. It's the morning of the show. What are we going to do?'

'Calm down, darling, just think *cool wet grass*. This is where the good news comes in. The first part, as I believe Papa has already hinted to you, is that he is willing to reprise his role as Sabrina. And the second part of my good news is the reason for me not playing the part: it's because I'm finally pregnant, I'm certain. It was that third mug of iced water last night that did the trick. Your little chappie finally got through to Mrs Egg. I felt a "ping" as you expired inside me last night, and I'm sure that must be it. Mother always said she knew that Papa had finally rung her bell when I was conceived.'

I gurned at her.

'It's all right, I've already cleared the substitution with Wence and Tatum. And Sir Lionel Dingwallace will be on the barge with the King, so it's all rather cosy. You know Sir Lionel played Attendant Spirit to Papa's Sabrina at Eton, don't you?'

'Let me reventilate . . . Okay, I'm somewhat reassured. All Pops has to do is drag up, mince down the pier and out above the lake at the anchor point, take the spotlight, cue the water nymphs and lead the singing of the welcoming hosannas.'

'Piece of cake, really,' said Sarah. 'I would have carried on, but Papa thinks it unseemly for the future Holy Mother to have been on the stage.'

A late-flourishing bluebottle settled on her collar.

'Sarah?'

'Yes, darling?'

'It's super news about the baby. But we can carry on making love, can't we? We don't have to stop because you're pregnant?'

'Lingus, my wedded husband, I shall always submit to you as a good wife should. Through the first two trimesters, certainly. After that, when I'm in full sail, we'll have to be careful not to hurt the baby, so we'd be wise to avoid penetration. And you're excused the iced water from now on.'

20⑦

The stallholders had set up during the night and were now in position, waiting for the ten o'clock gun to fire, which would signal the opening of the fayre. Cat-calls and ribald banter flew between them.

Bartleby must have persuaded Tatum on the leper issue, and a convincingly made-up specimen lurked between the stalls, leaning on a stave and jingling a warning bell. A brown muslin rag masked his face.

'Alms for a poor leper! Alms, for the pity of Jesus Christ!'

'Buy your blooming lavender, lavender here!' shouted a neighbouring stallholder.

'Souvenir Trafalgar tea towels!' shouted another.

I preened with satisfaction, looking on the spectacle I had helped to shape and smug in the knowledge that I was now the expectant father of two. By different women, granted, but that was a relatively minor consideration. I did a quick count-up: Jude was due . . . It dawned on me she must have been brought to childbed and delivered by now. I wondered if Sarah and Jude could both accept me as their husband in a polygamous relationship, and live together in harmony for the sake of the children. Mormons and Mussulmen could get away with it, so why not me? The only problem I could foresee was the friction we might have with two Messiahs in the same family.

The ten o'clock cannon barked and the revels began.

20 ⑧

I spied Father Michael Crosby, the Convent's confessor, perched on a stall. He'd expanded his range of clothing, and it was mostly medieval sports-casual he was offering these days – falconry jerkins, bear-baiting tunics, black-and-tan archery gloves – but there were two fine examples of chasubles with matching surplices, superbly stitched. Stitched, no doubt, at the cost of the eyesight of Shanty Town helots, but business is business, as he was quick to remind me.

'We can't afford ethical just yet. Now look here, son, did the underpants I gave you bring you luck, like I said they would?'

'It's difficult to say. I only got the chance to wear them once, and I've had so many bewildering turns of fortune since then, I don't know what to think.'

'Ah, now, you should see these,' he said, holding up a pair of silk drawers. 'A real bargain, from the Tristan and Iseult range. I'll be frank with you: there was a mix-up in the ordering and the pious motto on the seat was done in Albanian. It should have been a mix of Welsh, Breton and

Cornish for the market niche I'm aiming to occupy, but never mind, I can let you have them at a discount. Ten shekels a dozen pairs, that's less than a shekel for a fine pair of drawers. What do you say?'

'I'm well supplied in that department since I married. But I'll take a dozen. I can use them as end-of-show thank-you gifts for the crew captains.'

'Glory be. To tell the truth, I'm thinking of going back to doing the whole output in Latin again. I can shift more of them than all your vernacular underpants put together.'

Further down the line of stalls some early-bird punters, already well-drunken, kicked over the leper's begging bowl and pushed him to the gravel. They ran off laughing. I saw Andrew, the burned-out case, help the leper up. They spoke together then embraced.

'Look at that,' said Father Michael. 'You'd almost think he was a real leper, wouldn't you? He was round here before, wanting to try one of my chasubles, but I didn't think it right. Not quite the image I'm trying to promote. Now you son, I always thought you'd make a fine model.'

I had one of the chasubles on now, and was running my fingers over its rich, smooth silkiness. The chasuble was a superb garment of costly and gorgeous raiment, blue and gold, green and silver, with a copper sheen, and the legend 'HIS' in blood-red on the back. Father Michael nodded approval as I fingered the cloth, trying in vain to find a seam.

'Do you have a mirror?'

'But of course. Ah son, you look grand. Do you think you might have a vocation to the priesthood?'

I disrobed and handed him back the chasuble.

'I don't think so. My family have always been in the Reformation camp. It would be treason to convert to Rome, let alone become a papish priest. Anyway, I'm married. And agnostic.'

'And truly, wasn't Saint Peter married? And isn't the Archbishop of Durham an atheist? Tell me you'll think about it. I can feel from your aura that you have a real flair for spiritual marketing.'

'I can do you a package – instruction, baptism and confirmation, fifty shekels the lot. And I can make enquiries, pull a few strings, and get you the seminary of your choice, abroad somewhere, a nice warm spot where the wine flows free, the señoritas have dark, laughing eyes and the course is a mere two years rather than the usual seven, leading to a copper-bottomed vocational qualification and employment prospects anywhere in this world – or in the next, come to that. How about it? Come on, what have you to lose?'

'My soul, perhaps. Tell me, what's the Holy Father's position on polygamy and the priesthood?'

'Truth to tell, you wouldn't be the first. No, if you were encumbered with two motts, or a whole harem even, that would be fine with us.'

'I'll think seriously about it.'

'Now don't be teasing an old man, son. Say you really mean it.'

'Don't worry, Father. I promise.'

I suddenly noticed that he was no longer wearing his orthopaedic shoe. Father Michael danced a jig, rolled back his sleeve and spat on his left hand.

'Come in with us, son, and anything is possible,' he said. 'Shake.'

We shook, and the bargain was struck.

20 ⑨

There was a slew of punters in the park now, swarming round the stalls and booths, shying at coconuts, sniping at tin-plate ducks in the shooting gallery and cramming food and drink into their gaping maws. Not many of them looked like the kind who would bother following the trail through the woods to get the benefit of Tatum's vision of *Komus*. We should have offered some sort of incentive, although I was stumped to think what, unless it was the casks of Johnny and the Trojans Wence was saving for later. But there were a few serious souls who had some idea of seventeenth-century aristocratic entertainment, and they earnestly quizzed me about the adaptation. To these, I presented it as rather more high-falutin' and less sensational than Tatum made it. One old man, who had the look of a defeated and castaway schoolteacher, took me to task about the decapitation of Komus.

'There is no decapitation in Milton's masque. I can assure you, most emphatically.'

'Well, it is only an adaptation, true to the spirit of Milton's work, perhaps, rather than the letter. And if we don't cut his head off we can't stick it on a pole.'

He curled his lip and sneered.

'Quite the logician, aren't we?' he said.

Orlando was entertaining a ragamuffin crowd with his juggling and conjuring tricks. In a break, I reminded him not to go on too long with the sideshow; the masque was what I was worried about. I was concerned about the Sons of Onan. Some of them had been a bit too indulgent with the Good Oil. A couple of Sons had got into a serious ruck with the Coven and come off worse, one with a broken arm.

'Don't worry, they're good-hearted lads. They'll do what I say. Or else.'

I wasn't so sure. But Orlando was a pro, and managing the Sons was his gig, not mine.

I went down to the assembly area, where the floats and trucks for the pageant were getting ready to go. There was a float dedicated to the Coven, and another with thesps hired to represent the Flagellant Faction. They had their hoods off, to get the benefit of the breeze, and were laughing and joking. Their scourges weren't the real thing but strands of twine threaded through corks. Playfully they teased each other with light strokes. Most of the genuine flails were now in the hands of collectors of Commune memorabilia. Last I heard they were fetching serious money.

The Army and Navy occupied a float each and the Texas Rangers gallantly stepped in at the last minute to represent our American partners in liberation, the Big Red 1 having been mobilised at short notice for service somewhere East of Eden.

Ahead of the Army was the Women's Royal Voluntary

Service, whose part in the pageant reflected their role in the suppression of the Commune. The women kept the home fires burning for our gallant soldiers, sailors and airmen, while they got on with duffing us up with bullet, bomb and bayonet. The float sported a banner with the legend, 'Shall stay-at-homes do naught but snivel and sigh?'

A giant teapot filled with dry ice, white vapour steaming from its spout, squatted on the lorry's cab.

The defence of the 'Alamo', the South Bank barricade, was commemorated by another tribe of actors, representing the Little Sisters of the Circumcision. The original Little Sisters had been tumbled into a mass grave and covered with a car park. Wence's choirboys were on this float, ready to sing their prepubescent hearts out.

I saw Wence and Andrew walk towards the Martyr's Torch float. Wence had an arm round Andrew's shoulders. He gave him a sudden squeeze. Andrew winced. His scars stood out starkly under the slanting October sun.

There were torches on each corner of the float, cabers covered with felt, cotton and tarred paper, steeped in paraffin to burn with a colder flame. Two huge manikins were set up above, one for Errol Sachs and one for Manley Stanley. Later, the manikins would be set on fire and punted into the lake. In the middle, atop another pole, was a precarious looking perch, and on this Andrew was to sit, dressed in a short white tunic which let his legs and arms go bare, allowing maximum exposure to his scars.

I helped Andrew out of his smock and into his tunic, while Wence muttered banal endearments and jock-type exhortations to 'go get 'em'. Andrew started to cry.

'Don't blub, boy,' said Wence. 'Remember, you're a survivor and you're up there today to represent all the brave guys who torched and died.'

'I don't want them looking at me,' said Andrew.

'The whole point is that they look at you, and look at you real good. You're part of the spectacle, part of the show, part of the healing, part of the family.'

'I'm not getting up there, it's too high.'

'Listen, you crusted crisp,' said Wence. 'If you don't get up on that pole, tonight you'll be back in the hulks.'

I stepped away a couple of feet, to distance myself from Wence's menace. Andrew rubbed his eyes with the backs of his hands and allowed us to lift him up on the lorry. Other hands assisted him to his perch. The torches were lit and the pageant moved off slowly, wheels gradually getting traction on the straw-mat road laid out round the lake. The crowd cheered.

'That was close,' said Wence. 'Listen, Lingus, these guys will do ten laps. On lap nine, you're opening up the *Komus* trail, right?'

'It's all in the scenario. No problem. I just hope we get a good turnout for the hike through the woods.'

'Yeah, so do I. It would be nice for Tatum especially. But it's got to finish so that everyone is back at the lake for the royal barge coming in, so make sure you close the trail on time.'

'Understood. Have you tested the lock gates?'

'All done. What about the flags?'

'Yes, they're all stacked up and ready to hand out.'

Wence took my hand and said, 'I heard the news, about you and Sarah. So it worked out, after all. I was wrong. You young people know your own hearts.'

I blushed. 'She shouldn't have said. It's still early days.'

'It wasn't Sarah who said. Orlando told me he'd had a vision. He's been at the chicken giblets again.'

Two security goons walked by with Caligula, intent on the crackling from their radio. Caligula pulled out a copy of the scenario and checked a detail. He spoke into the mouthpiece. 'Roger that. Yeah, giant teapot, flaming cabers, gimpy geek with half a face, it's in the script. Over and out.'

'See you later, at the party if not before,' said Wence. I gave him a mock-heroic salute and turned to the next item on my clipboard.

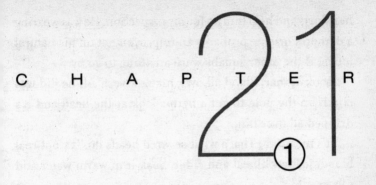

CHAPTER 21

Dusk was seeping into the park, under a rising moon, when the last few punters made their way from the *Komus* trail and down to the lakeside. They bickered over how to interpret what they'd witnessed. The actors followed, cigarettes in hand and oblivious to controversy, noisily congratulating each other between deep lungfuls of smoke. No sign of Orlando or the Sons. A family of fat mum, fat dad and fat rowdy kids passed by.

Seeing my clipboard and radio earpiece, fat mum took a chance to complain.

'Not much for the kiddies, was there? Some of it is quite disgusting, men dressed as animals, doing the business up the back passage. And doing operations on themselves and cutting each other's bits off. If we'd wanted that, we could have stayed in Romford.'

It didn't sound much like *A Masque Presented At Ludlow Castle* to me.

Fat mum said, 'They all seem to be on drugs. And look at this.'

She hauled one of her stinking children out from under

her skirts and held him up for my inspection. He was wearing a demon's mask – probably an improvement on his natural looks, if the other squabs were anything to go by.

'Look at that. Blood all over his new vest. All he did was climb up the pole to get a better look at the head and it's dripped all over him.'

'It's meant to. That's what severed heads do. It's not real blood, just cochineal and cider. Soak it in warm water and salt,' I said.

They went off grumbling. I had to admit, despite Komus' malcontent, misfit crew being in the guise of tigers and leopards, goats and monkeys – transformed by the magician's charming-rod – bestiality, buggery and mutilation weren't in the scenario. But I supposed the Sons of Onan had been carried away on a tide of Dionysian intoxication, immersing themselves too completely in their orgiastic role as Komus' posse. And they'd never had much to do with women.

There was a whistling in my earpiece and Bruiser spoke.

'Lingus, we have a report. Arnie got jiggy with a punter. His trousers are torn and he's threatening to sue – the punter is, not Arnie. And there's a light flashing in the woods. It's not in the script. Get up there and check it out. Over.'

'Roger. Will do. Over and out.'

I swivelled my spyglass. Yes, there was a green light, shining steady now, above the site of the barbecue pit. I looked to the east. Out on the river, leaving the main navigation channel and steering for the canal, came the royal barge, her bow pointed towards the Refuge and her port and starboard lights shining red and green. The Royal Standard flew from her poop.

On the lakeshore the Cunt Coven were gathered by the pier, transformed to water nymphs with charming-rods in hand and making ready to board their motorised lily pads. Reverend Bartleby made his way to the changing tent.

I shut the spyglass and went into the wood where the trail finished. I saw the head of Komus, on its pole, dripping red. The actor playing Sir Lionel Dingwallace was wiping his broadsword on an old tea towel. He was ready to leave.

'Wotcha mate,' he said. 'Glad this bit's over. I'm nearly hoarse, explaining to the great unwashed what it's all about. Ask your mate Tatum if next time we can have a story everyone knows.'

I asked if he knew what Orlando and the Sons had been up to.

'No idea. There's been a few complaints about what's going on further up, some sort of orgy it seems, but there you go, no pleasing some. I'll get down to the lake and watch the barge come in.'

He went off towards the shore, broadsword balanced on his shoulder.

The lamps set to mark the trail for the benefit of any late stragglers lighted up with a faint blue glow. Ahead, the green light flashed twice and went out. The recorder quintet spooled out their rich counterpoint, to the last bar of the final 'Courtly Masquing Air'.

I followed the trail upwards, under a canopy of rustling leaves, past the now abandoned tableaux sites, where the props and sets were turning spectral in the deepening twilight.

I followed the trail while it twisted across the rise. An

overgrown path, with bramble and creeper, led down to the barbecue pit. I left the trail and pushed through the scrub, holding the clipboard over my face to ward off thorns. I tripped. I put my hand out to save myself from falling and tore a finger on the brambles. My earpiece crackled and cut out.

In the pit, among Alsatian skulls and bones, Orlando squatted on a log. A pot of rendered fat was seething over a low light on the propane gas burner.

Orlando fingered his flageolet. He put it to his lips and blew.

From above, I heard what I thought was a throaty sigh and looked up. A limelight switched on its beam. Above me, hanging in the tree, was a torso, split vertically from gullet to sphincter, lungs torn open, ribs bent towards the backbone. The skin had been flayed and it flapped in the wind. The limelight went dark. The moon appeared behind the tree.

Transfixed on the smaller branches, intensely black against the moon, were organs harvested from the body cavity – heart, spleen, kidneys and liver. The white tripes hung down from the paunch. I stared and then ducked as they plummeted and slithered through my hair. A length of slippery bowel scarfed my neck. I dropped my clipboard and retched.

Orlando unscarfed me, tossing the bowel into a bush.

'Sorry, Lingus. That was unforgivable. We've been gutting a Saracen. I think we're getting quicker. Here's Arnie.'

Arnie, flanked by two muscular Sons of Onan, stepped from the bushes. All three were naked. Their glistening skin

276

was anointed with fat. Their eyes were glowing and spinning with drug-induced frenzy but their carriage was calm,
almost stately. Arnie held a spear. On its tip a bloody head
dripped, prick and balls stuffed in the mouth, dead eyes
open and staring.

I turned away, then looked back and met the dead gaze of
Caligula.

21②

There wasn't much I could do just then except sit on a log,
heave up what was left of my stomach and watch vacantly as
Orlando and Arnie set off with their trophy. Twenty Sons,
all naked, greasy and glistening in the moonlight spilling
through the leaves, stole from the bushes and gathered in
step behind. Orlando sang the opening phrase of their dirge
and Arnie called the response.

'The mightiest hand of God is always down upon us.'

'My own small tongue is but a stone in size.'

The Sons processed through the scrub towards the trail,
crooning softly.

I waited a minute and then tried to get Bruiser on the
radio. After a bout of static he came on.

'Lingus here, over,' I said.

'Roger, Lingus. Bruiser here. Over.'

'It's all a bit strange. I don't know where to start. Over.'

'Roger. Sorry Lingus, but we sent you on a wild-goose

chase. We checked the script, everything's fine. Over.'

'Even the bloke tearing his trousers and being buggered by Arnie? Over.'

'Roger the buggery. Pocock's not best pleased but there you go. Over.'

'Question. Two heads on poles, not one? Over.'

'Roger two heads. Reverend Bartleby showed us Tatum's latest scenario. There's meant to be two heads, the false Komus and the true Komus. Over.'

'Roger the binary opposition between false hero and true. Standard folk-tale motif. Over.'

'Roger the folk-tale motif. Bartleby says that's what Tatum said just before he passed out. Our Laureate doesn't seem able to hold his liquor any more. Get yourself down here on the double. The barge is just going through the final lock. Over and out.'

21③

I stumbled out of the wood and into the press of the crowd. I was aiming for the watchtower, over to my left, where Wence was megaphoning his pomp to the gathering multitude, but my way was blocked by a jam of baby-buggies and cursing mums and dads. I was thumped in the back by a collapsing drunk and staggered forward. A surge of bodies enveloped me and carried me down to the lakeside, a good two hundred metres from the tower. A toothless crone grinned and stuck a Japanese flag in my paw.

'Go to it, dearie, you have a nice wave like the rest of us,' she said, whirling a Rising Sun around her head.

I found myself fitfully waving the flag of Nippon, shouting for Sham and Tatum, Bruiser and Sarah, but my cries went unheeded, baffled in the clamour of the crowd. The floodlights came on, drenching the park in white light. I saw a clear space open up around an ice-cream van and I pushed through. I hoisted myself up to the serving hatch. The vendor slapped my legs, shouting, 'Get off, arsehole.' I looked up, judged the distance and clambered up to the plastic ice-cream cone and its honey-candy glow. The vendor leaned out and pelted me with lollies. I wrapped my legs round the cone and held on tight, embracing the flake.

The royal barge was steering out of the canal, on course for the centre of the lake. Reverend Bartleby, now in the guise of Sabrina the river goddess and wearing one of Father Michael's chasubles, was mincing along the pier, tippy-toeing out to its furthest point. The floodlights dimmed and a super-trouper blazed and followed him, lighting up every detail of his drag. He looked quite tasty but a bit flat-chested. His blonde wig was immaculately groomed and the tresses, adorned with silver ribbons, flowed over his sumptuous vestments. He teetered over the water with his arms outstretched and called, 'Welcome to our King!' His amplified voice swelled over the lake and the echoes swirled around us.

The water nymphs sparked the motors of their lily-pads and the water frothed and bubbled as they surged out from the shelter of the pier. One lily-pad accelerated and went into the lead, and I recognised Rasp, stretched out prone, waving her arm to the Covenanters behind. The engine notes of the others rose in pitch as they throttled up.

Forty metres from the barge the Covenanters opened fire. They stood up on their pads and hoisted charming-rods to their shoulders. Blue-white incandescent tracer bullets hosed the barge.

'Welcome to our King!' shouted Bartleby as the shots struck.

But the Covenanters shot low and the rounds sparked off the armour-clad hull. From the barge came the word of command and a battery of water cannon spouted. A salvo hit the nymphs and swept them into the lake. Just a few crucial metres ahead, Rasp escaped being hit and tried to get off another shot. But her lily-pad was out of control and crashed headlong into the barge. Rasp and her lily-pad vanished in a sudden flame of fire.

I saw a sailor quickly lay his water cannon on Bartleby. The spout caught him in the gut and Bartleby sailed out and up, towards apotheosis, arms outstretched, hands scrabbling at the moon. His chasuble blazed gloriously in the web of limelight which held him suspended for a calm moment before he took a dive towards the water, tresses and silver ribbons streaming behind. A fountain of spray rose and broke in a shower of lime-green drops where he fell.

Wence's voice megaphoned from the watchtower.

'Our revels now are ended. Time to party! Party-party! Welcome to our Sovereign! Hosanna to our well-hung King!'

The limelight cut out and Wence touched off the fireworks. An emerald snake stretched her coils from one shore to the other and rockets climbed high and burst, silver and gold. We heard bangs in the sky and oohs and aahs expired from the crowd. Where Bartleby had been standing there was now a spinning, spitting Catherine Wheel. Out on the lake, bobbing on a raft, the manikins of Errol Sachs and Manley Stanley burned hard with a gem-like flame.

I let go of the flake and climbed down. The lexically challenged vendor called me an arsehole again. I wasn't in the mood to argue. So, sugar being good for shock, I asked for a 99 with raspberry sauce, forked over a shekel, took my change and went to find Sarah.

21 ④

I couldn't see her. I swept my spyglass over the darkening grounds; no luck. But in the distance, beyond the causeway, in the light of a bonfire, I saw the glistening Sons of Onan as they passed by with Arnie in the lead, holding aloft their totem, the newly severed head. Riotous punters whooped and cheered them on.

Now that the fireworks were done the crowd began to thin. Weary punters trudged out of the park and over the causeway, where charabancs and pedishaws were waiting to take them into the city.

Stallholders and caterers began packing their shoddy goods, their pots and pans and paraffin lamps, stacking them on barrows, ready for the off. Garbage trucks moved slowly round the lake, picking up litter and lost kiddies.

I saw Father Michael, stowing the remains of his medieval sports-casual in a rather smart Italian-made estate car. He'd had a pretty good day.

'Great show; fantastic finale. Just one thing: Reverend Bartleby still owes me for the chasuble. Will you see to the invoice?'

'Give it here; I'll make sure you're paid.'

'Thanks, son. I just hope he doesn't get too much shrinkage with the vestment. I told him dry-clean only. It says so on the label. Was he expecting to take a dip?'

'A dip? Oh, yes, all part of the show.'

The lie came naturally to my lips. All over the park, Wence and his acolytes pushed the same line.

I found Tatum before I found Sarah. He was sitting with Bruiser and Sham under a parasol at a table on the terrace, his head in his hands, groaning. He'd missed a couple of hours, having passed out, like Bruiser said. Last thing he remembered was Makepeace offering him a hot Thermos of custard and Bartleby topping it up with a vial of what he claimed was Norwegian damson brandy.

'My head feels shredded. I'm completely fucked. The vicar slipped me a Mickey.'

'You don't know that, Tate,' said Sham, mopping his brow with a Japanese flag.

'It's got to be. I can tell you, firing live ammo at the royal barge was not in the scenario.'

'It was only small-calibre stuff,' said Bruiser. 'No harm done. Maybe it was just they were, you know, overenthusiastic. Improvising. That's what Sham and I told the police. They'll want to speak to everyone, but they're being very discreet and low-key. They don't want to spark a panic, and after all, there's no real damage. Look, if you're feeling better I'll slip off, the party's starting in half an hour. I want to take a shower. And if you don't mind me saying, Lingus, you could do with a shower yourself. You smell like you crawled out of a septic tank.'

'Yeah,' said Sham, 'but it's kind of funky on Lingus. Well, that's it for me. I've got police clearance and there's a car waiting to take me and my bass fiddle to Plymouth and on to Spain. I left the address of my new billet on the refectory wall. Check out Goliath's left buttock.'

Shamela leaned across and kissed me quick. Then she was gone.

I fetched a rug from the house and covered Tatum's shoulders. Sarah came running up.

'Oh, Lingus, there you are, thank goodness. I thought you were dead. Someone said they saw your head on a pole with your organ of generation stuffed in your mouth. And Papa's half-drowned and been taken into custody.'

She began to sob. Her tears seemed genuine enough. I reached out and put my hand on her shoulder.

'Sarah, tell me you had nothing to do with any of this.'

'I helped Papa get dressed, that's all. I thought he looked quite beautiful. Before he went on, he gave me this envelope and told me to open it after the show. I thought it was some tickets for our honeymoon in Albania. Now I'm scared it's not.'

A tall, moustached man in trench coat and Homburg stepped from the shadows. He tipped his hat.

'Quite so, miss. Inspector Truscott at your service, and

here's my warrant card. We'll all take a peep at Papa's billet-doux, shall we?'

Truscott took us to the library. Tatum was still pretty groggy. Wence was already there, looking confident, giving last-minute instructions to minions about the party. They scurried off. Outside the window I could hear the sound of casks of Johnny-Jump-Up being tapped and packets of Trojan being torn open.

'Pretty successful show, wouldn't you say?' said Wence. 'Kind of improv at the end but none the worse for that. What does Andy One say? Anyone seen the King?'

'I am told that His Majesty is still on the barge,' said Truscott. 'Our advice is that he should only join the party once a few things are cleared up and the situation is secure.'

'Well, don't keep him waiting too long,' said Wence. 'I know for sure Andy is a real party animal.'

'This shouldn't take too long, sir. I feel the answers we seek are contained in the envelope the young lady is holding. I know it's addressed to you, miss, but will you mind if I open it?'

'Not at all, Inspector,' said Sarah, handing it across. 'Papa said it was a voucher for a free holiday for two on the Albanian Riviera. A sort of delayed honeymoon for Lingus and me.'

Wence gave Truscott a paperknife and he slit open the envelope. He quickly scanned the pages and said, 'Ah yes, here we are.'

The letter was intended to be Bartleby's Last Will and

Testament, although it wasn't styled as such. But Bartleby hadn't expected to live. However, being trounced by a water cannon wasn't in his scenario. He thought he'd take a bullet clean to the head or heart, or at the worst have his backbone shot through like his hero Nelson, and linger, but not too long. So the letter said.

'Nelson?' said Wence, interrupting Truscott's flow.

Sarah kept her eyes on mine, to steady herself, as she explained to the company how much her father had admired Lord Nelson. Nelson, a hero of Bartleby's from boyhood, was regarded by him (and the poet Tennyson) as the greatest sailor the world has ever known. Nelson had been the inspiration for Bartleby's enthusiastic adoption of scuba-diving.

Truscott asked if Reverend Bartleby had perhaps occasionally confused Admiral Nelson with Commander Cousteau? Sarah said she didn't think so but anything was possible. Truscott said, 'Thank you, miss,' cleared his throat and carried on.

By robing himself in sumptuous vestments Bartleby was making ready for the sacrifice of his own life, just as Nelson did on the quarter-deck of *Victory*, when, at Trafalgar, dressed in Admiral's regalia with ribbons and stars across his breast, he laid himself open to death through the French sharpshooter. Bartleby's sacrifice, like Nelson's, was offered to the Liberty of Old England.

He cleared Sarah of any involvement. Yes, like him, she was inspired by High John's visions, but for Sarah the spiritual realm alone signified. After all, High John's doctrinal precepts were a mere modification of the Thirty-Nine Articles of the Anglican Church, whereas he, Bartleby, knew that a blow must be struck ('strucken' was the word he used) against the hydra-headed, eight-legged, jack-booted octopus of perversion that was the Anglo-American Empire. Such a blow could be no more than symbolic, but it would germinate the seed-corn for decades of agitation and the eventual manifestation of the Godhead at the end of historic time. He was taking the long view.

Truscott paused to answer a query from Wence. I glanced at Sarah, who was sitting now with perfect composure. There was a touch of special pleading on my wife's behalf in Bartleby's testament, but as no one else doubted his words I kept mum. I thought of the new samplers I'd recently found lying around, however, with mottos such as, 'Slay the hydra-headed eight-legged jack-booted octopus of perversion!' – an uncanny foreshadowing of Bartleby's letter. Then there was the sampler I'd found hidden under our mattress. For an emblem, it boasted a pair of crossed machine-guns arched over a grenade. The legend read, 'Jeremiah Brandreth Memorial Suicide Commando, Saint Sepulchre's-in-the-Mire Chapter'.

Truscott continued with Bartleby's testament.

Our vicar went on to praise the same 'Jeremiah Brandreth Memorial Suicide Commando', a necessarily clandestine organisation, hastily formed and scarcely trained and who, without the benefit of prior work experience, had carried out the assault on the barge. He referred to the water nymphs as the Cunt Coven, not Front Bottom.

A few people winced at Bartleby's employment of the C-word and Truscott apologised for offending sensibilities. Howsoever, he felt that euphemism was not appropriate in this case, as that's what they were, a shower of cunts.

Bartleby made no mention of the Sons of Onan. To me, this was no surprise. They were acting independently, out of Dionysian impulse – no doubt prompted by dear old Dad and an excess of Good Oil – but they were not within the ken of Bartleby.

Bartleby's testament concluded with a hymn of praise to High John the Conqueror, with whom Bartleby hoped soon to be sitting at the right hand of God the Father, from whence they would come, mob-handed, to judge the living and the dead, through the promise of Jesus Christ Our Lord, Amen.

'I wondered when Jesus would get a mention,' said Truscott. 'I expect better from a Church of England vicar. Well, that's all. We're sending a snatch squad into Shanty Town now. We'll pick up this High Johnny Conquadine, if he hasn't done a bunk, and if he has it makes no odds. We'll track him down if we have to cross the ocean and ride to Kansas.'

'Awfully flat, Kansas,' said Tatum.

I knew my father – up to a point – and I thought it likely he was still in his anchorite's hutch, flailing away at his back and making the best of a confined space. Like some starry field marshal he had made his several dispositions – the Suicide Commando, Cunt Coven and Sons of Onan – doing what he could in a logistical role, then he'd retired behind the lines to flail away the hours until the fight was decided. I had no doubt we'd find him there, in his hutch, unless the moon and tide were right for an Albanian submarine.

'So that's the story,' said Truscott.

Sarah took my head in her hands and kissed me.

'What a relief,' she said.

The door opened and two figures stepped into the library: Andrew, the burned-out case, and the leper. The leper tinkled his bell.

'Get those freaks out of here,' shouted Wence. He began flicking pretzels at them.

Andrew and the leper, now arm in arm, stepped closer. The leper pulled away the brown muslin rag covering his face, while Andrew, acting as valet, stripped the pustulant robe from his new best friend. Before us now was no leper but our anointed King, Andy One, clad in a grimy night-shirt.

Inspector Truscott genuflected then stood to attention, his head bowed. 'Your Majesty!' he said. Wence and Tatum, being American, weren't sure what the form was – although he was now as much their King as mine – and shuffled about nervously, while Sarah dropped a dainty curtsy. I gave my Sovereign a vague half-salute, touching two fingers to my brow.

After the salutations it was Andy's privilege to speak first. His voice was strong, clear and steady, as befits a monarch.

'My loyal subjects, we are come among you, first as a leper and an outcast and now as your anointed King. Just as Harry Five, in disguise, walked among his men on the eve of Agincourt, the better to take their measure and try their mettle, so we . . . Oh, bollocks to formality, I . . . have been among you today. I have found much that is good among my subjects – witness this young man here, my namesake Andrew, led astray by political manipulators in his early days and who has suffered so much for his misguided ideals. What an example of kindness and reconciliation he is to us all.

But I have also learned that much is amiss. Our nation may speak of hope, and of healing the fracture between mind, body and spirit. We can speak of bridging the divisions of class, gender and sexuality. Our nation may seek reconciliation after years of strife. We can embody these aspirations in our artistic representations – as you have so spectacularly proven today – but if we lack love and charity, and act towards our fellow subjects as if they were objects, in crude, cold and mechanistic fashion, then what hope for our realm? What hope for reconciliation, for the consummation we so devoutly wish?'

Wence hung his head. Andy One put his arm round Andrew and kissed him full on the mouth for a good half-minute. Andy came up for air, caught Tatum's eye and slyly winked.

'And now that we're all reconciled,' said the King. 'Let's get consummated!'

When I got up the next morning, with Sarah still snoring, I felt clear-headed and — a surprise to me — glad to be alive. Yes, there were worries and problems ahead, but so what? No one ever promised me a rose garden.

The night before, news came in of Dad's capture in Shanty Town. As for Arnie, Orlando and the rest, they had four heads up on their totem pole by the time they got to Aldgate, but there they'd been challenged and secured by one of the trained bands of yeoman militia. This was the news that most people were quietly waiting for, what they needed to hear before they could fully relax.

Andy One, Andrew, Wence and Tatum went full speed ahead and got royally slaughtered on a kaleidoscope of pharmaceuticals and alcohol. So much for the lessons of abstinence Tatum had learned in captivity. But failure in that line was Tatum's bag, and his alone. One thing I'd learned in recent months was moderation, in most things. I wasn't about to make the same mistake. I was only too pleased that none of the Trojans royally employed had turned out to be one of Cockeye's booby-traps.

I came downstairs to a solitary breakfast. From a cheerful waitron I ordered freshly squeezed orange juice, three eggs scrambled, bacon cooked crispy, fresh rolls with unsalted butter and a pot of strong coffee. I'd just finished, and was burping discreetly, when Bruiser came in.

'I'm surprised you're awake and up,' I said.

'No, listen, man, there's someone to see you. A wizened old nun. She won't say what it's about. I took her to Wence's study. Do you think I should go and wake him?'

'No, it's me she wants, let him sleep. I'll talk to her.'

Sister Vincent was leafing through a folder of erotic prints when I entered.

'I must share some of these postures with Archbishop Cyril,' she said. 'He's outside, waiting in his limousine. It was good of him to bring me over. And I have news for you, young man, about Jude, although I don't think it's good news.'

I said nothing and waited for her to go on.

'Perhaps I'd better give you some background.' She rubbed her eyes. 'That awful man, that awful awful man. I know he's your father . . .'

'Please don't spare me because of him. I have no particular reason to obey the Fifth Commandment on his account.'

'Well, you can honour it for your mother at least, should you ever meet again.'

Sister Vincent straightened her wimple.

'First of all, we arranged through the Church and the Red Crescent for Jude and the baby – she gave birth to a girl, Perdita – to be repatriated from Albania to England. It took some doing, and the journey was lengthy and circuitous, but she arrived in the country three days ago and we lodged her at the Convent.'

'I must see the baby. My daughter, you know. And Jude, of course.' As I said this, I couldn't help feel just a twinge of disappointment that Perdita was not a boy.

'I'm afraid that while the paternity issue may be clear in your mind, there's little doubt about Perdita being your father's child. The doctors are as certain as they can be without a genetic test. Jude gave instructions on arrival that nobody should be told, and we have honoured that request until this morning.'

'So what's changed?'

'I'm afraid the milipols came last night and took her and the baby away – we don't know where, but possibly to the Tower. I was on a sleep-over at Archbishop Cyril's and no one thought to let me know until I got back this morning. I know your father has been arrested, it was on the radio earlier, so I can only think that the two events are connected.'

The coffee I'd drunk prompted clear thinking.

'His Majesty the King sleeps here today. I'm sure I can speak to him and explain. I'll crave a boon as a loyal subject and get Jude and the baby released. But before I do that, tell me . . . What has my father done to Jude?'

'We heard the story bit by bit in a letter and over the last few days. You remember her postcard?'

'Wettest summer in memory, frightful humidity and poor post-defecation hygiene. With sailors dancing the hornpipe.'

'Well, the Tirana post office noticed it. There's no official censorship in Albania, as you know, but nearly everyone works for the Government there again these days, so I'm told. They let the card go, but they had Manley Stanley severely admonish your father for not keeping a tighter hold over his woman and allowing her to slander the Albanian people. Your father was incandescent with anger. He took the cat-o'-ninety to Jude and flogged her mercilessly – with her consent, she says, although I would call it uninformed consent, and she bears the scars.'

'Don't you mean the cat-o'-nine?'

'Oh no, there's been inflation in that detail. The upshot was, she was so badly flogged, she went into premature labour. It was only thanks to the devoted care of the nurses at the Tirana cottage hospital that she and the child survived. So you see, they do wash their hands.

'He abandoned her and the child in Tirana and took ship for England. At the last, he told Jude a girl child could not be the new Messiah and, as she had given birth to a girl, a non-Messiah, he could not be the father, since he . . . well, I'm sure I don't need to spell it out any further, except to say that he called her a whore.

'And now I think you'd better go and have a word with His Majesty, crave your boon and see what he can do to help Jude and her baby. Now I'll be off. I don't want to keep Cyril waiting too long.'

We went out to where the limousine was waiting. Archbishop Cyril offered his hand through the window, for me to kiss the ruby ring he wore. I stooped and kissed, not wanting to hurt his feelings.

'Mickey the priest sends his regards,' said Cyril, 'and says how would Spain suit you?'

They drove away. I rose on my toes and clicked imaginary castanets — tik-tik — then went back in to see if Andy One and Wence were awake. But I didn't hurry as much as I might have done, had the paternity issue gone my way.

22②

When Jude came home the baby wasn't with her. I saw the Homeland Controller's car pull up in front of the house, with Wence and Jude inside. Wence got out and held the door for Jude. She sat a while in the car with her legs out on the gravel, then she hauled herself forward and Wence lifted her out — tenderly, I thought. She looked sick and bloated. I ran out to say hello. She didn't know me. Wence shook his head, warning me off. I watched her hobble into the house, clinging to Wence's arm. I looked in the car to see whether there were any bags. There was nothing but a small bundle of blue baby clothes.

Bruiser came out as the car drove away.

'Where's the kid?'

I shrugged. I showed him the bundle.

'Better burn these,' he said.

22 ③

Rumour was that Jude had tumbled into psychosis. Wence had her shut up in a padded cell refurbished for *Boys of Bedlam*, his next show currently on the stocks. Tatum spent an hour with Wence in his study, trying to persuade him to call a half-decent doctor. According to Wence, Jude needed spiritual healing, not psychiatry. He'd do the job himself. When she quietened down and the scars faded he'd set her to a little withy-bending and basket-making. She needed to use her hands again.

Tatum and I sat in the library, nursing beakers of non-alcoholic fruit cup. Tatum had galleys of *The Commune Cantos* in front of him and was making corrections. He lit a cigar.

'Wence is an arrogant bastard. He knows jack shit about spiritual healing. I'll give him forty-eight hours and then I get my croaker out here.'

'Wence will go crazy if you smoke in the library.'

'Fuck Wence. Want one?'

'No thanks. I haven't smoked since yesterday morning. I think I've really cracked it this time.'

'I wish I had a silver dollar for every time I said that. You know, since I was locked up I don't miss any of it — alcohol, hash, speed, opium, downers. Haven't touched acid in years. You know, the after-show party was just an aberration. But this, this is truly the Devil's weed.'

He puffed his cigar. A Hogarthian maidservant came in and bobbed him a curtsy.

'Telephone call for you, master, on your private line.'

'Thanks. And look, quit all the master and genuflection garbage. I'm a poet and a Greek, an American and a Republican, see? Got that?'

Tatum went out with her, taking his proofs with him. I drank some more fruit cup and watched a rain-squall whip the darkening lake. Tatum came back.

'Bad news. I suspected foul play so I got a gumshoe to nose around. He ran down a US Navy doctor, name of Levine. The way she tells it, Perdita is on her way to the States for adoption. Levine had to check her over for the bill of health. Now she's drunk and sore at herself.'

'Any idea who she's going to?'

'Someone in the Pentagon, a high-ranker with gonad trouble. Levine says she'll find out if she can. It's tough on Jude. She knows the baby's been forcibly adopted, but what she doesn't know is that Wence set it up. He gets the money, minus local sales tax. As far as she knows, it's a simple unfit-mother rap.'

22④

Monday morning, at breakfast time, Wence, Leah and Sarah sat around the television in Wence's study, watching an outside broadcast from Hyde Park. Leah sat in the nursing chair, breastfeeding little Lionel. I stopped by to borrow a book and take a quick look at the set-up. I had no intention of staying for the climax. The prisoners were still on their way to the park. A roving reporter was canvassing the crowd. Everyone thought the condemned men had it coming. A huge, free-floating, blood-orange moon face boomed its mystery.

'Crying shame, doing all that up the back passage where a kiddy was bound to see.'

Back to the studio, where a presenter filled us in on the fate of what she chose to call Front Bottom. Due to the fact that they'd been led astray by Bartleby and High John, and because of their sex, the King in his mercy had decreed the Front-Bottomites must suffer ten years' hard labour in Camp Stroppy-Woman in Cumbria. There was some discussion among the studio pundits over the true sex of the bodily dysmorphic and transgendered Rasp, and the condign punishment due, but as she'd been killed crashing into the barge they had the grace to admit that such discussion was rather academic.

The presenter came back on screen to say that, as usual, true to custom, Mister Rumbold was refusing all invitations to be interviewed, although there was a hope that afterwards he might be persuaded to speak, given rumours of a radical break with the heritage of centuries in his choice of assistant. She reported that the Homeland Controller was exerting his considerable influence.

'Bullshit,' said Leah. 'Daddy wouldn't presume.'

'Not sticking around, Lingus?' said Sarah. 'Papa wouldn't mind. He's finally getting the martyrdom he craved.'

I knew she was relieved he hadn't cracked under torture, and that today would see the danger of Bartleby 'fessing up her involvement finally gone for good.

'I'm loath to see poor old Pops hanged. And my own father, for that matter, much as I'll be glad to see the back of him. And poor Orlando too. Even Arnie, who's never been one of my favourites, although I gather he's being saved for tomorrow, with Pocock. Why Pocock, for goodness' sake?'

'He's a creepy homophobe and he was getting on my tits with his constant smoking around Leah and the baby,' said Wence, 'so I suggested they put him in the frame to make it up to a lucky number. It's Chinese numerological psychic astrology, with a twist.'

The camera, back in the park, picked up a long shot of Rumbold and his assistant approaching the gallows in the back of an open lorry. Rumbold acknowledged the cheers of the crowd by lifting his trilby. The assistant was hooded.

'Hey,' said Leah, 'that certainly is a chick he's got with him, I swear. Look at those tits!'

I said to Sarah, 'Right, I'm off. You can fill me in on the details later.'

She grunted and stretched out her hand to me, still staring at the screen. The camera panned across the scaffold, halting three times to zoom in on the crowd through the loop of each noose.

'I wonder is he giving them a drop?' said Sarah.

'Yeah. It's before the watershed,' said Wence, 'so they can't have them choking. Before you came in they had graphs and stuff, to show you the weight and drop for each man. I guess only Rumbold knows for sure, but that's journalists for you: they have to speculate.'

Wence popped the cork on a bottle of champagne.

'Here come the condemned men. Say, Orlando looks pretty chirpy. Champagne, anyone?'

'Well, I'll be off.'

'Hey, there's my dad,' said Leah.

Sir Lionel Dingwallace was shaking hands with Rumbold at the foot of the gallows. They froze while flashguns went off, but the photographers were mostly interested in the hooded assistant with tits. I studied her closely. She made me think of Pirate Jenny: same build, same swagger, same . . . Then I knew for sure it was her. She ran briskly up the ladder to escape the photographers. I saw Rumbold, still at the foot of the ladder, frown at this breach of etiquette, but it was only a passing cloud and he quickly followed her up to take command. The camera closed on Jenny whispering something in Dad's ear. The hood was not yet over his face. He turned his head to look at her. He tried to spit but his mouth was dry. She pulled the signet ring from his finger and strapped his hands behind his back. Then she bent to tie his ankles.

'Golly, doesn't Papa look white?' said Sarah. 'Perhaps it's the set?'

She started punching buttons on the remote.

I went to look for Jude. She was out of the padded cell now and allowed to wander where she pleased. Wence had lost interest in her again. The last few mornings, early, I'd walked her round the lake to cut withies and skim stones.

The weather was cold and raw. Down on the shore I could see no sign of Jude. I strolled some way along the bank.

Hanging on a willow tree was her parasol. I looked over the lake and saw her floating, half-submerged, six metres out, with her arms and legs spread wide and her royal blue dress billowing about her. I waded out. She was face down. There were stones in her pockets. I dragged her to the shore and did what I could to breathe life back into her, but it was no use.

The wind scattered a shower of sleet. Something caught my eye among the shivering reeds. It was a round basket, made watertight with red sealing wax. In it lay a corn dolly. It was a boy.

22 ⑤

I covered Jude with my coat and ran back to the house. I had trouble getting anyone to take notice. They were gathered round the screen, cheering and clapping their hands. Sarah squeezed me tight and said, 'You really did miss something. It was fantastic! One minute he was standing there with the others, waiting to be strapped up, and the next he was shinning up the rope like a monkey. There was a bit of a dazzle at the top, like a flashbulb going off, and he was gone.'

'Orlando, I presume?'

'Who else?' said Wence.

It seemed true enough. Two ropes stretched taut from the crossbeam, the bodies out of sight beneath the trap. One empty noose dangled slack.

Sarah had been right about the colour contrast on the set. Now I could see clearly that one rope, the Reverend Bartleby's, was braided in the colours of his old school tie.

'Yes,' said Sarah, 'and Mister Rumbold had a dark blue hood for him too. That's what I call attention to detail.'

The camera crept up on Jolly Roger, sitting on a beer keg with a guitar in his lap, crooning 'The Ballad of High John the Conqueror'.

I tapped Wence on the shoulder.

'Uh, Wence, there's something you ought to know. Can I have a word, now? Please? Wence? Sir Wenceslas? Lord Wenceslas?'

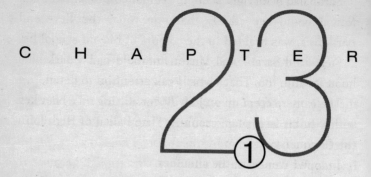

CHAPTER 23

Sarah sat fully dressed on the edge of the bed. It was after midnight.

'Lingus, dear heart, I know why you're going. But please understand, I can't possibly come with you, even though the Roman Catholic Church will accept you as a trainee priest with me as a wife, or even with two wives from what you tell. I must say, it's all rather sudden. You weren't even a Protestant this morning.'

'Father Michael Crosby, "Bing" to his friends, fixed it for me. He's very obliging. He thinks there may be a fine career opportunity for me in spiritual marketing when I'm ordained. He thinks I have flair. He offered me the accelerated programme – religious instruction, baptism and confirmation. Forty minutes, forty shekels. He wanted fifty, but I beat him down. Are you sure you won't come with me?'

'No, Lingus, I am sorry, really I am. But the thought of spending the next two years in a seminary in Spain doesn't appeal to me. Why Salamanca anyway?'

'Father Michael rang round. Salamanca was the only seminary that had places left for this year. There's been a huge upsurge in vocations, it seems. You won't change your mind?'

'No.'

I didn't press the point any further.

Sarah said, 'I "came on" earlier, so me thinking I was "up the duff", as you call it, was all a false alarm. That's a relief under the circumstances, isn't it? I suppose it's more difficult for you now, with only one thingy. I'm glad we'll still be friends. We can get an annulment easily enough because, if you remember, Papa began our wedding by reciting the opening of the funeral service. Apparently that invalidates the marriage. And signing what Pocock called "the marriage chitty" was invalid too, not much better than scrawling on a fag packet. And you're sure you don't mind about the new relationship between me and Bruiser? It was all down to the excitement of this morning and then the terrible news about Jude. I needed comfort but you'd dashed off to see Father Michael, so you weren't around when I needed you most, and Bruiser was. Hurting you is the last thing either of us wants to do. You know that, don't you? And I suppose if it hasn't killed you, it will make you so much stronger.'

'Please don't worry about me. It was a bit of a shock at first, coming across you and Bruiser mooning and spooning and planning a lifetime of ugly-bumping, but I'm not in a position to complain. "Let he who is without sin cast the first stone" is what I say these days. If you wanted to come with me I wouldn't mention your adultery ever again, but you've made your choice. And now I really must examine my conscience, say my prayers and get to sleep, if you don't mind. There's a lot to do before I go. Castanets to buy, for one thing.'

'Darling Lingus, you're so terribly sweet. Kiss kiss?'

'Kiss kiss. Goodnight.'

23 ②

Tatum came down to the dock to see me off. It was a foggy night in November.

'Thanks for fixing everything.'

'That's little enough to do for my good buddy and amanuensis. *El Capitan* is an old flame of mine. He owes me one. He ain't a bad guy, but if he comes to you covered in goatdung and fish-glue it means he's on the rut, so watch your ass. Lock the cabin door. When you get to Bilbao, hang your hat at the Hotel Esmeralda and ask for Inez. She has a brother with a seltzer truck who can take you on to Salamanca. If I find out anything about Perdita in the States I'll let you know through Inez. I'll do it through her, because I don't think you'll go the distance on the priestly gig. So wherever you wander, check in with Inez once in a while.'

A sturdy urchin came by, pushing a soapbox cart with a crude, stuffed rag doll wedged in it. There was a placard pinned to its chest, with the legend 'Little Johnny Conquadoo'.

'Penny for the guy, guvnor?'

Tatum tossed him a shekel. The urchin disappeared with Little Johnny Conquadoo into the fog.

'Way to go. I have some good news for you. I took that old

picture from your daddy's flat down to Sotheby's. Seems that Dutch Noah's Arks are leading in a rising market. They reckon half a million. If I take ten per cent does that sound fair? The rest through Inez. Don't worry, she can be trusted. I can give you five thousand now on account.'

Tatum handed me a wad of notes.

'Watch yourself with that. Get a money belt as soon as you can. Hey, that klaxon is for you, they want you aboard.'

A Spanish sailor beckoned from the gangway. I picked up my grip.

'Thanks again. One last thing. Who's taking over as Laureate, now you've resigned?'

'It's that old bum Makepeace. He's developed a rare form of senile dementia — it's turned him into a foolproof clone of Sir John Betjeman. It's like those guys, idiots savants, who do impossible feats with numbers. With Makepeace it's poetry. He has the whole of Sir John's repertory by heart, and he's writing new stuff too. Not even an expert can tell it from the original.'

'Maybe he's possessed?'

'Now don't be too hasty with that mumbo-jumbo — I reckon that's been a lot of the trouble round here. No, I talked to a shrink. There's a rational explanation, properly documented in the learned journals. Even got a name for it.'

'What's that?'

'For now they call it Makepeace Syndrome, since he's the first recorded case, but my shrink friend tells me there will be others — poets, dramatists, novelists; Chaucer, Milton, Cervantes, Menard, Keats. Maybe even Liotes one day.'

We shook hands and parted. When I got on deck I looked back, but Tatum was lost in the fog. The sailor fidgeted anxiously beside me, keen on showing me my cabin so he could get hauling on the bowline or whatever. He led me below.

'You must share with another boy. A good Catholic boy like you. He is persecuted for his faith, like you, so he too flees abroad. I pray for the conversion of England.'

'You'd better pray hard, it's one sinful place. Maybe we need another Armada?'

'Good idea.'

He opened the door on a narrow, two-berth cabin. A youth was lying in a bunk, reading a pornographic magazine and eating tortilla. It was Arthur the catamite. He looked up and beamed.

'Well hello! I saw you and Tatum on the quay. How is he these days? You'll never guess what I've been up to. Gomez, a bottle of *Vittoria Siempre*, another glass and two more tortillas.'

We were outward bound for Bilbao, by way of Zeebrugge, where I said goodbye to Arthur, the London agent and chief procurer of martyrs for what was now the Esteemed Guild of the Blessed Society of the Martyr's Unquenchable Torch.

'Business has been a bit slow lately, and the authorities have been cracking down since the lakeside caper. I've got to make myself scarce for a while. Manley Stanley has fixed me up with a job at Radio Tirana. I'm going to be a disc jockey. I've got a programme called *Freedom Folk* starting the week before Christmas. Tune in, why don't you?'

'I'm not sure what reception is like in Salamanca but I'll listen if I get a chance. All the best.'

'And you.'

23 ③

I had a few days to kill while the ship lay in Zeebrugge harbour, awaiting a delayed cargo of salted eel. Gomez the sailor had a night's liberty and took me on the town. He was well-known in these parts. He introduced me to a local Godfather called Daddy Hoot, who took a shine to me.

'You're a Scottish boy, eh? Kiltie lads, ladies from Hell. Good soldiers. The best.'

He offered to take me on a tour of the Flanders battle-fields. He was a battle buff with a collection of souvenirs from Malplaquet to Vimy Ridge and beyond. He also had an armoury of firearms from the last four centuries, plus repro items, many of which he kept primed and loaded, ready to shoot.

I declined the offer and bought another round.

'Maybe you'd like to shoot wildfowl? There's good sport round here. Come out tomorrow.'

Next day, towards dusk, after a hard day's slog through the marshes and some desultory shooting, we were near the seaside. Daddy Hoot showed me his pride and joy. Where the marsh met the dunes there was a tiny hunter's cabin, little more than a hide, made of wattle and daub. Beside it, jutting into the marsh, was a jetty made of barrels and covered over with planks. Moored to the jetty was a punt, with a long punt-gun, a fearsome blunderbuss, mounted in the bow. Daddy Hoot stroked the barrel. He laughed.

'My thunder-gun. Birds land on the water soon, many ducks and geese, then BOOM!'

'Sure-fire. I'm going over the dunes to look at the seascape.'

'Careful of the tide. Here, take this, in case you see something interesting. Or if you need to put a trapped and suffering animal out of its misery.'

He rummaged in his bag. He pulled out a flintlock pistol.

'Repro and mint condition, from an eighteen-ten flintlock by Blake. My ancestor found the original under the body of a Scottish Cornet-of-Horse on the field of Waterloo. I had this copy made in Antwerp, by one of our finest gunsmiths. Not the best for wildfowling, but we give the birds a chance now and then, eh? Here. She's primed and ready for cocking. Don't trip.'

Holding the pistol carefully in two hands, I crossed the dunes. The wind blew strong from the east, drifting the sand against the spiky clumps of reed. There was some sort of track here at one time, and traces of a broken-down dyke. I walked on a little way. Hunched among the dunes, black against the setting sun, was a ramshackle wayside shrine, a makeshift hutch on top of a crooked post. The paint had weathered from the Madonna's face and there was no trace of her eyes. The sun was nearly down. A vee of wild geese flew in from the north. Over the sea, below the horizon, Jude lay drowned among the reeds, arms and legs spread wide.

I cocked the pistol. I stood sideways like a duellist, aiming at the setting sun and the last of England. I tripped the trigger and hove a bullet across the sea. At first behind, with a crack, then booming all around me, the blunderbuss of Daddy Hoot rolled over the Flandyke shore.